Betrayal at Ravenswick

A Fiona Figg Mystery

BETRAYAL AT RAVENSWICK

A Fiona Figg Mystery

by KELLY OLIVER

First published by Level Best Books March 10, 2020

This novel is entirely a work of fiction. The names, characters and incidents portrayed in it are the work of the author's imagination. Any resemblance to actual persons, living or dead, events or localities is entirely coincidental.

Kelly Oliver asserts the moral right to be identified as the author of this work.

First edition

ISBN: 978-1-947915-28-2

This book was professionally typeset on Reedsy.
Find out more at reedsy.com

For Mom.
I wish she could have met Fiona Figg.

Contents

Praise for Betrayal at Ravenswick

"With a novel approach and unforgettable charm, Kelly Oliver gives us an enticing mystery with unique characters who bring the World War I era into sharp focus. Fans of Susan Elia MacNeal will gobble up this series! Highly recommend." —L.A. Chandlar, author of the *Art Deco Mysteries*

"Take a plucky sleuth, a handsome soldier, a shady stranger, add mystery and a dash of espionage, shake well, and you have *Betrayal at Ravenswick*. Fans of traditional mysteries will root for Fiona Figg as she navigates the treachery of London and a seemingly bucolic English country manor at a time when everything in England was changing." —Liz Milliron, author of *The Homefront Mysteries*

"*Betrayal at Ravenswick* is a riveting start to Kelly Oliver's World War I mystery series. After a devastating divorce, the brilliant but insecure Fiona Figg throws herself heart and soul into espionage, and almost immediately finds herself investigating a murder. Oliver skillfully balances Fiona's wry humor and occasional downright comedy with heartrending reminders of the appalling casualties of war. Readers will find this story impossible to put down and will eagerly await the sequel." —Barbara Monajem, *USA Today* Bestselling author of the *Lady Rosamund Mysteries*

Chapter One: The Beginning of the End

I should have poisoned him. If only I'd had the chance. By the time he confessed to loving another woman and asked for a divorce, it was too late. When he left me, he took my desires with him, even my desire for death. If it weren't for an article in the *Daily Times* about a certain South African war correspondent living near Wickham Bishops, I might still be languishing in my bed, wishing I'd never been born.

I'd been such an idiot. Everyone knew Andrew was having an affair with his secretary—everyone except me. Clueless, I'd marveled at his tenderness when he brought me my headache powders last night—the night before I discovered the truth. That morning, he was off to work before I awoke.

The sun streaming through the window of our second-floor flat woke me, which was unusual because we rarely saw the sun in London, especially these days with the war dragging on. Bad news from the Front put a damper on even the brightest day. Today I was not going to think about the war. It was my day off, my headache was gone, and I was going to make the most of it.

I stretched out and enjoyed having the bed all to myself. "You're burning daylight," I heard my father's voice in my head. As always, he was right. I threw off the blankets, got up, fetched my robe, and trundled into the kitchen to make my first cup of tea for the day.

Andrew and I moved into this flat when we first got married. I'd just turned twenty and was happy to be out of my parents' house and setting up one of my own. Hard to believe it was 1916 and we'd been married for four years already.

I'd immediately fallen in love with the modest two bedroom with high ceilings and large windows facing Warwick Avenue, which was always bustling with life. The kitchen had the newest appliances—an enameled Smith & Philips gas stove, new paraffin lamps from Liberty's, and of course a telephone mounted on the wall. The glow of the double burner lamp reflecting off the black and white mosaic floor tiles gave it a cheerful feel, and, even then, I knew I'd be happy here.

Then the war started. And everything changed.

This morning, the war seemed far away as I sat at our small kitchen table, hands wrapped around my cup, enjoying its warmth. As I sipped the strong black tea with just a splash of milk, I recalled Andrew's cool hand on my throbbing forehead the night before. He'd been so sweet and caring, and I'd been such a wretch. I gulped down the rest of my tea and resolved to take the train into town and sweep him off to luncheon at the Criterion. It was my day off, so why not? I clasped my hands together. Wouldn't he be surprised?

I set about picking my wardrobe. I wanted to look casually appealing, not trying too hard, mind you, just naturally elegant and charming. I settled on a silky brown, low-waisted frock with black panels down one side. When I put on the matching hat, I looked like a nun in a floppy wimple. That wouldn't do.

I went back to the top shelf of my wardrobe where no less than a dozen hats reposed. I admit I have a weakness for hats. A hat added an air of mystery to even the plainest face. And mine was indeed one of the plainest faces in Northwick Terrace, if not all of London. Sometimes I wondered why Andrew married me when, with his fine features, silken hair, indigo eyes, and supple lips, he could have had any girl. Thank goodness for hats.

Given the constant threat of rain squalls, I reached for one of my all-purpose hats, a tan felt number that matched nearly any outfit. I went back to my dressing table, tried it on, and examined it in my hand mirror. I turned the brim up and then down. No, this was not the look I wanted. Too country house and not enough chic.

I went back to my wardrobe and replaced my country hat in its proper place. I picked up a round bandbox and removed my favorite hat, which was brown with gray feathers. It was a bit too fancy and formal for luncheon, but it brought out a certain feminine quality in my otherwise square-jawed countenance. I put it on. Yes, this was the one. It fit close to the head and was more durable than it looked. I reapplied my cherry lipstick, touched up my rouge, dabbed rose water on my wrists and neck, and smiled at my reflection. Andrew was in for a surprise...and, as it turned out, so was I.

By the time I reached Andrew's office at Imperial and Foreign Corporation, I was perspiring. August in London is not for the faint of heart. I kept my arms glued to my sides for fear my dress had puddles forming under the arms. As I approached the heavy wooden door, I suddenly felt ridiculous. I considered bypassing the IFC and going next door to Liberty's to buy a new hat. I should have listened to that little voice urging me to go shopping instead of continuing to Andrew's office.

After two flights of stairs, I was panting and my hair was plastered to the sides of my face. I stood on the landing, rearranged my skirt, blew the hat's feathers out of my face, then took a deep breath, forced a broad smile, and made a beeline for Andrew's office at the end of the hall. As I turned the doorknob, I heard laughter—really more like giggling. I stopped to listen, which was my first mistake.

"Don't worry, darling," said the familiar voice. "I'll take care of you."

He had said the very same thing to me the night before.

I flung the door open. There was Andrew, his arms around the little tart of a secretary, who was nibbling on his ear. He pulled away, but Nancy clung to him like a wet undershirt.

"How could you?" I cried.

Andrew came toward me, the curvaceous shadow trailing behind him. "I can explain—"

He'd only been home from the Front six months and already he'd taken up with his secretary?

"Sack her!" I shouted. "She goes or I will."

"Fio, don't get hysterical."

"Hysterical!" I stepped backward, my second mistake. I was backed into a corner. "Don't call me hysterical, you cheater."

Nancy giggled nervously and held onto the sleeve of his suit jacket. Her amber eyes flashed at me like a hungry cat's.

If I were a man, I'd have socked her in her pretty little nose.

How could he? How could Andrew do this to me? With that simpering imbecile no less? I didn't know which was worse, his infidelity or his insulting taste in women. "It's her or me," I shouted. "Take your pick." The ultimatum was my third mistake. As they say in America, three strikes and you're out.

"Fio, I've been meaning to tell you for weeks now." He glanced back at the little tart, and she smiled sweetly. "Nancy and I are in love. We want to get married."

My hand flew over my mouth. I pushed past him and ran out the door. *How could he? How could I have been so clueless?* What a nightmare!

Getting home was a blur. I remember I tripped running down the stairs and an army officer helped me to my feet. I don't know how I got myself to the train station, on the right train, and back home to our flat. I couldn't see through my tears.

Andrew must have stayed at his club...or with *her*. Every evening I waited for him to come home and apologize and beg me to take him back. But he never came. The next Tuesday when I got home from work, he'd cleared out. Two weeks later, I was served divorce papers. The barmy thing was, the papers said *I* had asked for the divorce for his infidelity with someone named Sarah Sample, not Nancy Nettles. At first I was confused. It took me a while to work out he didn't want his darling Nancy's name dragged through the mud. Never mind me or my reputation...as a first-class dupe. I was devastated.

For the next four months, I got out of bed only when I had to go to work. I barely ate or slept. I lay on my four-poster bed memorizing the outlines of every leaf on the pale pink ceiling paper, wondering what I'd done wrong. *I'd been a good wife, hadn't I? Was it because we couldn't have a baby?* But that might have been his fault, not mine. *What did she have that I didn't?*

All right, she was fleshier and a whole lot prettier. But she was a moron, whereas I was the head filing clerk at the War Office's top-secret Room 40, helping to decode military telegrams and win the bloody—I mean, blasted—war. Andrew claimed he'd always been attracted to smart women.

Maybe the war had affected his mind along with his body. Men were coming back from the Western Front unable to function, nearly catatonic, with what doctors called shell shock. Could shell shock make a man cheat on his wife of four years? Four blasted years! I rolled over and buried my head in the pillow. Andrew wasn't the only one suffering from shell shock. The war was taking its toll on us all.

Thoughts of war roused me from my bed. It was time to get to work. I suspected Andrew resented my taking a job at the War Office. But with so many men at the Front, women needed to keep things running back home. He should have been glad I didn't take a job at a factory or become a canary girl at a munitions plant. Anyway, his beloved Nancy was a working girl.

I glanced at the bedroom clock. I'd have to rush or I'd be late for work. I'd always prided myself on my punctuality. Since the divorce, I'd been slipping. I grabbed the matching gabardine skirt and blouse I'd worn the day before and slid them on. I removed my hairnet and tugged my felt hat over my mess of curls. I didn't have time to properly redo my hair. I'd have to remember not to remove my hat. No time for face paint either. When I glanced in the mirror, for a moment I saw my Uncle Frank looking haggard and wearing a woman's hat. Ridiculous. I blinked and he was gone.

When I was young, I wanted to be an actor just like Uncle Frank. I'd dress up in my father's hats or my mother's heels and act out the characters from my detective novels. By the age of eighteen I'd grown taller and ganglier, but not a jot prettier. In my final year at North London Collegiate School for girls, Mrs. Benson, the drama teacher, said to me, "Sorry to be blunt, dear, but with that face, you'll never make it as an actress. You'd be better off putting on trousers and passing yourself off as a man."

Taking her advice, I gave up my dreams of acting. Although I admit, in my marriage, I'd employed my acting skills on many occasions, especially when entertaining Andrew's military colleagues and his school chums from

Clifton College or the Royal Military Academy.

I gulped down a quick cup of tea, grabbed a biscuit, and headed to the train station. I'd be lucky to make it to the War Office on time.

The War Office occupied several rooms in the Old Admiralty, a grand U-shaped brick building that housed government and military offices along with the top navy brass in well-appointed flats on the top floor. I arrived at Room 40 late—only by five minutes, but still late. Room 40 was a cavernous warehouse of a room with rows of drafting tables and desks. Men and women manned the desks, which sat one after the other, and were set up with teletypes, typewriters, and desktop file cabinets. The room was so long and narrow that if you stood at one end, you could barely make out the other. Amidst the clicking of typewriter keys and shuffling of papers, people talked in whispered voices.

A group of men huddled over a drafting table near my desk. I whisked past them and busied myself at my filing cabinet. Absentmindedly, I filed a stack of papers. A photographic memory came in handy when filing while eavesdropping.

The excitement in the men's voices piqued my curiosity. Using the ruse of offering them coffee, I went to investigate. I darted into the kitchenette to prepare the coffee. Luckily, it was on the same end of the long room as my desk. You never knew what you'd find in the kitchen area. I steeled myself for bits of week-old sandwich and crusty teacups. Ruth must have cleaned up, because to my surprise it smelled of fresh pine instead of old cheese. I made a fresh pot of coffee, filled three cups, and put them on a tray.

"No thank you, Mrs. Cunningham," Mr. Montgomery said with a bow of his oblong head. "I just had a cup of tea." William Montgomery was the head of cryptography. Before the war, he had been a Presbyterian minister and an expert translator of German theological texts. Now he was one of Britain's premier code breakers. He still looked more like a preacher than a spy.

"Thank you, I'll have a cup," Mr. Grey said. The men called him "the door mouse" because of his small stature and quiet demeanor. He gave me a sympathetic look. "Are you quite well, Mrs. Cunningham?"

"By all means, Mr. Grey." I forced a smile. "Don't worry about me."

The third man in the group was Dillwyn "Dilly" Knox, a former classics scholar and papyrologist at King's College, Cambridge. He was the most gregarious of the bunch, and was said to have a notorious personal life that included both men and women lovers. He was the proverbial ladies' man, man's man, man about town. Not that I'm much for gossip, mind you. But with his full lips, sultry eyes, and thick hair, he didn't look like any professor I'd ever seen.

Mr. Knox nodded at me and took the cup from my hand. "The issue now is how to tell the Americans without them thinking we're spying on them, too," he said to the other men.

"This could be the turning point that brings the Americans into the war," Mr. Grey said, his small hand gripping the handle of his cup.

"And with the Americans on our side," Mr. Montgomery said, "we're sure to finally win this damn war. So many lives lost and for what?"

Ears pricked, I lingered around the table straightening some file folders. I had a reputation for sticking my nose where it didn't belong. The men wouldn't admit it, but I'd helped them crack code and plan espionage on several occasions.

"The devil is if the Americans find out we're intercepting their diplomatic communications, they might turn against us," Mr. Knox said. When he glanced my way, I busied myself shuffling some papers stacked on the end of the drafting table.

"It's a sticky wicket," Mr. Grey said. "On top of that, we have to prove to the Americans it's authentic. And to do that we have to give them cipher 13040, which risks the Germans discovering we've broken their code."

Picking up an empty coffee cup, I glanced down at the Western Union telegram they were decoding. It was issued from a Herr Zimmerman of the German Foreign Office to Ambassador Heinrich von Eckart, the German ambassador to Mexico. The entire telegraph was a laundry list of numbers. *What did the Germans want with Mexico? Were they trying to bring Mexico into the bloody blasted war?*

"We have to find a way to get word to the Americans without them knowing how we got it." Mr. Montgomery held out his empty cup as I passed by.

A light went on in my brain. "What about telling them you stole it in Mexico?" I blurted out. "Everyone knows corruption and bribery are rampant down there." *Horsefeathers! What had I done?* The impudence. I'd be sacked for sure. Not to mention, I really didn't know what went on "down there."

"Fiona, that's not a bad idea!" Mr. Knox said. "Hohler could pull it off."

My face grew hot. *How did he know my first name?* He *was* a forward chap.

"Yes, Mr. H could intercept the telegram in Mexico using whatever means necessary. And then we could tell the Americans we got it in Mexico." Mr. Montgomery beamed at me. "I say, it just might work."

"What about the Germans?" Mr. Grey asked. "Won't we still have to decipher it for the Americans? Then they'll know we've broken their code."

"What if your Mr. H stole the telegram already deciphered?" I asked. Glancing around at the men's rapt faces, I continued, "Surely someone has to decipher the code for the German ambassador to Mexico."

"Why, Mrs. Cunningham, that's genius." Mr. Grey gave me a full-faced smile.

"You do have a knack for espionage." Mr. Knox winked at me.

My cheeks burned. Still, I couldn't help but smile. It was the first time I'd felt useful since Andrew left.

A week later, when I arrived at Room 40, the men were celebrating.

"Mrs. Cunningham, congratulations." Mr. Grey exclaimed. He gestured me over to the planning table where they were gathered.

"What for?" I asked as I joined them.

"Your jolly clever scheme for the Zimmerman telegram worked." Mr. Knox flashed a toothy smile, the kind that made nuns blush.

"It's only a matter of time until the Americans join the allies and we finally end this bloody war." Mr. Grey tucked his pencil behind his mousy ear. "And it's all thanks to you, Mrs. Cunningham."

"We should make you an honorary consultant," Mr. Montgomery said, stroking his beard. "You've been cracking code and coming up with creative solutions with the best of them."

"Oh no. I couldn't—" I broke off. Why not? Why couldn't I? *Because I'm a woman?* Nonsense. I could match wits with any man. Anyway, it was true. I had been helping out a great deal, and it was nice to finally get recognition for my schemes instead of the men passing them off as their own.

"That's a jolly good idea," Mr. Knox said. He extended his hand to me.

I took it firmly and shook. He held my hand a bit too long for my liking. I gave him a stern look of reproach. Served him right. Cheeky devil.

"Welcome to Britain's premier intelligence-gathering agency." Mr. Montgomery extended his hand and gave me a polite handshake. "You can officially consider yourself an honorary consultant to the world's best code breakers."

"Surely now the Americans know what the Germans are up to in their own back garden, they will have to join the war. And when they do, it will be curtains for the Huns," Mr. Knox said, and then disappeared into the kitchenette. He returned with a bottle of wine. "This calls for a celebration. I was saving this for the end of the war. But today marks the beginning of the end." With great fanfare, he popped the cork. "Fetch some glasses, will you, old girl," he said to me.

I scooted off to the kitchenette, which to my dismay was already a disaster area. Ruth and I were the only ones who even tried to keep it tidy. Cleaning up after men at war was a full-time job. I wiped out an odd assortment of glasses, put them on a tray, and brought them back into the planning room.

Mr. Knox poured wine into the glasses and the men each took one. "Where's yours?" he turned to me. "Silly girl, go get one for yourself." He pointed toward the kitchenette. "And quit calling me Mr. Knox. It's Dilly."

"Yes, sir."

I obeyed.

Mr. Grey raised his glass. "To the beginning of the end."

"To the Americans joining the Triple Entente!" Mr. Montgomery clinked his glass against each of the others'.

"To Fiona!" Mr. Knox downed his entire glass in one gulp.

I tightened my lips. The nerve! Using my first name without permission.

"Yes, to Mrs. Cunningham," Mr. Grey said and held out his glass to me.

I clinked and took a sip. The wine was sour, and I didn't particularly like it. I hadn't drunk wine since my last wedding anniversary. The memory stabbed me like a dagger through the heart.

"Are you sure you're quite well, Mrs. Cunningham?" Mr. Grey asked again.

"Yes, yes."

"You know, you might have just changed the course of the war."

"Really?"

"Don't underestimate yourself, Mrs. Cunningham," Mr. Grey said. His soft eyes offered added encouragement. "You may have just helped us get the Americans into the war."

Mr. Knox refilled his glass and then raised it again. "To the new and improved espionage team."

"Mrs. Cunningham is an *honorary* consultant," Mr. Montgomery said to Mr. Knox as if in warning. "Not officially part of the team."

Honorary or not, I raised my glass. *Goodbye, Mrs. Andrew Cunningham,* I made my own mental toast. *To the new and improved Miss Fiona Figg.*

Chapter Two: The Assignment

For the next month, every time I heard about Andrew's exploits at the Front, or ran into one of our old friends, I'd collapse back into my bed. Every place we'd been, everyone we knew, everything we'd done reminded me of him and his betrayal.

How could he have been so brutal? In the beginning, I'd found his brutality irresistible. Now the same qualities I'd so passionately loved I just as passionately despised. I hated him. I'd never hated anyone before, and the seed planted in my heart threatened to grow into a suffocating vine beyond my control. As much as I'd loved him, I loved being in control even more.

If only I could get out of London and everything that made me think of Andrew... or worse, Nancy. The first time I ran into her was a dreary Saturday in February. I was on my way to the hospital to tend to soldiers when the sky opened and it started raining buckets. I'd forgotten my umbrella, so I ducked under the awning of Fortnum & Mason to wait out the downpour. Who do I run into coming out of the store? The little husband-stealing tart! I did an about-face and headed straight home to bed. The hospital would have to do without me.

On my days off from the War Office, I volunteered at Charing Cross Hospital, a teaching hospital with five wards commandeered by the War Office. All the local hospitals were overflowing with casualties, but given its location near the train station, Charing Cross was an arrival point for thousands of injured servicemen. Caravans of canvas-covered lorries arrived daily. Many times, the hallways were full of cots where the wounded awaited treatment.

My greatest fear was one day I'd be looking into the terrified eyes of my former husband, crippled by the war. Or worse, find him in the morgue…not that it wouldn't serve him right. Andrew had been called back to the Royal Flying Corps shortly after he married *her*.

But it wasn't seeing Andrew lying on a gurney that put me over the edge that day. It was seeing her. On another dreary Saturday a month later, I ran into her again. She had just started working at the hospital dispensary where I volunteered. She didn't seem to recognize me in my white uniform and cap. I gasped and my hands flew to my mouth. She was pregnant!

In my head, I counted the months since the divorce. *Damn him!* My heart sunk. I turned on my heel and vowed to leave town at the first opportunity.

My opportunity came sooner than I expected.

The Zimmerman telegram may have been the beginning of the end of the war, but that end was slow in coming. The Americans still hadn't joined the Allied Powers. And, the war continued. I settled into my role as honorary consultant to the team in Room 40. I kept improving my filing system, helped break code, fetched tea, and on occasion did field work. Given women could go some places men couldn't, from time to time they'd send me off to trail a new arrival from France or Belgium, a refugee they suspected might be doing more than taking refuge in Britain.

Following women of interest became my specialty. I could pass unnoticed in department stores, cafes, and schools. Following my female targets, I discovered how much more of the world belonged to men than to women. For there were many places where it was simply not proper for an unaccompanied woman to travel alone. And those were usually the more interesting places.

I'd just returned to the office from trailing a young woman mathematician who fled Brussels but had spent time in Berlin as a student. She ran me all over Mayfair before returning to her flat. Exhausted, I headed for the kitchenette to put on the kettle for tea. I was enjoying a strong cup with a dash of milk when I spotted the article that would change my life.

Sitting at my desk, sipping my tea, I passed my eyes over last week's *Daily Times*, looking at the pictures more than reading. A picture of a rugged young swashbuckler wearing a slouch hat, duxbak jodhpurs, and pencil mustache caught my attention. A leather bandoleer filled with bullets crisscrossed his chest like a trophy adorned with tiger's teeth. I pulled the paper closer and began to read. The man was a wounded war hero and famous shooting instructor who had taken the American President, Theodore Roosevelt, big game hunting in Africa. A true renaissance man, he was also a war correspondent for an American newspaper. These days, he was recuperating from his war injuries at our very own Ravenswick Abbey. I studied the photograph, surprised that a grainy black-and-white photograph could stir such intense sensations in my torso.

"If this chap is a famous big game hunter and a war hero," Mr. Knox said over my shoulder.

"Don't sneak up on me like that," I gasped.

"Why is he living at the mercy of a wealthy English lady? The upper brass want to know what he's doing here." Mr. Knox peered down at the newspaper. "They've put a tail on him."

I should have known the mysterious hunter, hero, cum war correspondent was already a person of interest to Room 40.

"Apparently, there isn't an animal he can't track," I said, glancing up at Mr. Knox.

He gave a little snort. "Great White Hunter, my eye."

I put my teacup down. "Listen to this." I read from the paper. "He wrote an article titled 'Fire Hunting with the Congo-Cannibals'." I immediately took an interest in the outrageous fellow and hoped to meet him one day.

"Why is this Tarzan gadding about, taking tea with ladies, and shopping for expensive mustache pomades?" Mr. Knox asked, arms akimbo. "He must be up to no good. He could be a German spy. He could even be the notorious Dionysus."

"Or a French spy," Mr. Montgomery said, joining Mr. Knox at my desk. "He has been living in Paris, and not so long ago, France was our mortal enemy—"

"He's South African," I interrupted. Although, according to the newspaper article, he was born in England, fluent in five languages and graduated from the Royal Military Academy in Brussels. On second thought, even the newspaper article didn't identify his origins. "Who's Dionysus?"

"A myth invented by the War Office. Something about a super spy." Mr. Grey chuckled as he approached my desk, cup and saucer in hand. "Just a lot of rubbish and nonsense."

"I say he's working for the French." Mr. Montgomery lifted the newspaper from my desk.

"They're our allies," I said.

"Now they are, but we've been enemies for much longer than we've been friends." He dropped the paper back onto my desk.

It was true. A lot of people felt very uneasy about putting our lot in with France after all they'd done to us over the last century.

I studied the photo and its caption. "What an odd name—"

"French or not, he's a journalist and Kitchener has banned all reporters from the front lines," Mr. Montgomery said.

Mr. Grey's mousy nose twitched. "Complete censorship, that's what they want."

"National security, old boy," Mr. Knox said. "Churchill doesn't want us to read about our troops chewing barbed-wire in Flanders. Too demoralizing."

"That's not right—" I started to say.

"It's a rum do about that chap who was to go to Essex and tail the newsman," Mr. Knox interrupted. "He's broken his leg, slipped getting on the train to go up there."

I wish these blasted men would quit interrupting me.

"I heard his cover was posing as a foreign gynecologist on holiday for his nerves." Mr. Grey snickered. "I thought that sort of thing only happened in the theater."

You'll never make it as an actress. Mrs. Benson's words came back to me. *You'd be better off putting on trousers and passing yourself off as a man.* Was it such a daft idea?

"I'll do it!" I blurted out.

"What?" Mr. Montgomery's eyes widened.

"Do what?" Mr. Knox asked.

"Take the fellow's place…" I said, my voice trailing off.

"You want to impersonate a doctor and spy on the huntsman?" Mr. Grey dropped his spoon onto his saucer. "Are you mad? No one will believe a woman is a real doctor, not even a foreign one."

"I can do it," I said, dropping my deep voice another octave. "I've been told I make a passable man." I stood up, feet apart and hands on my hips.

Mouths open, the three men stared at me for several seconds.

"I say," Mr. Montgomery said.

Mr. Grey sat his saucer down on my desk and fetched his hat from the rack. "Here," he said, handing it to me. "Say something doctorly."

I took the hat and placed it on top of my hair, which luckily I always wore tightly pinned to my head. "The leg bone's connected to the ankle bone."

They laughed. But I was serious. *Deadly serious.* This was my chance to get out of London, to go on an adventure, and to meet the mysterious huntsman cum war correspondent.

I closed my eyes, inhaled, and slipped into character. Conjuring the words of Dr. Cornwall the last time he examined me, I said in a low voice, "Madame, you are suffering from an anxiety neurosis, most likely hysteria. I recommend bed rest, bland food, and seclusion. I will have some bromide powders prepared to help you sleep."

The men all quit laughing and gaped at me again.

"I say, it just might work!" Mr. Montgomery was the first to speak.

"Indeed, I've never seen anything like it," Mr. Grey said.

Mr. Knox gave me a wink. "You're a natural, old boy." When he clapped me on the back, I nearly fell over.

I had to bulk up if I was going to pull this off. "So, you'll recommend me for the job?"

"The head office *is* in a pickle." Mr. Montgomery scratched his head. "Oh, why not?" He chuckled.

"Thank you." I wanted to hug him.

"There's many a slip between the cup and the lip," he said. "Let's wait and see what they say in the head office."

After work, I walked directly to Foyles to buy some books on bodybuilding. The rain had finally stopped, and I was encouraged by a hint of sunshine warming the sky. Although as Mr. Montgomery had warned the gap between cup and lip could be a doozy, I was happier than I had been in a long time. The chance of tracking the Great White Hunter had cheered me considerably.

My new bodybuilding book in hand, I checked my timetable for the next train to Shaftesbury Avenue. Next stop, Angels Fancy Dress, London's go-to shop for costumes. I'd been there many times as a child, begging my mother to take me there whenever we were in town.

As usual, the train was packed with people on their way home, most dressed in cream-colored trench coats holding black umbrellas like so many piano keys packed in a box. I was sandwiched between a bulky woman who smelled of garlic and an elderly gentleman wearing a top hat. I took a seat, opened my book, and admired the physiques of the muscular men who had competed in the Great Competition at Royal Albert Hall sixteen years ago. *My word!* Sir Arthur Conan Doyle was one of the judges of the contest. As a child, I'd loved Sherlock Holmes. My mother had subscribed to the *Strand Magazine*, and after she'd abandoned them to be used as kindling, I'd sneaked the magazines to my room to devour Sherlock Holmes stories in private.

When I looked up from my book, the gentleman next to me gave me a sly smile. I slapped the book shut, my cheeks burning. *What must he think of me looking at pictures of scantily clad men?* For the rest of the trip, I stared straight ahead, refusing to make eye contact with anyone.

I was so relieved when the train reached my stop that I jumped up and the blasted book slipped off my lap onto the floor. The gentleman bent to pick it up. I blushed as I snatched it away from him and scurried off the train. I didn't look back until I reached Angels Fancy Dress shop.

With racks of brightly colored costumes and countertops covered in false mustaches, beards, and wigs, Angels Fancy Dress shop was the perfect antidote to my awkwardness. I'd always felt more at home dressed as someone other than myself. You could be anyone you wanted at Angels. A shop girl could become a duchess, and an errand boy, a duke. A duchess could become a harem girl and her duke a sheik. From masquerade balls to motion pictures, Angels was the place for make-believe.

As I headed to the men's department, I passed a wall of eye masks, some with elegant colored feathers. Inhaling the musty smells that reminded me of my childhood, I tried on topcoats, hats, trousers, and bushy eyebrows, and I considered a set of false teeth. I settled on a great black beard and two reasonably priced outfits, one navy and one brown. I hoped I would grow into them with a steady course of weightlifting exercises prescribed by Eugen Sandow in the bodybuilding book.

Of course, I wasn't in possession of the dumbbells and pulleys recommended by Mr. Sandow. Although I didn't need it, I bought a sack of flour instead, which I could barely lift. I would have preferred a bag of sugar—which I did need—but with war rations, sugar was scarce. One advantage of the flour sack was if times got really tough, I could sew the fabric into a dress like they did in the wilds of North America. I hoped it wouldn't come to that as my flour sack was a ghastly shade of cement gray, sure to turn my complexion the color of stale porridge.

Another two weeks went by and no word came from the head office about the assignment. Seeing significant progress from my flour-sack exercises, and eating an extra half tin of biscuits a day, I continued my bodybuilding even though I was sure they'd given the assignment to someone else. Probably to a man. On the other hand, men were almost as scarce as sugar—all of the able-bodied ones having been sent to the Western Front. Many didn't come back. And those who did come back were broken, bent, or barmy from witnessing the carnage of war.

The following Saturday, my day off, I took the train to Charing Cross to volunteer once again at the hospital. Five stories high and a city block long, the hospital was an imposing structure. Its flat, unadorned façade made it look almost two-dimensional. I pushed my way through the crowded walkway, past the dark maw where the ambulances entered into the inside court, and slipped in through a side door. Two flights up, down an endless hallway, and I was at the dispensary, a quiet corner filled with bottles, tonics, and pills, tucked away from the masses of tangled flesh and missing limbs.

In addition to helping repair damaged men, these days I had another motive for going to the hospital. Still hoping I'd get the job spying on the huntsman, I was using my time in the dispensary to learn everything I could about tonics and poisons. The cover story already in place for the agent assigned to the case was a doctor specializing in toxicology.

Whenever there was a lull at the dispensary, I took the opportunity to study the medicines, which stood in neat rows in cabinets lining three of the four walls of the room. My tutor of sorts was a character named Daisy Nelson, a self-proclaimed "cunning woman" and practitioner of white magic, who ran the dispensary and was an expert on chemical tonics along with home remedies and medicinal plants both common and rare.

That afternoon, I was alone, standing next to one of the medicine cabinets, sniffing a bottle of mercury bichloride. I'd read it was colorless, odorless, and highly toxic. It was used to treat syphilis, more fallout of war judging by how many soldiers were suffering the consequences of visits to French *maisons tolérées*. Not quite odorless, the poison had a faint scent of daffodils. I recorked the bottle and carefully set it back on the shelf in the medicine cabinet.

"Planning to poison someone?" A woman's voice came from behind me. "Or do you suffer from the French disease?"

Blimey! I swung around and was face-to-face with the new Mrs. Andrew Cunningham. Her shiny black hair was perfectly coiffed in close curls, and her red lips formed a small heart in the center of her disgustingly symmetrical face. Her uniform accented her post-baby hourglass figure. I pulled my lab coat tight around my flat chest and wallowed in my deficiencies. I was half tempted to grab the mercury and gulp it down.

"I can think of a couple of people who deserve it," I spat out. I didn't specify whether I meant poisoning or syphilis. Either would do. I pushed past her and exited the dispensary. I didn't stop until I was out of sight of the hospital. Directionless and fractured, I stood on the curb shaking. Spitting rain mixed with my tears. I didn't want to go home. But I didn't know where else to go. Without thinking, I headed to the War Office.

On the train, people stared at my sopping wet clothes, but I didn't care.

In a daze, I nearly missed the conductor calling out the Whitehall Station stop. I walked to Horse Guards Avenue and stood across from the imposing building, wondering what to do next. It was unlikely anyone would be in the office and probably the doors were locked. As I crossed the street, a motorcycle swerved to miss me, and in the process sprayed my skirt with mud. Could this day get any worse?

I picked up my pace to avoid getting run over. Taking shelter in the doorway, I considered my options. Since the door was locked and I didn't have a key, I couldn't get inside. Too bad I didn't bring the mercury bichloride with me, then I could just be done with it. I could go throw myself in the Thames. But frankly, after the trek from Charing Cross, I was exhausted. I leaned against the stone wall. I was even too tired to cry.

Looking down at the state of my attire, I decided I'd better go home before someone from the War Office saw me. My boots were wet and the leather was split; my skirt was covered in mud, and my coat was sticking to me. I was shivering from the damp. I took a deep breath and steeled myself for the trip home. I was not looking forward to encountering more ghosts of my dead marriage.

As I turned to go, the door opened and Mr. Montgomery stepped outside. At first, he didn't seem to recognize me. I stared down at my ruined boots, hoping he wouldn't. A sudden rain squall made him hesitate. I peeked up at him, and he glanced in my direction.

"I say, Miss Figg, is that you?"

"Mr. Montgomery—"

"Don't you look a sight." He took my elbow. "Come on, we'd better get you inside for a nice cuppa before you catch your death."

He removed a hefty key ring from his pocket and used one of his dozen keys to unlock the door. "Are you quite all right?"

"A cup of tea would be nice." I could barely force the words out, and they were nearly inaudible at that.

"Come on." He held the door open. "And if the tea doesn't fix you up, I've got some news that will."

I glanced back at him and he smiled.

The bitter black tea revived me a bit. Mr. Montgomery refilled my cup. I added a bit of milk and took a biscuit from the tin when Mr. Montgomery offered it. We were sitting at the little table in the kitchenette behind the planning room. It was a disgusting mess as usual, but I didn't have the energy to tidy up. Anyway, in my present state, I was in no position to criticize a blooming mess.

To my surprise, several men were working at their desks and a few women were manning the telephones. The hushed rhythm of their voices was comforting.

"Don't you take a day off?" I asked.

"The war doesn't take a day off, so neither do I." Mr. Montgomery ate a biscuit in two bites.

My biscuit still sat, untouched, on my saucer. I had no appetite for biscuits or anything else.

"You could have knocked me down with a feather when I got the news." Mr. Montgomery smiled. "The head office has approved my recommendation. You're to take that poor chappy's place at the abbey...you know, following the huntsman."

Stunned, I sat there blinking.

"The cover was already set, I'm afraid, a doctor named Vogel. Don't worry. You'll get intensive training for the next two weeks and then off you go."

I stared at Mr. Montgomery, unable to believe my ears.

"You're to report back to the War Office once a week. If your position is compromised, then they'll find a way to extract you."

I gaped at him, unable to speak.

"That's what you wanted, isn't it?" He had a concerned look on his face.

I nodded. "Yes. Thank you, Mr. Montgomery. You've saved my life."

"You do have a flair for the dramatic, Miss Figg." Mr. Montgomery laughed.

I was deadly serious. The next encounter with my cheating ex or his fertile wife would have pushed me right over the edge.

Chapter Three: Ravenswick Abbey

Two weeks later, after a crash course in espionage—and cutting off my most feminine feature, my beautiful auburn locks—I descended from the train at Wickham Bishops. Suspended above lush pastures and country paths, the platform was so small it could hardly be called a station. A lovely young woman was waiting on the platform. Her slim silhouette against the bright sunshine resembled a burning matchstick. She introduced herself as Lady Mary Elliott.

"My mother-in-law sent me." She took the smaller of my two bags from my hand. "She would have come to welcome you herself, Dr. Vogel, but she's just recovered from a stomach malady, and she still has to prepare the house for a bazaar to benefit the Red Cross."

"I'm sorry to hear she's been ill."

Lady Elliott narrowed her eyes and stared into my face. I vowed my countenance would not betray the fluttering of my heart. *Had she found me out already?* The black beard itched and the bushy eyebrows threatened my lids. I lowered my voice to the limit of its depths. "Is something wrong, Lady Elliott?"

"Please, call me Mary. I know you're here on holiday." Her astonishing emerald eyes transmitted intelligence and warmth. "But I wonder if I might have a word with you about a delicate issue?" She blushed. "Not today, mind you. But whenever you have time."

"Of course." I nodded. "As I'm on holiday and have no schedule whatsoever, I'm at your beck and call." If she wanted me to treat her mother-in-law's sour stomach, I could think of no better cure than fresh ginger root tea.

She smiled and then piloted me out to the car.

"Thanks to my mother-in-law's charitable activities, and my work with the land girls, we get a limited supply of petrol. Our chauffeur was called up, so I'm afraid you've got me instead."

"I could drive if you like," I said, hoping she wouldn't take me up on it. Still, it seemed the manly thing to say.

"Oh no. Don't be silly. Women are just as capable as men, you know."

"Yes, I know." *Don't I just.*

She took the wheel, and I climbed into the passenger's seat.

"You volunteer as a land girl?" I was surprised an aristocratic lady would drive her own car, let alone do manual labor.

"At the abbey, they call me Cinderella of the soil. I have an awfully green thumb. And everyone should do their part, don't you think, Doctor?"

"Indeed, they should."

I was so used to the gray skies and smoky air of London that the brilliant blue sky and sweet country breeze took me by surprise. I'd forgotten what it was like to breathe fresh air. An energy so vibrant and alive emanated from the green pastures and flowered fields, it made me forget the death and destruction of the war.

"So you were delayed? We expected you a month ago," Mary said as she piloted the motor.

For a moment, I gaped at her like a cod out of water trying to remember my cover story. "Yes, well… I had a longtime patient take a turn for the worse, poor dear. I couldn't leave her, you see."

"And how is she now?"

"I'm afraid she died. Poor Nancy Nettles." I sighed. "I did everything I could for her."

"Oh dear. That can't be good for business."

"No, I suppose not."

After that conversation stopper, we both stared straight ahead for the rest of the journey.

We must have traveled about four miles before we reached the village of Wickham Bishops with its green grocer, chemist shop, and, of course, public house. We passed a few ladies wearing hats and pleasant floral country frocks, holding parasols against the bright spring sun as they strolled along the side of the road. It was a nice change from the crowded streets of London and the hustle and bustle of the city. A trip to the country was just what the doctor ordered, if I did say so myself.

As we turned in at the manor house gates, Lady Mary said, "I hope you don't mind. My mother-in-law has invited you to tea. Your cottage is just down the road." She pointed to a row of small stone houses. "It's very quiet down here, Dr. Vogel. I hope you find it restful."

Beyond the massive gates lay the estate grounds, and in the distance, I saw a huge house, which I assumed to be the abbey. My heart sped up.

"I'm sure I will," I said, knowing I was on the adventure of my life, hardly a restful holiday.

"I'll walk you to your cottage after tea. In the meantime, I'll have Earl or Alfred take your cases down," she said as we drew up in front of a fine old house. "I hope you don't mind staying amongst the refugees and other bits and bob my mother-in-law collects."

"Bits and bobs?"

"She's practically running a guest house. She's taken in refugees, wounded soldiers, and famous London doctors on holiday." She smiled.

"Refugees, soldiers, and doctors?" Oh right. She meant me. The so-called famous doctor on holiday.

"The abbey is a wonderful place to rest and recover." She led the way to the grand manor.

The three-story stone building had no less than six chimneys and a railing around the roof. I wondered if past lords of the manor facing financial ruin or scandalous affairs had thrown themselves off and the railing was installed to prevent the current occupants from doing the same. A circular drive was ringed by thick green grass, in the middle of which sat a sculpture of a giant vase. Perhaps before the war, the vase had held some magnificent plant or bush. The entrance to the manor house was crowned with four pillars that started above the ground floor. Judging by the garden, which was in bloom with roses and neatly trimmed shrubbery, the gardeners had not been called up.

A lady in a sailor blouse with a thick black belt who was staring into a fishpond waved as we approached. Lady Mary introduced her as Miss Gwen Bentham, secretary and lady's companion to her mother-in-law.

"I heard you're here to rest. We don't get many famous doctors. Female maladies, is it?" Miss Bentham sighed and took my hand in her slimy gloved palm. She was a fleshy woman in her forties with squishy blue eyes in a moon face and an ample body balancing on tiny booted feet. "All the fish have died. There's no one to clean the pond, you see. I don't suppose you—"

"Only too happy to help, Miss Bentham." I bowed my head slightly in her direction and nonchalantly wiped the pond scum from my hand. The pond water had an oily sheen, and I sincerely hoped I wouldn't have to put my own hand into that muck.

"Are you coming to tea?" Lady Mary asked Miss Bentham.

"You know me. I never miss tea." Miss Bentham chuckled and pulled off her rubber gloves. "Annabelle made a seed cake. And I plan on a generous slice."

With her abundant freckles and doughy face, Miss Bentham resembled a generous slice of seed cake.

I followed Lady Mary around the house to the back garden. With sculpted shrubbery and rows of chrysanthemums giving off an earthy tobacco scent, the back garden was even more impressive than the front. And the back of the house, with its french windows and cheerful shrubs, was less intimidating and more charming.

Under an ancient beech, tea was spread out on a long table covered with a checkered tablecloth. Three men and a woman were seated at the table. They were already tucking into a delicious-looking seed cake. One of the men rose from a wicker chair and wiped his hands on a serviette.

"May I present my husband," Lady Mary Elliott said. "Ernest, this is Dr. Vogel, who is visiting us from London."

Lord Ernest Elliott was handsome in a country squire sort of way. He wore his affability on the sleeve of his well-pressed linen jacket. His handshake belied a man who hadn't done manual labor in his life. He gave me an appraising look as if sizing up an opponent in a game of cricket. I hoped it didn't come to that as I'm hopeless at sports.

"Do you shoot?" he asked.

"I'm afraid not," I said.

"But you ride?"

"No, not really."

"Do you play the ponies?"

I shook my head.

"The War Office has taken over Aintree, but you could come with me to the track at Gatwick if you like." He glanced over at his wife, who was sitting on her hands, teeth clenched. I surmised she did not approve of her husband's visits to the racetrack.

"That's very kind, but I'm not much of a gambler." Of course, coming to Ravenswick dressed as a man, pretending to be a doctor, and chasing a possible German spy, was the gamble of my life.

"Oh well, my wife can entertain you then." He snorted and went back to the table, probably wondering what kind of man didn't shoot, ride, or gamble.

A well-dressed, white-haired woman with the air of a virtuoso, opened a french window and stepped out onto the terrace. I assumed she must be the lady of the house, the dowager countess. From my espionage preparations in London, I'd learned that the dowager, whose Christian name was Edith, had been married to the late Lord Elliott, and had only recently married Mr. Derek Wilkinson. Technically, that meant she was no longer a countess, but her regal countenance and commanding demeanor assured me, she was still very much a countess in her own home.

I assumed the pucker-faced, red-bearded man following her, head bowed, must be Mr. Wilkinson.

"Take the invitations to town when you go, Derek, darling. But first, let me write to Lady Bracegirdle," she said in a commanding voice.

Her husband nodded.

The countess rushed over to me. "You must be Dr. Vogel. I'm so happy you've come to Ravenswick." She nodded toward the man at her side. "Derek darling, this is our new doctor. Doctor, this is my husband Derek Wilkinson."

Staying one step behind his wife, with feigned deference, the bearded man bowed.

"Actually, I'm here on holiday." I returned his bearded bow.

"Yes, I know." The countess extended her limp hand and then turned back to her husband. "Derek darling, will you fetch my shawl?"

Derek darling obeyed like a well-trained dog. Indeed, he had the look of a wirehaired terrier wearing clothes and a gold-rimmed monocle.

Lady Elliott introduced me around the table. The dowager countess's niece, a bright-eyed, freckle-faced, young woman named Lilian Mandrake tossed her cap to the ground and flung herself down on the grass next to the chair of a melancholy man who looked to be in his late thirties, and was introduced as the dowager's younger son, Ian. I knew from my preparations that Lilian Mandrake was the orphaned child of the dowager's younger step-sister, who like a fool had married their gardener's strapping son and then died in childbirth. The beefy gardener had been banished to the hinterlands of Wales.

Now, after seeing them in action, I surmised that the dowager would not allow her youngest son, Ian, to make the same mistake. Although judging from the clandestine caresses passing between Ian and young Lilian as they sat on the grass, heads together, giggling, it was already too late.

Another clean-shaven man of about forty, with a receding hairline and long angular face, sitting legs crossed, wearing a wool suit—in spite of the heat—and fancy Italian lace-ups, rounded out the pretty little party. He was introduced as Lieutenant Clifford Douglas, a wounded soldier just home from the Western Front, and a schoolmate of Lord Elliott's.

I filed each person's name and biography into my mental filing cabinet. "What will you do after the war ends, Lieutenant Douglas?" I asked.

The lieutenant eyed me suspiciously before answering. I instinctively touched my beard to make sure it was still attached. Something about the way he stared made me uneasy. I puffed up my chest and stood with my legs farther apart than necessary to compensate. I adjusted my eyeglasses and cleared my throat with a deep grunt.

The countess gestured for me to sit down. Feeling rather a spectacle standing before the rest of the party, I gladly complied.

"Before the war I worked at Barclays," Lieutenant Douglas said. "But I'm tired of banking. Maybe I'll try something new."

Lady Mary Elliott sat her fork on the table. "Like what?"

"I've always wanted to write."

"You mean for a newspaper?" Lilian asked.

"Promise me you won't laugh."

"I might," Lady Mary Elliott said with a wink as she poured me a cup of tea.

"I'd like to try my hand at writing detective stories." The Lieutenant's thin lips turned up into an embarrassed smile.

"Sir Arthur Conan Doyle or Edgar Allan Poe?" I asked, taking a biscuit from the serving tray.

I was about to take a sip of tea when the lieutenant gave me an odd look. I tucked my little finger into my palm and concentrated on manly slurping.

"You mean Sherlock Holmes or what's-his-name?" He'd stopped mid-bite and held a half-eaten biscuit in the air.

"Dupin." I sipped my tea. "Le Chevalier C. Auguste Dupin. Of course that was before the word detective had been coined."

"I say, aren't you clever." The lieutenant popped the rest of his biscuit into his mouth. "But I want to write true crime."

"Right. Holmes and Dupin weren't real detectives." Lady Mary Elliott stirred her tea with a tiny spoon. "Not like Scotland Yard."

"Perhaps you could join Scotland Yard to get material for your stories," I said, although I couldn't see the tidy man sitting across from me chasing down violent criminals, at least not in those shoes. "Have you tracked criminals before?"

Lieutenant Douglas chuckled. "Well, no. But I've had a lot of practice tracking animals. Tracking criminals can't be so different. You see, years ago, I met a great hunter in South Africa, and he taught me his technique. Only, I plan to apply it to stalking murderers instead of rhinoceroses. I've heard he's convalescing at Ravenswick and I'm hoping to renew our acquaintance."

Aha! Lieutenant Douglas knew the Great White Hunter. I'd have to stick close and see what I could find out. I wondered why the famed hunter was not part of the tea party. Perhaps his manners were too coarse for polite society.

"You think criminals can be tracked down like animals?" I sipped my tea in as manly a fashion as I could muster. "You must have a very low regard for human beings, either that or a high regard for animals. Or do you think all criminals are animals? Even petty pilfering to feed one's family?"

"Well I suppose…" The lieutenant looked flustered. "Perhaps not all criminals."

"Technically, human beings are animals too," Lilian added.

"Jolly good." Lieutenant Douglas smiled. "And they leave tracks just like other animals."

"So you plan to track criminals looking for their paw prints and scat?" I asked playfully.

"Scat." The lieutenant blushed. "Good lord." He gave me an odd look, examining my beard as if *it* were some rare mammal.

"Tell me more about this great hunter and his methods," I said, avoiding eye contact with the unsettling man.

"I guess you could say he's a sort of Sherlock Holmes of the bush. It's a funny story how we met—"

He was interrupted by the appearance of Derek Wilkinson, who had returned, carrying his wife's shawl. He placed it around her shoulders and she patted his hand. Miss Bentham sneered. The rest of the party fell silent. Mr. Wilkinson descended on the tea party like a thick fog. The dowager seemed not to notice the damping effect of her husband. All the gayness of the afternoon dissipated as he installed himself in a basket chair next to his wife.

"Dr. Vogel." Lady Mary's clear voice startled me. "You must know a lot about poison. Toxicology is your specialty, is it not?"

She'd caught me completely off guard. "Why yes, it is. Some poisons are very difficult to detect. And some are remarkably easy to procure. Some are common household chemicals."

"You mean to say, anyone can commit murder?" Lieutenant Douglas asked. "Present company excepted," he said, turning to Lady Mary and then nodding to Miss Mandrake.

"Why except us? Poison, you know, is the weapon of choice for women," Lilian said. "Even *I* know about poisons from working in the dispensary. If I wanted to poison someone, it would be easy."

"Lilian, don't be so morbid!" The countess stared into her teacup for a moment. "Surely you're not capable..." Her voice trailed off.

"Almost anything can be poisonous in the right dosage," I said.

"Everything in moderation, eh?" When Ernest laughed he sounded like a goose taking flight. "Even arsenic?"

"The war is bad enough without talk of poison." The countess let out a disgusted scoff. "I wish someone would poison those warring Huns."

"What about the Saxe-Coburgs?" Ernest asked. "You and our king are descended from warring Huns."

"I thought you were proud of your German ancestry, mother dearest," Ian said in a mocking tone.

"Your mother is a patriot," Derek Wilkinson said, defending his wife.

"Enough talk of war," the countess said abruptly. "Lilian, dear, could you help with the invitations?"

"Of course, Aunt Edith."

When Lilian jumped up, her comportment made me think her position as a dependent was something the benevolent dowager relished, in spite of her terms of endearment toward the girl. It was obvious the orphaned girl was beholden to her aunt.

After the matron and her niece had disappeared into the house, Lady Mary rose from the table.

"I'll show you to your cottage. I'm afraid it's very modest."

"I'm sure it will suit me fine."

We bade farewell to the rest of the party, and Lady Mary led me through the garden out toward the main gates. I admired the rose bushes, wishing I had a green thumb. I was too much of a city girl to grow anything except my hair, which was the only thing I missed about Miss Figg. It was a beautiful day for a walk, and the fresh country air and brilliant sunshine chased away all the dreariness of my life in London.

We were still within earshot of the house when Lord Elliott shouted, "Mary."

We turned to see him chasing after us.

"A damnable inconvenience," he said rushing to catch up. "Gwen's had a row with Derek and she's going."

"What do you mean going?" Lady Mary asked.

"She's leaving. You see—here she is now." Ernest worried a button on his jacket.

Fleshy lips pursed, Miss Bentham stomped up the path carrying a small suitcase.

"I've told him off!" She set her case down. Her flushed cheeks and damp eyes suggested a jealous lover rather than a mere ladies' companion.

"My dear Gwen," Lady Mary cried. "You can't go!"

Miss Bentham's jowls wobbled as she shook her head. "I warned him. He's just after her money. A gold miner, that's what he is."

"You said that to his face?" Ernest asked, a sly smile spreading across his lips.

"I don't trust that man as far as I can throw him." Miss Bentham shook her head. "Either he goes or I do."

Sounded familiar. Not so long ago, I gave the same ultimatum to Andrew.

Miss Bentham picked up her suitcase and took off down the path. We stood staring after her.

"Why not wait until morning?" Lady Mary called after her.

Without stopping or turning back, the portly woman gave a dismissive wave.

Ernest started after her, and Lady Mary and I followed. By this time, Lieutenant Douglas had joined us.

At the gate, Miss Bentham turned back and said, "Please look after poor gullible Edith. The cad only married her for her money." Then she did an about face and marched out the gate.

"She's right, you know," Ernest said with a sigh. "Wilkinson is just after

Mutti's fortune, which rightfully belongs to me. After all, it was my father's."
Ernest shook his head ruefully. "Why he left everything to Mutti, I'll never
know. It's not right. The son should inherit. The fortune must go with the
title. Otherwise, how can I be expected to manage Ravenswick?"

Yes, and thirty-five years ago, wives were considered their husband's
property. I thought it rather brave of the late Lord to leave everything to his
wife.

Ernest excused himself and went back to the house. Lady Mary, Lieutenant
Douglas, and I continued on the path through the plantation toward the
cottages. Scattered clouds dotted the sky and more gathered on the horizon.
The few clouds were so low they cast great round shadows that danced
across the fields.

We came upon a group of charming stone cottages at the edge of the estate.
They formed a neat line officially separating the estate from the village.

"Who lives here?" I asked.

"My mother-in-law is hosting several refugees and wounded soldiers on
the estate."

"Very generous of her." I wondered where she'd put the Great White
Hunter. Captain Douglas confirmed the huntsman was staying at
Ravenswick Abbey.

"Yes, she is very generous," Lady Mary Elliott said in a rueful tone.

"You know they've had it damned difficult with the Germans using
Belgium as a welcome mat for France," Lieutenant Douglas said. "This war
is horrid for all of us." He touched his leg. His limp was barely discernible.

"Indeed," I said, wondering about what was happening at the War Office.
Being a spy was jolly exciting but a bit nerve-racking.

As Lady Mary opened the wooden door to my cottage, a strapping figure
of a man exited the cottage next door and tipped his hat when he saw us.
Thick sheepdog locks fell over his handsome forehead and he jerked his
head to move them back into place.

"Is that one of the refugees?" I asked, although I recognized him instantly
from the photograph in the newspaper, the famous huntsman with his broad
chest, pencil mustache waxed to perfection, oversized tweed riding jacket,

swagger stick, and knee-high black boots.

With his strong nose in the air, the Great White Hunter brushed imaginary dust from his sleeve and replaced his slouch hat on top of his ample head of dark hair.

I peered at the chunky gold ring on his pinky finger, wondering what the insignia meant. Was it a tiger?

"No, that's a wounded war hero, Fredrick Fredricks. He's a war correspondent now," Lady Mary said. "A dashed brave one too."

"Why, I say!" Lieutenant Douglas said, rushing up to the resident war hero. "If it isn't my old hunting partner."

Fredricks blanched. "Do I know you?"

Lieutenant Douglas laughed. "Why Fredricks, it's me, Clifford Douglas."

"*Ma foi!*" the swarthy man said, coming toward us. "I didn't recognize you. Of course, Clifford." He gave his friend's hand a hearty shake. "*Quelle surprise!*"

Had the War Office gotten it wrong? Was Fredricks actually French and not from the South African Republic?

"I'd heard you were here," Lieutenant Douglas said.

"Madame Elliott," the man said, bowing gallantly to Lady Mary.

He turned to me. "Permit me to introduce myself."

"I know who you are," I said, mustering my courage. "You're Fredricks, the famous big game hunter and reporter for the New York Herald."

"*Oui, Monsieur.* That's me." He smiled broadly, both pointy edges of his mustache turning up. "I'm flattered that my reputation precedes me. My friends call me Apollo."

"I bet they do," I said under my breath, trying to avoid staring at the smooth tanned skin revealed by his open shirt collar.

He held out his meaty palm as if it were a cricket bat.

I didn't know whether to duck or shake it.

"Fredricks and I met hunting elephants in Africa." Lieutenant Douglas said.

Yes, he'd already regaled us with the story of his hunting prowess over tea. I must say, hearing the gory details quite ruined my appetite.

"Fredricks is the greatest big game tracker in the world," the lieutenant continued. "Why, once, he—"

Fredricks interrupted him with a hearty slap on the shoulder. "I'm a reporter now. A lowly war correspondent, just continuing to do my part after my injury in the battle of the Somme." He cradled his wounded arm like a baby. "And I'm sure these good people don't want to hear about our exploits in the barren plains of Africa." He turned to Lady Mary. "Our stories of heathen cannibals are not fit for the delicate ears of such a beautiful lady." He bowed again to Lady Mary.

The way he ogled Lady Mary turned my stomach.

He turned to me. "I've actually made a bit of a name for myself in America as an investigative journalist."

From what I'd heard at the War Office, American neutrality had protected correspondents from the harsh censorship of the British and French press. Now that they had entered the war too, I expect that had changed.

The way the huntsman looked me up and down as he spoke, made my blood run cold. I knew I'd better get away from his keen gaze as quickly as possible. I felt as if he could see right through me. I shook his hand again with a firm grip, then ducked into my cottage and resolved to watch the eagle-eyed hunter from a safe distance.

Chapter Four: Foul Play

The next few days, I settled in and took the lay of the land. Trying not to arouse suspicions, I chatted up the village merchants about the presence of the Belgian refugees and the dowager's "other guests," hoping one of them would tell me something about the Great White Hunter.

Young Mr. Sage at the chemist shop was more than happy to tell me about the expensive mustache pomades the "over-sized frog" asked him to special order, and the girl at the cash desk at the greengrocer told of the "Aussie's" fondness for sweets. Another shop girl practically swooned, insisting the handsome stranger was an American film star. There seemed to be sufficient confusion over Fredrick Fredrick's origins to make it difficult to glean much information from the townspeople.

The rest of the week passed pleasantly with Lady Mary visiting me daily. She invited me to the manor house for dinner, and we enjoyed leisurely walks through wooded paths. As long as we avoided the heat of midday, we had lovely strolls through the vast estate, which included the beautiful gardens surrounding the manor house, hardwood forests outside the gardens, and then farmlands beyond the forests.

Given my cover as a doctor specializing in poisons and female maladies, Lady Mary confided in me about her troubled marriage. She complained about her husband's interest in a certain recently widowed shepherd's wife, reportedly a robust beauty. Although she admitted marrying Ernest Elliott more to escape the confines of her father's suffocating household than for passion, she had grown to love him and didn't want to lose him. In my opinion, her husband's wandering eye seemed more in line with male maladies best cured by poison.

Of course, I kept my opinion to myself, and comforted her with gentle soothing words and recommended a mild bromide sleeping powder available at any chemist. She showed her appreciation by grasping my arm and listening to my made-up stories about my early days as a doctor in North London.

Thanks to the attentions of Lady Mary Elliott, I was happier than I had been since before my divorce. In some ways, our time together reminded me of the halcyon days of Andrew's courtship and the first months of our married life. If I weren't binding my chest and wearing a great itchy beard, I imagined Lady Mary and I could be fast friends.

Early one afternoon, I met Lady Mary on the forest path. She was in a state, her eyes puffy and face blotchy. I suspected she'd been crying.

"What's wrong?" I asked.

She broke down sobbing.

I put my arm around her shaking shoulders. "There, there. It can't be that bad."

Just then a buxom woman with long flowing hair wearing a dusty split skirt galloped past us on a beautiful chestnut horse. I withdrew my arm for fear we'd cause a scandal. I'd almost forgotten I was a man escorting another man's wife along a secluded footpath.

"That's her," Lady Mary whimpered.

"Who?"

"Mrs. Roland, the shepherd's widow. Ernest's mistress." Her whole body was shaking now.

"Her? Why you're ten times more attractive." I took her by the shoulders. "She's coarse and smells of horse manure. I'm sure Ernest would never—"

"Really? Ten times—"

When she looked up at me with those startling eyes, now flooded with tears, for a moment I thought she might kiss me. I released her shoulders and patted her hand.

"Really," I said, starting down the path. I was quite unsettled and nearly tripped over a sycamore root.

"What if I had proof he was having an affair?" Lady Mary wiped her eyes with the backs of her hands.

"What kind of proof?"

"My mother-in-law received a letter. I'm sure it's about Ernest."

"How can you be—"

"I know it. Edith was very upset about it. She and Ernest quarreled. The horrible woman visited the house on the pretense of delivering a basket of fresh-picked chanterelle mushrooms. The nerve!" Lady Mary stomped her little foot into the ground. "It was then that she delivered the letter. She's trying to ruin my marriage and get Ernest for herself." She stared down at a clump of grass.

"I asked to see the letter, but Edith won't let me read it," she continued. "Edith locked it in her handbag and told me it has nothing to do with me." She moved closer and seized my elbow. "But it has everything to do with me. I must see that letter." She looked up at me with desperate eyes. "At the risk of seeming forward, might you help me retrieve it?"

"What? You want me to help you steal a letter?" I nearly laughed out loud.

"The uncertainty is making me crazy. I just want to know. And you're the only one I can trust."

Me, the only one she can trust. In that case, I felt sorry for the poor dear woman. After all, my whole persona was a lie.

"If the letter is addressed to the countess, then you have no right to read it without her permission." I sounded like a fussy schoolmaster.

"I have a right to know if my husband is unfaithful, don't I?"

She had a point. For months before my arrival at Ravenswick, I'd kicked myself every day because I hadn't even suspected my own husband's infidelity. What kind of dupe was I? Could I allow Lady Mary Elliott to suffer the same fate?

"I'll make you a deal," Lady Mary pleaded. "You help me get the letter and I'll tell you everything I know about that ruddy hunter you're always asking about."

I'd almost forgotten I was here to gather information on the huntsman.

Was I that obvious? I'd better be more circumspect in future. I nodded. "What's your plan?"

"Come to the house this evening after dinner, and I'll distract Edith so you can sneak into the study and take the letter from her handbag."

"And how shall I do that?"

"I'll make sure the window is open."

"You want me to crawl through a window?" My voice rose an octave before I caught myself. I cleared my throat loudly.

She shrugged, and a forlorn shadow fell across her pale countenance. I thought she might start to cry again.

"All right. I can't promise. I'll see what I can do." Of all the crazy plans. I couldn't believe I was even considering it. What kind of spell had she cast on me?

Later that evening, I strolled along the dirt path from my cottage to the big house. It was a lovely walk through a meadow with a stand of sycamore near the manor house gate. The sun setting behind it formed a halo of orange and the big house looked majestic. As I approached the circular drive, I glanced around and, seeing no one, I quickened my pace and made my way across the grass to the side of the house. I paced back and forth in front of the study window before darting into the bushes underneath it.

Breathless, I listened for voices. Nothing. Not a sound. I pulled myself up onto the window ledge. My weightlifting had paid off. I swung one leg over. I was just swinging my other leg over when I heard footfalls from inside nearing the study door. I lurched backward and toppled into the shrubbery, slid down, and landed face first in the flowerbed. Blast! Sitting up, I patted my beard and adjusted my clothing. I crawled on all fours through the bushes, glanced around, and then stood up, hoping no one saw my graceless descent, not to mention my illicit ascent.

Wiping mud from my suit, I walked quickly back toward the gates. Double blast! I only had one other suit.

I hadn't gone far when I was intercepted by Derek Wilkinson.

"Why Doctor Vogel!" he said. "What happened to you?"

"I-I-I saw an unusual herb there." I pointed in the vague direction of the garden. "The bell-shaped flower put me in mind of *belladonna*. I was trying to reach it to examine it when I slipped in the mud." I thought of Daisy Nelson's lessons on poisonous plants.

"You'd better come to the house and have a brandy." He strode ahead. With red hair covering his head and chin, and a cranberry striped vest, bright polka-dotted tie, and high-top olive green boots encasing his outsized feet, he resembled a Christmas tree. And I thought I was the one wearing a costume.

"They say nightshade is dangerous, and now I know why." A nervous laugh bubbled up as I followed him.

Wilkinson insisted I accompany him into the house. He led me into the drawing room, where the family had retired for tea.

"I must look a sight. I'm not fit for the drawing room," I said, wiping my forehead with the back of my hand.

"What happened, Doctor?" Lady Mary rushed to my side.

"I'm terribly sorry to impose," I said. "Mr. Wilkinson—"

"Dear me, Vogel, you are a sight." Lord Elliott strolled in from the hall. "Come in. Have some tea and dry off."

I repeated my story about the dangerous herb and everyone laughed—everyone except Lieutenant Douglas, who shot me a nasty look. He seemed to have come to dislike me. I couldn't for the world figure out why.

"I'm afraid I'm a mess," I said, hoping my beard was holding up.

"Oh, I almost forgot," Derek Wilkinson said turning to Lord Elliott. "The fetching Mrs. Roland was around looking for you earlier." A sinister sort of grin made his beady eyes glow.

Poor Lady Mary stared down at her hands folded in her lap.

Lord Elliott cleared his throat. "I wonder whatever for." He fumbled with his teacup.

"Lilian," the countess called from the hall.

The girl jumped up and dashed out.

"Can you bring my handbag, dearest? I don't feel well. I'm going to bed." Holding her tea cup, the countess started up the stairs. "Bring my shawl. I'm freezing."

"Certainly, Aunt Edith." Lilian followed behind her.

She was freezing? It was beastly hot for only the first week in May. Perhaps she had the chills. Lady Mary had mentioned her mother-in-law had been ill. I hope I wasn't called upon for medical advice.

I was about to take my leave when Lady Mary pulled me aside and whispered, "Please come back tonight. I'll get her handbag. You meet me in front just before dawn."

I tried to protest, but I didn't want to make a scene.

"I can't bear it alone," she said, her lip trembling.

I nodded.

As I ducked into my cottage, I had the sensation of being watched. The huntsman's cottage was next door, and I had the distinct impression that the Great White Hunter was watching me like a hawk from his first-floor window, which looked down at my stoop. I quickly went inside, shut the door, and exhaled a sigh of relief. Finally, I was alone and could go back to being plain old Fiona Figg instead of a fancy London doctor whose face was covered in spirit gum.

The charming stone cottages were scattered at odd angles as if someone had thrown them like dice. With just one room, mine was the smallest of the lot. Dark wooden beams and whitewashed stucco walls made a cozy retreat from the anxiety of playing my part. And given I took at least one meal a day at the big house, my tiny kitchen with its ancient gas stove was perfect for making a cup of tea. My only complaint was the heat. Unless I opened my front door, in the afternoons my room was stifling.

Relieved to be back inside what had become my own little sanctuary, I changed into clean clothes and then removed my beard. Every time I took the blasted thing off, a layer of skin went with it. Underneath, my face was so red with rash I looked like a radish. No matter how slowly I pulled it off, it hurt like the dickens. I carefully washed my irritated face and applied Pond's Extract Vanishing Cream. My experience with the muddy ponds of Ravenswick Abbey almost made me wish I could vanish back into my own life in London.

Sleeping with one eye open, I lay on my bed with my head at an angle to see the clock on the mantel. I watched the arms slowly tick off the time and again wondered if the countess was quite well.

I must have fallen asleep because the sound of a dog barking woke me shortly after four. I dragged myself out of bed and reluctantly glued my beard back in place. I replaced my spectacles, which were nothing but clear glass. I placed my straw boater on top of my head and then set out for the manor house at a good clip. I wasn't used to wandering about before dawn. Luckily, there was a full moon. By the time I reached the gate, I was panting, whether from exertion or fright I couldn't say.

To my surprise, a car was leaving the manor house gate. I jumped back to avoid getting run over. The driver stopped, rolled down the window, and shouted, "Hurry. It's the countess. She's having some kind of fit. I'm off to get Dr. Booth."

I ran to the house as fast as I could. Although I wasn't a real doctor, maybe I could be of use. I had worked in a hospital after all.

The front door was wide open. I dashed inside. Voices drifted down from an upper-floor. I took the stairs two at a time and followed the voices to a bedroom at the end of the hall.

Clad in nightclothes and robes, the entire family—except for Mr. Wilkinson—was gathered around the dowager's bed.

I strode to her bedside. The front of her nightgown was covered in dark stains, as were her bedcovers, and her body was bowed in convulsion. I stared down at her, helpless to do anything.

Her eyes glued to me, she cried out, "Der... Der..."

"Derek?" I asked.

"Derspitzel," she gasped and then she fell back onto the bed and began convulsing again. Was she calling for Derek or trying to tell me something?

"Help me move her to the floor," I said to one of the servants. Again, I was glad for my bodybuilding. She was a substantial woman.

"Bring me those pillows," I shouted at another servant.

I waved at the onlookers to give us some space. The dowager's body went rigid for a second and then limp as an empty glove.

Using the Silvester method of artificial respiration, I elevated her shoulders and allowed her head to drop backward. As I knelt behind her head and grasped her wrists, I smelled the sour scent of daffodils mixed with the acrid smell of vomit. Crossing her wrists over her lower chest, I rocked forward, pressing on her chest and then backward, stretching her arms outward and upward. I counted to myself, making sure to repeat the cycle twelve times per minute. After several minutes, I stopped. It was no use. She was dead.

I glanced up at the terrified family and shook my head.

Buried faces and muted sobs met my gaze.

"Help me get the countess back on the bed," I ordered the servants.

Just then, Dr. Booth, the dowager's own doctor, rushed in and began fussing over the old woman. A plainspoken and kind little man, I'd met him several times while taking tea at the house. He obviously was very close to the countess. The blood drained from his face and his lip quivered as he stared down at her lifeless form.

"Oh dear. Oh dear. Oh dear," Dr. Booth whispered. "She had a weak heart. I told her to slow down, but she cared more for others than for herself." He looked as though he would break down at any minute. "Her heart finally gave out."

"I don't think it was her heart," I said.

Dr. Booth blinked. The others huddled nearby, mouths agape.

"Perhaps someone should make tea." I turned to Lord Elliott. "It's been a shock, especially for the ladies." As one of the ladies, I knew it had been a shock for me.

"Of course." Lord Elliott stretched out his arm and led the family out into the hall, leaving me alone with Dr. Booth.

"The countess has been poisoned," I said. "She displayed the classic symptoms of a toxic dose of mercury bichloride." I glanced around the room. A tea cup was overturned on the floor. "I suspect it may have been in her tea." I pointed at a brown stain on her gown and the carpet. I had conducted a thorough study of all known poisons to prepare myself for my assignment as an expert in poison, and this case was clearly one of poisoning, and given the violent nature of her fit, most likely mercury bichloride.

"Vomiting is also consistent with cardiac arrest." Dr. Booth was wringing his hands. "It could have been her heart. Poor dear woman."

"She suffered a very particular kind of convulsion before she died, a seizure more in line with poisoning than heart attack." I knelt down next to the stain on the carpet. "It will be difficult to get a sample of the tea. But we should perform a postmortem to confirm my hypothesis." By we, I meant Dr. Booth. I was ready to do what it took to maintain the integrity of my cover, and I had worked in the morgue at the hospital, but actually performing a postmortem was going a bit too far, even for me.

"Yes, under the circumstances, I suppose you're right," Dr. Booth said. "Poor dear lady." He wiped at his eyes with his handkerchief.

I surveyed the room for any more clues as to how the countess had been poisoned. A saucepan sat on the chest of drawers near the fireplace. It was half-full. I sniffed the milky amber liquid. Milk and rum.

"I should get a sample of this milk." Obviously, the countess was not a teetotaler. In fact, if I were a betting man—or any kind of man—I'd say she liked a regular nip.

I slipped a small vial from my waistcoat pocket, dipped its dropper in the liquid, and depressed its black bulb to suck the milk into the dropper. Given my recent study of poisons, I always carried a spare vial or two in case I ran into an interesting plant specimen.

The fireplace reminded me of the dowager's chill, and I stooped down to examine the ashes. A corner of torn paper caught my eye. I debated whether or not to remove it. We would certainly have to call the police. Perhaps even the famous huntsman turned newsman would get involved. I'd best leave undisturbed what was surely a murder scene.

I bent closer to examine the bit of paper without touching it. I held my breath to avoid the acrid smell of the fireplace. The paper was torn into such small bits that I could barely make out the word *Will* in bold letters on one scrap of the thick paper. Curious. The countess made a point of telling us at tea not a scrap of paper was wasted. Yet, she had ripped up a perfectly good piece of paper.

"What is it?" Dr. Booth asked.

"Nothing," I said and stood up. "We should tell the others of our suspicions. We will need to notify the police."

"The police!" Dr. Booth looked insulted. "Certainly we can spare the family scandal on top of tragedy."

"Under the circumstances, I don't see how," I said. "The countess has been murdered."

"Poor dear lady," Dr. Booth murmured, wringing his hands.

"You go down and tell the family. I'll be right behind you."

I patrolled the rest of the bedroom as quickly as I could. The only other items of interest were a small medicine bottle and a box of Ryno's Hay Fever and Catarrh Remedy, both in the washstand drawer. Without touching anything, I bent to examine them. I sniffed the bottle, which had a slight bitter smell. I could see through the blue glass the medicine bottle was almost empty except for two fingers of cloudy liquid and crystals settled at the bottom, and I dared not sniff the Ryno's Remedy, which I knew from my days at the dispensary was almost pure cocaine snuff.

I was about to exit the death chamber when I saw it. The dowager's handbag. I thought of the letter Lady Mary Elliott had asked me to retrieve. Had she taken it already? She wouldn't have murdered her mother-in-law to get it, would she? I slipped my handkerchief from my pocket and turned the tiny key in the lock. The only contents were a neatly folded letter and an ornate corked bottle. I slipped the small bottle into my waistcoat pocket and unfolded the stationary.

Just as I was about to read it, Dr. Booth called out from the hallway. "Vogel, are you coming?"

"Yes, I'll be right there." I didn't have time to read it, and I couldn't keep it on me. I glanced around the room. A gorgeous caramel-colored hat with a birdcage veil resting on a hat stand caught my eye. Then I got an idea. I carefully folded the letter into a tight accordion and tucked it inside the hat's luscious velvet band. It should be safe there until I could get back and read the letter myself. I didn't want Lady Mary to see it until I knew its contents. No doubt she was already distressed after the shock of her mother-in-law's death.

To ensure the murder scene wasn't disturbed, I locked both adjoining doors, placed the keys in my waistcoat pocket, and then shut the main door and locked it on my way out.

Dr. Booth was waiting for me.

"What have you been up to?" he asked.

"Just looking for clues as to how the poison was administered. I didn't touch anything, though," I assured him. Then I remembered the bottle in my pocket. Blast! It could very well be the damning evidence, but I couldn't very well replace it now with Booth watching me. I'd have to sneak back and replace it later... after I'd examined it, of course.

The family was solemnly assembled downstairs in the drawing room, the very room where just the night before we'd enjoyed a laugh together.

"Lord Elliott," Dr. Booth said. "I recommend an autopsy."

"Why?" Lord Elliott sucked in his breath and grimaced as if he'd been pricked by a pin.

"Surely it's natural causes," Ian said. He was sitting in the window seat, fiddling with a tassel on the curtains.

"Probably not," I said.

"You can't think someone..." Lord Elliott's voice trailed off.

"Under the circumstances, it would be best to do a postmortem, so we could issue a proper death certificate," I said. Technically, of course, I couldn't issue a death certificate under any circumstances.

Lord Elliott bent his head and gave a slight nod.

"You should prepare yourselves for the police." Dr. Booth held his hat in both hands, gently caressing the band with his thumb.

"Why do we need the police?" Lady Mary asked, her voice trembling. "Wasn't it her heart?"

"I fear the countess has been poisoned," I said, glancing at Dr. Booth. There was no reason to be coy.

"Poisoned!" Lady Mary gasped. "Oh no!" Tears pooled in her eyes and she put both hands over her mouth.

"Rubbish," cried Ian. "You see poison everywhere, Vogel. Dr. Booth had no idea of poison until you put it into his mind. Mother had a heart attack, and that's the end of it."

I was surprised by Ian's reaction. Usually so quiet and unassuming, I'd never seen him so worked up.

"The postmortem will tell us soon enough," I said, drawing the bedroom keys from my pocket and handing them to Lord Elliott. "I've locked the countess, er, Mrs. Wilkinson's, rooms until the police inspect the premises."

"Police? Come on, old boy," Ernest said. "You can't really suspect one of us killed Mutti?"

"Where is Mr. Wilkinson?" I asked. "Gwen Bentham warned us about him."

"Indeed," Ernest said. "If anyone poisoned Mutti, it was that dodgy cad."

"Is there a will?" I asked, thinking it might give us a clue as to the murderer.

"How can you talk of such things at a time like this!" Ian stormed out of the room, and Lilian ran after him.

"I suppose I'm to inherit everything." Lord Elliott sighed. "At least that was father's wish. Heavens, does that make me a suspect?"

"What about calling on the famous investigative journalist staying at your cottages?" I asked, hoping I'd get to see him in action. "Perhaps he could get to the bottom of this."

"You mean call in a reporter?" Lord Elliott looked incredulous. "Are you mad?"

At that, I took my cue and bid them farewell.

Chapter Five: The Great White Hunter

For the next three days, the Great White Hunter was constantly about the manor investigating the murder and interviewing the staff. I made myself scarce for fear he'd find me out. It wasn't just his reputation that had me worried. I'd seen something in his eyes the day we met, a discerning flash of brilliance, which threatened to reveal me as a fraud.

The last thing I wanted was for the astute reporter to interview me. If I thought I could get away with it, I would very much like to interview him. I'd heard about the "brilliant hunter and war hero" from his friend Lieutenant Douglas, who was a great talker and loved to tell stories and waffle on about how he'd first met "the brilliant Fredrick Fredricks." *What kind of name is Fredrick Fredricks?* It had to be a false name… more evidence he was really a spy.

I came away from my one-sided conversations with the lieutenant having learned more than I wanted to know about his trips to Africa and his exploits in the trenches, but very little about his famous friend—except that "Apollo" Fredricks had helped President Theodore Roosevelt bag a lion. Thoroughly disgusting, if you asked me. To top it off, I still had the feeling Lieutenant Douglas disliked me. He practically held his nose every time I approached.

Every evening back at my cottage, I wrote notes about what I'd learned during the day, which so far wasn't much. I'd purchased a special leather-bound notebook and a new fountain pen before I'd left London. I loved the feel of the cool smooth leather in my hands. And the ink flowed onto the page like silk.

Tonight, I reviewed my notes in anticipation of my weekly report, which was due in two days. Given I was avoiding the manor house and hadn't seen much of the Great White Hunter or Lord and Lady Elliott, I hadn't much to add to my notebook. Pen in hand, I stared at the blank page. I had to get more information on the huntsman, or the War Office might take me off the case. I couldn't go back to my life in London...at least, not yet. The country air and my renewed sense of purpose were reviving my spirits. Returning now would just bring me back to that dark place of despair over Andrew's affair.

I decided to review everything I'd discovered about Fredrick Fredricks so far. In the margins, I would add my speculations and conclusions.

Fredrick Fredricks seemed completely out of his element living amongst the Belgian refugees, most of whom were down on their luck and availed themselves of the charity of women like the countess. They'd arrived in England with only the clothes on their backs and whatever they could carry in a knapsack. Given the way he dressed, the newsman, on the other hand, must have had a duke's closet full of expensive hunting outfits and evening wear. Even the most successful big game hunter and war correspondent couldn't afford Mr. Fredricks's wealthy lifestyle...imported chocolates, expensive mustache pomades, ivory and gold handled swagger sticks. Some people in Wickham Bishops speculated he was South African or Australian royalty disguised as a newspaper reporter. Others, less generous, surmised he must be a German spy. Most agreed he was well mannered and exceedingly charming, especially with the ladies, if also annoyingly perceptive.

In the past two days, sequestered in my cottage, and living amongst the refugees, I had a chance to interview several of them. To my surprise, all the women loved Fredricks, who spoke to them in their native languages, whether French or Flemish. He lent them money while they were waiting to get work at the nearby munitions plant. With so many of our own men fighting at the Front, the war effort at home needed any and all willing laborers.

I thought of the Lord of the Admiralty, Winston Churchill, writing "Belgians ought to stay there and eat up continental food and occupy German policy attention...This is no time for charity." Fortunately, the public disagreed. At the start of the war, when the refugees first fled the Germans, wealthy English families wanted to take in the "plucky little Belgians" who were treated like exotic pets and put on display as evidence of British patriotism. At first, refugees from the "rape of Belgium" were welcomed with biscuits and tea. Now in 1917, after almost three long years of war, it seemed they'd worn out their welcome.

I admired the countess for continuing to take in refugees at a time when the tide of public sentiment was changing and refugees were seen as lazy at best or spies at worst. Riots had broken out in factories where locals claimed refugees lived in luxury while they suffered.

Somehow, the Great White Hunter remained above all the turmoil. With his indistinct accent, he was sometimes mistaken for a wealthy French or Italian gentleman, and at other times an American cowboy or Australian bush baron. The Englishwomen swooned over him. I had to admit, he was a handsome devil. And if the English gentlemen treated him with resentment, it was not for being a foreigner—if he was a foreigner—It was for being a bombastic braggard.

Dilly Knox was right. Great White Hunter, my eye. Indeed the sobriquet alone set my teeth on edge.

I was finishing up my notes when there was a knock on my door. Perhaps the Great White Hunter had come to interview me. My heart raced as I went to the door. I was about to open it when my hands flew to my chin. My beard! I'd almost forgotten I wasn't wearing it. I rushed to my dressing table, applied the glue and the beard, patted it into place, adjusted my spectacles, and took a deep breath.

To my relief, Lady Mary Elliott stood on the stoop. She visited more often these days than she had before the murder. Her forlorn countenance warned me something was wrong. She asked if we might go for a walk, so I fetched my hat and off we went.

"Has that nosy reporter found out who poisoned the countess?" I asked. She shook her head.

Every time I mentioned poison, Lady Mary flushed and went silent. I wondered once again if she had poisoned the old lady to get the letter. With that ruddy newspaper reporter constantly about, I hadn't gotten back to the dowager's bedroom to retrieve the letter from the hatband. And the bottle! Having given up wearing a waistcoat in this heat, I'd completely forgotten about the evidence tucked into my waistcoat pocket. What a fool. That bottle could have contained the deadly poison. I needed to have it analyzed as soon as possible.

"Is something wrong, Doctor?" Lady Mary asked.

I shook my head. I wasn't about to tell Lady Mary about the letter until I'd read it and could help her take it in. If her husband was cheating on her, and the letter was proof of it, she'd need a friend, which I knew better than anyone.

Lady Mary didn't want to talk about the murder, and so we walked in silence. I admired the countryside with its lush green meadows and wildflowers in bloom. In the distance, a wood pigeon cooed its lamentation, joining the symphony of buzzing, whistling, and twittering of its fellow rural inhabitants. Again, I was struck by the contrast with the city's blaring horns and clacking hooves.

Finally, I broke the silence. "Who would want to kill the countess?"

"It's my fault," she said. Overcome with emotion, she stopped and buried her face in her hands.

"Why do you say that?" I sincerely hoped she wasn't confessing to the murder of her mother-in-law. I'd come to like her a great deal, and I'd hate to see her hanged.

"I made the tea, you see," she said.

"Yes, but that doesn't mean you poisoned her." I put my hand on her shoulder. "Did you?"

"Not intentionally," she whispered.

Did she accidentally poison her mother-in-law? I raised my glued-on eyebrows.

"Go on," I said encouragingly.

"Well, I added sleeping powders to her tea so I could take the letter after she went to sleep." She started sobbing. "I killed her—"

"Now, now, don't cry. My conjecture is the countess was poisoned with mercury bichloride, and in any case, not sleeping powder. The tea didn't kill her." I gently shook her shoulder. "*You* didn't kill her." I thought again of the bottle in my waistcoat pocket, and longed to return to my cottage to examine it properly.

"It was horrible, Doctor." She sobbed. "She was screaming and writhing in pain."

"There, there, it's not your fault." I surmised Lady Mary Elliott had found the countess in the throes of the poison when she went to retrieve the letter just before dawn.

"Elliott thinks Derek did it," Lady Mary said, sniffling. "He and Gwen think Derek married Edith for her money and now has disposed of her to get it."

"Won't everything go to Elliott and Ian now that the Countess is dead?" If Derek stood to inherit, that would be motive enough. Where was he the night of the murder? Had he poisoned his wife and flown the coop? Were his wife's dying words a declaration of love or an accusation? "Has her solicitor read the will?"

"That's just it. There's a rumor Edith made a new will favoring Derek after…" Her voice broke off. She continued in a whisper. "Receiving the letter from Mrs. Randall."

"You mean she cut Lord Elliott out of her will for his…" I tried to think of a delicate way of saying infidelity, dalliance, or betrayal, but I couldn't. If she had made a new will, then Derek Wilkinson had a motive. Indeed, it occurred to me that Derek Wilkinson had been the one spreading the gossip about an intrigue between Mrs. Randall and Lord Elliott. Perhaps he planted the poisonous seeds in his wife's mind to turn her against her oldest son.

"Mr. Fredricks has been snooping all through the house, interviewing the staff and everyone. He even questioned me."

"And what has the famous reporter found out?" I was dying to know. I only wished I could see him in action. "They say he is a student of human nature whose method is to dissect the human heart the same way he would dissect the organs of any other animal."

"This morning he stormed past me like a tornado. He's really a brash fellow."

I tried to imagine the Great White Hunter as a tornado, but a tepid squall was the best I could do. "What upset him?"

"From what I hear from Ernest, who gets most of his information from Lieutenant Douglas, originally Mr. Fredricks found the handbag locked and pocketed the key. Only now it turns out someone has forced the lock and the handbag is empty."

I gaped at her. "What?"

"It wasn't me," she said. "I did go to get the letter, but Edith started having that frightful fit and it scared me and I dropped my candle. Luckily the carpet didn't catch fire. Then I hurried into Lilian's room. After that, everything's a blur."

Someone had tampered with the handbag after I'd taken its contents. Were they after the letter or the bottle? Perhaps the bottle contained the deadly poison. Or, maybe the letter was more important than I'd realized. I was tempted to tell Lady Mary about the letter hidden in the hatband but restrained myself. It wouldn't do to have her sneak back into the bedroom to retrieve it and then find herself in a faint.

"What else did Mr. Fredricks find?"

"Well, Ernest says he made quite a scene about a piece of paper in the fireplace. He seems to think it was a new will Edith had just made out and the murderer destroyed it."

"A new will?" That explains the word "will" I saw on a torn corner. *But why would she make a new will, and who knew she had done so?* "And her existing will?" I asked.

"Apparently, she had recently drawn up a will leaving the house to Ernest and her fortune to Derek Wilkinson!"

"So Wilkinson had a motive. Did he have the means, I wonder?"

"Haven't you heard?" Her face lit up. "Mr. Sage from the chemist shop says Derek purchased strychnine to poison the stray cats. He signed for it and everything."

Poisoning stray cats. What a disgusting fellow.

"Strychnine?" I could have sworn the symptoms were those of mercury bichloride poisoning. "Is that what the postmortem revealed?"

"Yes. She had strychnine in her blood." She kicked at a rock with her small booted foot.

I caught myself about to scratch at my beard and diverted my hand to my ear. "Wilkinson signed for strychnine, you say? That's very convenient, isn't it?"

"What do you mean?"

"Let's say Derek Wilkinson goes to the trouble to poison his wife with strychnine…in some devious way that delays the effects so he will be out of the house. Very clever. But that same clever man openly buys strychnine and signs for it? Seems unlikely, doesn't it?"

"Maybe he didn't think anyone would find out."

"With that great red beard, gold monocle, and striped waistcoat?" I stroked my own great black beard. "No, he was sure to be noticed. And signing the registry is as good as a confession. It just doesn't make sense."

"If he killed her, he should hang for it." Her voice rose.

"In my opinion, he should hang for poisoning stray cats, but will he?"

"Cats are one thing, a human being is entirely another." She looked indignant. "If he's guilty of murder, he should be punished."

"Agreed."

The thought crossed my mind, if Wilkinson was out of the way, Ernest would inherit everything. Lady Mary had always been eager to get out from under her mother-in-law's thumb. No, Lady Mary wouldn't have poisoned her mother-in-law and tried to pin it on Wilkinson… now I was imagining things.

"Does he want to get caught?" I asked, more to myself than Lady Mary.

"Who wants to get caught?" she asked, a puzzled look on her face.

"Never mind. Tell me more about Mr. Fredricks's findings."

"He suspects some foul play with the tea, and Lieutenant Douglas suspects the milk. They seem to have some competition going to see who can solve the case. It's quite funny, really." She chuckled.

"We know the tea was tampered with, do we not?" I asked, giving her a knowing smile.

She blushed. "I suppose we do." She stopped and gazed out at the cool glades. Even the chirping of the birds was faint and subdued. "I have a confession," she said suddenly. "I also put sleeping powders into Lilian's tea. After Edith died, I ran back to the drawing room, retrieved Lilian's cup and dropped it into that hideous Japanese vase in the hallway."

I couldn't believe my ears. This lovely lady was capable of much more than I'd given her credit for. "Did you also throw the dowager's cup on the floor?"

"No. I assumed Edith dropped it when she had the fit."

"Interesting. As I recall, it was about eight in the evening when she went up with her tea and it wasn't until just before dawn the next morning when you found her suffering the effects of the poison." I scratched at my beard.

Mercury bichloride in toxic doses was a quick acting poison. So was strychnine. Yet the countess succumbed just after five in the morning. Had the countess been unable to sleep and gotten up to make herself some poisoned warm milk? Or had the tea been the offending medium and for some unknown reason it took several hours for the poison to take effect? Then again, perhaps the murderer had administered the poison by some other means entirely. Or, maybe the poison was neither mercury bichloride, nor strychnine, but something else. I thought of the cordial bottle I'd collected from the dowager's handbag. Could it have contained the poison?

"You should really just cut that thing off if it bothers you so much," Lady Mary said with a wry smile. "You'd look nice clean shaven. You have a handsome face."

No one had ever told me I had a handsome face, or even a pretty one. Now here I was, dressed as a man, wearing a beard and bushy brows, with a married woman telling me I had a handsome face. I stared at my boots. What would a real man do in this situation? I dared not think...

I turned us around and headed back in the direction of my cottage. We'd been so engrossed in our conversation I hadn't noticed how far we'd walked.

We were passing by the Roland farm, the last place Lady Mary needed to be. As I guided her back in the other direction, in the distance I noticed two figures standing beside the Roland's barn. One tall hourglass silhouette and one pyramid of manhood. There was no doubt. It was Mrs. Roland and the Great White Hunter.

What did he want with Mrs. Roland? What could she possibly know about the murder or the murderer? If Ernest was having an affair with the shepherd's widow, could that be a motive for killing his mother? Perhaps he wanted a divorce and needed money. He did play the ponies, after all. Presumably "Mutti" wouldn't give him an allowance to divorce Lady Mary and marry another woman, especially not one of her tenants' widows. Is it possible the mercury bichloride belonged to Ernest, who contracted "the French disease" from his philandering? I quickened my pace, hoping Lady Mary didn't notice her rival.

"Did Lord Elliott know about this new will leaving the fortune to Derek?" I asked.

"Oh no. It came as a great surprise to all of us."

"Ernest thought he would inherit everything?"

"That's what his father wanted. The earl left the house and the fortune to Edith on the understanding it would be passed to Ernest when she died."

"What about Ian? Was he to be cut out entirely?" That hardly seemed fair. Then again, English entitlements had nothing to do with justice, but only with wealthy men maintaining their privilege. What was astounding was the elder Lord Elliott left his entire estate to his wife and not to his sons. Not so very long ago, that would have been illegal. At least some things were changing for the better.

"Ian is convinced his mother died of natural causes. He studied medicine, you know." She stopped on the path and turned to me. "Not to contradict you, dear friend, but could he be right?"

I shook my head. Had she forgotten she'd told me the postmortem confirmed the countess was poisoned?

"Did Ian stand to benefit from the dowager's death?"

"Ian was to inherit a handsome sum. But the most recent will leaves the house to Ernest and the fortune to that interloper, Derek. Ian gets only a small allowance." She shook her head. "And then there's Lilian."

"What about Lilian?"

"Well, Edith didn't approve of Ian marrying Lilian." She tightened her lips. "In fact, she downright forbade it. Said she'd cut them both off without a penny."

"Really?" So Lilian and Ian had their own reasons for wishing the countess out of the way.

"She wanted Ian to marry into money. Poor Lilian's parents left her very little. That's why Edith took her in."

"Did Ian know about the new will?" I said, picking up a stick from the side of the road. "Perhaps he thought he was to inherit more."

Lady Mary thought for a moment, then tilted her head to one side and said, "Lieutenant Douglas thinks you did it."

"What?" I dropped the stick and stared at her in disbelief. I knew that man had something against me.

Chapter Six: The Lamb and Three Kings

That Friday, I was called to testify at the inquest. I'd never been more agitated in my life. This was a true test of my acting prowess, on stage for the whole village—including the astute reporter—to see. I felt as though I were the one on trial.

It didn't help that Mr. Montgomery had made it painfully clear I wasn't to call attention to myself, particularly not by involving myself in this murder case. In our last communiqué, he'd given me strict orders to watch Fredricks and nothing more.

The inquest was held at the Lamb and Three Kings in the village. The pub had a rough stone façade and sported a heavy wooden sign hanging from a post, featuring a friar in a black robe with a tonsure. The irony of naming a public house after biblical kings and Christ would have amused me if I had not been so nervous.

The air inside the pub was heavy with the lingering smell of stale cigarette smoke, intensified by the unseasonable heat and the presence of so many unwashed bodies. The villagers jostled to get front-row seats. A murder was unheard of in the tiny village of Wickham Bishops, and many establishments had closed for the day so their employees could take in the spectacle of wealthy landowners on trial. Low ceilings, dark timber beams, uneven door frames, sweating stone walls, and a slab floor illuminated by only two oil lamps gave the pub an eerie feel.

A couple of old farmers with few teeth and even less hair were jabbering loudly near the front of the room. And a group of women in rough dresses and caps on their huddled heads stood near the door gossiping.

The coroner pounded his gavel on the counter. It took several loud whacks before the crowd settled down. The coroner asked the proprietor to open the windows, and then called Lord Elliott to take the makeshift witness stand, which was really a wooden chair placed next to the counter.

Dressed in a tweed suit and crisp shirt, Lord Elliott sat in the designated chair and proceeded to describe the events at Ravenswick Abbey the night his mother died: Just before dawn, he heard a commotion coming from her bedroom and went to investigate. When he found her bedroom door locked, he hurried through Derek Wilkinson's adjacent room but found the connecting door was also locked. He noticed Derek hadn't slept in his bed. By this time, the rest of the family had awoken. They knocked on Lilian Mandrake's door because her bedroom also connected to his mother's. It took some time to rouse her, and they discovered the door between her room and his mother's was also locked. They had no choice but to break the lock and burst into his mother's room. She was moaning, writhing, and screaming. He called for Dr. Booth, but Vogel arrived first. It was too late. She died in his arms.

I was called next. I winced when the coroner referred to me as "the famous London specialist." The crush of bodies with their pongy smells mixed with smoke from the lamps was suffocating. The dark room started to close in on me, causing acute claustrophobia. My head was spinning as I made my way to the counter. A hush fell in the room as I took my seat.

Sitting on the hard chair, facing the entire village, I broke out in a sweat. I pulled a handkerchief from my waistcoat pocket and dabbed at my forehead. Why did men have to wear the full kit even when it was so bloody hot? At least women could wear skirts or dresses. I scanned the audience for Lady Mary's kind face, but instead my gaze landed on the inscrutable countenance of Fredrick Fredricks.

Trying not to swoon, I recounted how I ran into the house from the gate just before dawn to find the countess in the throes of a violent episode. I explained the distinctive signs of mercury bichloride poisoning's violent spasms.

"This is the first I've heard of mercury bichloride." The coroner frowned.

"Couldn't it have been strychnine?"

"Yes. I suppose it could have been." I swallowed hard. After all, I was not really an expert on poison, and Lady Mary had told me it was strychnine.

"The postmortem established the countess had strychnine in her blood."

"Right." My face grew even hotter. I wished I could rip off my beard and run for the exit.

"Is it easy to procure poison?"

"Mercury bichloride is sold at any chemists' as it has medicinal purposes." I cleared my throat. I hoped I wasn't asked what those were. "Strychnine, however, is not commonly used for domestic purposes, and there are restrictions on its sale." I twisted in the chair to face the coroner, who was sitting at the other end of the wooden counter. I couldn't look out into that sea of sweaty bodies. I placed one hand on the counter to steady myself. "I believe one must sign for either."

"Do you have a clue how the poison was administered?"

"No. I ruled out the warm milk. It came back negative for poison."

"It came back negative for mercury bichloride, you mean."

"Yes."

"Was it tested for strychnine?"

"Well, no, but—"

"And the tea?"

"We never could collect a sample of the tea. Then there is the matter of the timing. I suspect the poison was administered by some other means." I thought of the bottle hidden back in my room. I desperately needed to get that bottle back into the dowager's bed chamber. But how? It was locked. And, anyway, it was probably too late now. It would be deuced suspicious if it suddenly turned up.

"Couldn't the poison have been in her after-dinner tea?"

"Possibly, but both strychnine and mercury are fast-acting, with symptoms appearing one to two hours after being ingested. The countess took her tea around eight in the evening but wasn't affected until just before dawn." I was feeling more confident now that the nausea had subsided. The intrigue of the case had overpowered my urge to faint.

Finally, the coroner dismissed me. Much relieved, I moved to the back of the room. As I passed Lieutenant Douglas and Mr. Fredricks, they both looked up at me. I nodded, then quickly continued down the aisle and took a seat next to Lady Mary, who was sitting just two rows behind them. I was eager to watch the newsman's reactions to the testimony.

Dr. Booth was called next and corroborated my testimony. Sputtering with indignation, he repudiated utterly the suggestion that it could have been suicide. His patient suffered from a weak heart, but otherwise she enjoyed perfect health and devoted herself to good deeds, such as taking in Belgian refugees and wounded war heroes. He gestured toward Mr. Fredricks, who nodded in return.

Ian Elliott took the stand next. Fiddling with a pewter button on his waistcoat, he confirmed his brother's account of the night of his mother's death. Just as he was about to step down, he paused, and then, with hesitation in his voice, said, "With all due respect, my mother's death was from natural causes."

I thought he was going to push his heart attack theory again when he surprised me.

"For the past year, my mother had been taking a tincture containing strychnine for her heart."

The spectators audibly shifted in seats as tensions in the room increased. I glanced over to see Mr. Fredricks's reaction, but he remained unreadable as usual.

"Strychnine for her heart." the coroner repeated.

Seated alongside the far wall of the pub, the jury looked up as one.

"Yes." When Ian nodded, a lock of brown wavy hair fell onto his forehead. When he pushed it back into place, his hand was shaking. Ian was a sensitive sort, always moody and brooding. I had yet to figure out what made him tick. But there was definitely something odd about his behavior.

Dr. Booth was recalled to the witness stand and vehemently rejected the accusation that his prescription could have caused his patient's death.

"The cumulative effects of strychnine would have been noticed before they became lethal. She was in perfect health and had no complaints. The idea of cumulative poisoning is absurd." He was practically fuming. "As to an overdose, given the amount of strychnine in her blood, she would have had to take the entire bottle, which is nonsense." Dr. Booth seemed personally insulted by this line of questioning.

I wondered. I had heard of a case where a woman was accidentally poisoned with her own medicine, all the strychnine having settled to the bottom of the bottle. I glanced at the reporter again, who was scribbling on a small notepad.

The testimony of the next witness, the dowager's maid, refuted the possibility that the deceased could have taken the entire bottle of heart medicine.

"The med'cine weren't just made. It were nearly gone. She were on the last dose the night she passed." The maid sniffled and wadded her soiled handkerchief into a ball.

She testified to overhearing her mistress having a row with her eldest son, "master Ernest," on the day she died.

"She were mad 'bout some lady who come by earlier and somethin' 'bout marital discord."

The jurors' ears perked up at the mention of discord. Mine perked up at the mention of some lady. What lady?

"She shouted, give it to me."

"Give what to me?" the coroner asked.

"Dunno, sir." The maid shook her head.

Apropos of marital discord, the next witness was Lady Mary Elliott. Her demeanor didn't betray her, but I could sense she was nervous. Although she stared clear-eyed into the crowd, her cheeks had the slightest flush and her voice an almost imperceptible tremor.

"My alarm clock woke me at half past four as usual. You see, with the war, I do much of the work on the farm, milking cows and such." She was perfectly composed. It was uncanny. In my presence, she would cry at the drop of a hat, but under pressure she was cool and distant.

"As I was dressing, I heard the sound of something falling. Then the maid came running down the hall, and we all rushed to my mother-in-law's room, but it was locked—"

The coroner interrupted her. "Yes, we know. Could you tell us about the quarrel you overheard?"

"Quarrel?" She raised her hand to her throat and adjusted her necklace.

I noticed Lieutenant Douglas shifting in his chair. He whispered something to Fredricks, who ignored him.

"The maid testified she saw you sitting on a bench outside your mother-in-law's window at the same time she heard her and your husband having a row. From that vantage, you would have heard the quarrel too."

She hesitated. "I don't remember."

What was she playing at? I could tell she was lying. In fact, if this courtroom drama was any indication, the wealthy had no qualms about prevaricating. Was it only the middle-class children like myself whose mothers would wash their mouths out with soap if they were caught telling fibs?

"You don't remember?"

Her lip quivered as she answered. "I couldn't make out the words."

Lady Mary had told me the countess received a letter just before her death that she suspected spoke of her son's affair with Mrs. Roland. The maid had suggested the offending woman had visited the countess earlier that day. Lady Mary was jealous of her husband's relationship with Mrs. Roland, and even so, she was protecting him.

"You must remember something, a word, a phrase perhaps?"

The coroner pressed, but Lady Mary wouldn't admit to anything more. Finally, he dismissed her. She rejoined me in the back of the pub. Her face was pale, but she forced a little smile as she sat down next to me.

Next, a shop girl testified she'd sold the countess a will form. And then two gardeners swore under oath the countess had called them in to witness a document and sign it for her. *So, the old girl had made a new will.* But why had she destroyed it the very same day? Could it have something to do with the marital discord? Was Derek Wilkinson having an illicit liaison with someone? If he was, perhaps she'd cut him out of her will, and he'd discovered the new will, so he killed her and then ripped up the evidence.

But in that case, why hadn't he burnt it. After all, the will wasn't actually destroyed but just in bits.

The dowager's niece, Lilian Mandrake, was called to testify. She claimed she had gone to bed early and slept through the commotion, which fit with Lady Mary's admission to me that she had put sleeping powder in Lilian's tea. Young Lilian slept the sound sleep of a clear conscience...assisted by narcotics.

The next witness, Miss Bentham, was the most animated, all the while accusing Derek Wilkinson, the "blackguard," of murdering her dear friend Edith.

She pointed across the room at Wilkinson. "He's a murderer. Gold miner after her money." Her downy face flushed as she pounded her fleshy fist on the counter.

I began to wonder if Miss Bentham might not be overplaying her part. The violence of her hatred for Derek Wilkinson bordered on pathological. The shrillness of her testimony set the audience on edge, and the agitation in the room was palpable.

There was a sense of relief in the pub when the coroner dismissed Miss Bentham from the witness stand.

My head was pounding, and the heat in the room was oppressive. I had to get some air. Maybe I could duck out and get back in time for Derek Wilkinson's testimony. I whispered to Mary, "I'm going to step out for a bit." And then I picked my way through the crowd to the entrance and fled onto the lawn.

I loosened my tie and gulped in fresh air. How could I have forgotten about the cordial bottle I found in the dowager's handbag? It could be a crucial piece of evidence. With everyone at the inquest, perhaps I could sneak back to the house and replace it. How odd it would look, a bottle turning up after everyone, including the astute reporter, had seen the handbag was empty. If the murderer had gone looking to retrieve the letter—or the bottle—what must he have thought when he found it missing?

I glanced back at the entrance to the pub. How long could I disappear before I'd be missed? And how long did I have until Derek Wilkinson was called to testify? I didn't want to miss the moment of truth. I adjusted my wig and marched back to my cottage. If I couldn't replace the bottle in its rightful place, I could at least examine it. If only I could send it off to the laboratory at the War Office for testing. What an idiot. I'd been too caught up watching Fredricks to think of the evidence tucked into my own waistcoat pocket.

The street was deserted and most of the shops were closed. I quickened my pace lest some straggler noticed me. Even though it was only a five-minute walk, by the time I reached my cottage, I was drenched in perspiration. My mother always told me that ladies did not sweat, but she didn't know any who wore men's woolen suits in April. The Scottish were onto something with their kilts.

Once inside, I threw off my jacket, unbuttoned my shirtwaist, and unwrapped my chest. The gauze I'd used to conceal my femininity was soaking wet. I stripped down to my underclothes, retrieved the bottle from the pocket of my other waistcoat, which was hanging in the wardrobe, and then flopped onto my bed. I giggled, imagining what I must look like in women's underthings and a great black beard. Something from the circus no doubt.

Relaxing on my pillow, I held the clear bottle up to the light. It had beveled edges, curves in its neck, and lattice designs on its sides. The dregs of a dark liquid stained the inside of its corners. Around its neck was a small piece of thick paper attached with a tiny pink ribbon. I brought the bottle closer to read what was written on the paper. "To E. with all my love, J." was penned in an extravagant cursive, which suggested a lady's hand. If E was Edith, who was J?

Not Derek Wilkinson, unless they shared pet names. I uncorked the bottle and sniffed. The unmistakable sweet smell of sloe berries rode on the pungent current of liquor. Someone had made Edith Wilkinson a homemade aperitif, possibly a deadly brew designed to be her last.

I smelled the cork. Along with the berries and liquor, I sensed something dark and earthy, mushrooms perhaps, and the faint bitter smell of daffodils.

Did one of the tenants hold a grudge? Everyone gushed about how well the countess treated her tenants. Or perhaps one of the refugees actually resented the dowager's charity? On the other hand, if Derek Wilkinson purchased strychnine with the intention of killing his wife, this sweet cordial certainly could have camouflaged the bitter taste of the poison. Then again, if he used mercury bichloride, as I suspected, no camouflage would be necessary.

I jumped up from the bed and searched my room for paper or cloth in which to wrap the bottle. I settled on a strip of gauze from my chest-wrap and wound it around the bottle. I had to send it off for analysis as soon as possible. My weekly report was due to the War Office anyway. If only I could deliver the bottle along with my report.

Mr. Montgomery had already warned me not to get involved in the murder case and to stick to my investigation of the suspicious reporter and supposed war hero. So I definitely couldn't send the bottle to the laboratory at the War Office. I would need to get it analyzed elsewhere. But where?

Lilian Mandrake worked at a hospital. Maybe she could help analyze its contents. Of course, asking her would be problematic. "I stole this cordial bottle from the dowager's handbag could you analyze its contents?" Would anyone believe I accidentally removed it from the murder scene? If only I'd made more friends while volunteering at the hospital. If I hadn't been moping around pining for Andrew, I might have. Andrew. By some miracle, I'd gone two days in a row without thinking of Andrew...and his new wife. Nancy! She worked at the hospital. I could ask her... What an absurd idea.

Wait! What about Daisy Nelson at Charing Cross Hospital? She was the true expert in poisons both common and rare. But, could she keep a secret? I wrapped the gauzy bottle in butcher paper and tied the package up with string. I'd have to take my chances with Daisy. As a cunning woman, she was a practitioner of dark arts and white magic, and therefore no stranger to secrets.

Putting my damp clothes back on made my skin crawl. I glanced out the window before departing. My uncanny bearded reflection stared back at me, distorted further by the thick glass. Careful not to be seen, I dashed out the door and hurried to post my parcel on the way back to the Lamb and Three Kings. Hopefully, I wasn't too late to hear "Derek darling's" testimony.

When I arrived back at the pub, the whole of Wickham Bishops was milling about on the lawn. I was too late. The inquest was over. I spotted Lady Mary in a small group near the entrance. I made a beeline through the throng and landed at her side.

"You missed it!" She grabbed my elbow in excitement.

I stared down at her small white hand, which was still touching my wool jacket. She led me out to the road to get away from the crowd.

"It's obvious Derek killed Edith," Lady Mary said. "How dreadful. A husband poisoning his wife."

Yes, in the case of philandering husbands, it certainly should be the other way round.

"What makes you so sure it was Derek?" I asked.

"You should have heard the way he refused to answer the questions. And so arrogantly too!"

"Sounds rather brazen for a guilty man."

Our conversation was interrupted by the coroner calling us back into the public house. Once we were all seated, he concluded the inquest, announcing the verdict, "Willful murder by person or persons unknown."

Lady Mary was right. All the evidence pointed to Derek Wilkinson. He had the means, the motive, and ample opportunity to add the poison to his wife's tea. He'd also conveniently absented himself from the house later that evening and all night, so he wasn't at the scene when his wife succumbed. And yet, there was something too neat about all of it, as if there were too many clues, too much evidence against him.

I wished I could ask Fredricks what he thought of the inquest. But I didn't dare get that close to him. The astute fellow would ferret out my disguise *tout de suite*.

The next evening at dusk, there was a knock at my door. It was Lady Mary. She was flushed and agitated.

"It's clear Derek murdered Edith and is trying to steal Ernest's fortune!" She stomped her little foot. "What difference does it make if he has an alibi for Monday afternoon?"

"Alibi?"

"Yes. Mr. Fredricks found out he was in town with the land agent on Monday afternoon, so he couldn't have bought the poison."

"But someone bought the poison." *Someone disguised as Derek Wilkinson. Was someone trying to frame him? Miss Bentham, perhaps? She hated him and warned us against him.* Perhaps I wasn't the only female dressed up in a beard and trousers!

"Just because he didn't buy the poison doesn't mean he didn't use it. And just because someone disguised as Wilkinson bought the poison, doesn't mean Wilkinson is innocent."

"He did it. We all know he did it. He should be arrested." She looked up at me with indignation in those intense green eyes. "Why don't they arrest him?"

I stroked my beard. "Why indeed."

Chapter Seven: Miss Figg Reconnoiters

When Lady Mary came for our morning walk, she reported that immediately after breakfast Fredricks asked if the coachman could take him to Colchester, to the chemist where the countess had her tincture made up.

"Coachman?" I asked. "Not the chauffeur?"

"Ian had dibs on the car. So Mr. Fredricks had to settle for the horse-drawn coach."

"Even better!"

"Better? Why it will take four times as long." Lady Mary gave me a quizzical look.

"Indeed." I took her elbow. Given Colchester was a good eight miles away, I figured Fredricks wouldn't be back for at least another four hours. "Lady Mary, would you mind going on without me? I'm afraid my bad knee is acting up."

"Oh dear. But you're so young."

"Sports injury. From my college days, playing...ruggers."

"Rugby?" She narrowed her brows. "I don't believe you." She looked me up and down.

"I'm joking, of course." I laughed. "It was tennis." I turned toward the cottages and hobbled back along the path.

"Poor dear," Lady Mary called after me. "I'll come round this evening and collect you for dinner."

As soon as Lady Mary was out of sight, I dashed back to my cottage. I soaked a cloth, wrung it out, and applied it damp to my beard. After a minute, I pulled off the blasted thing, tore off my fake eyebrows, and applied cream to my poor inflamed face. I flung off my oversized boots, wriggled out of my trousers, jacket, waistcoat, shirtwaist, and then pulled off my socks. I unwrapped my bosom, such as it was, threw on my knickers, and stepped into my chemise.

I went to my suitcase and removed another costume I'd purchased for just this occasion. The black dress fell just above my ankles. Its little white collar was starched stiff. I sat on my bed and rolled on black stockings, and then slipped on black T-strap shoes. I lifted a white apron from the case and wore it over my dress. Luckily the white maid's cap covered most of my shorn head.

At the dressing table, I applied just a touch of kohl, rouge, and lipstick. I powdered my chin to cover the rash caused by that blasted beard. My transformation was complete. I'd gone from wiry bearded doctor to a proper English chambermaid. I smiled at my reflection in the hand mirror. The woman looking back at me wasn't a beauty, but at least she didn't have a beard.

Exercising my vocal cords, I sang a few notes from *Maid of the Mountain*, the last musical theater I'd seen before I left London. "Love will find a way..." I raised it up an octave and tried again. As the doctor, I'd been using such a low range, my voice was unaccustomed to the upper registers.

I peeked out the door of my cottage, looking both ways to make sure no one saw me. *Horsefeathers!* I didn't need to sneak around. I was now a chambermaid here to clean the cottages. Perfectly normal. No one noticed servants anyway. If I kept my head bowed and didn't make eye contact, I should be able to go about my business pretty much as if I were invisible. At least, that's what my brain said. My stomach was another matter altogether.

Carrying a couple of rags for effect, I walked across the dirt path to Leastways cottage, the one Fredrick Fredricks shared with the Belgian refugees. It was the largest of the cottages. Its thick brown-gray thatch looked like a saddle blanket draped over the pitched roof. Two dormer windows peeked out from under the thatch like sleepy eyes. Red roses climbed up the sides of the green front door, creating a festive contrast of color. I headed up the two stone steps, and then knocked on the door. When one of the Belgians answered, I curtsied slightly, and he gestured me inside.

"I haven't seen you before," he said with a thick accent.

"I'm new, sir," I said with my best cockney inflection. "Sent from the manor house."

"It's nice to see English girls working hard," he said.

"Yes, sir." I narrowed my brows but didn't ask what he meant. "I'll just go 'bout my work then."

I glanced around the front sitting room where two other men were playing a game of backgammon. Concentrating on their game, they didn't look up. I wiped off the fireplace mantel and dusted the tables. There was a heaviness in the room that couldn't be accounted for by the dark furnishings, thick drapes, or the men's pipe smoke. A sense of loss hung in the air mixed with sweet cherry tobacco. Although they were speaking French, I gathered from their conversation they were biding their time until positions opened up at the munitions factory. My ears perked up when one of the backgammon players mentioned Fredricks. I couldn't make out all the words, but his sentiment was clear—resentment.

"*Où trouve-t-il son argent?*" one of the players asked.

Where does he get his money, indeed.

"Excuse me, sirs," I said timidly. "Don't mean to eavesdrop, but Monsieur Fredricks has been up at the big house investigating the murder and I wonder if he's qualified. I mean they took him on without knowing his credentials." I hoped I'd read the room correctly and these men weren't fans of Mr. Fredricks. It seems only the women fancied him.

"What *do* you know about him?" I asked, still dusting.

"He puts on airs and looks down his nose at us," said the other backgammon player, a lanky middle-aged man with close-set eyes and slicked-back hair parted down the middle. "We have only the clothes on our backs. We don't know whether our families are safe. We are waiting for work so we can pay for our next meal. We have lost everything. And Monsieur Fredricks has everything."

"I'll pray for your families," I said, passing my cloth over the back of a chair. "Does Monsieur Fredricks ever talk about his family?"

A man with a bushy mustache looked up from the game. "Monsieur Fredricks treats us like children, always instructing us on how to behave in our new country. As an Englishman, this is his home, but we want to go home. We don't belong here." He puffed his pipe and blew out a cloud of smoke that hung in the air like a melancholy note.

But was Mr. Fredricks truly an Englishman?

"My woman and babies are in Folkestone working for rich lady cleaning house while I work here in weapons factory," said the one with the mustache.

"And Monsieur Fredricks? Does he have a wife and babies someplace?" I asked, wiping off a small corner table.

"Monsieur Fredricks is *une folle*," the lanky one said with a sly smile.

"*Folle?*" Didn't *folle* mean crazy woman? Maybe my French was rustier than I thought.

"*Une Countess*, how do you call them in English?"

"A countess, I see," I said with a blush, and went about pretending to clean. He clearly didn't mean a countess in the way Edith Wilkinson had been a countess, but another meaning altogether.

After a cursory dusting of the front rooms, I headed upstairs, wiping the wooden banister with a rag as I went.

I'd seen Fredricks open his bedroom window, so I knew his room was the second on the left.

I stopped on the landing when I heard voices coming from one of the rooms. I held my breath and listened. *Blimey!* I couldn't make out the words, but they were definitely speaking German. *Do Belgian refugees speak German?* I thought they spoke Flemish and French. Was this whole place full of German spies? Of course, speaking German did not necessarily make one a spy or sympathetic to our enemies.

I heard a doorknob turn and a voice getting louder, so I dashed past the door and slipped into the second room on the left.

Fredricks's chamber held a small bed and nightstand in one corner, a washstand and a writing desk near the window, and another small table and two chairs along the center of the interior wall. A tall armoire sat next to the table. Books organized from largest to smallest were neatly stacked at the back of the table against the wall, and a pen and a notebook lay in the center, all exactly parallel to one another. Similarly precise was his bed, made military style with every corner tucked in. I never understood how a fleshy three-dimensional person could slide into sheets so firmly fitted.

After surveying the room, I started my search at the nightstand. In its center was a small oil lamp and next to it, a chain of beads. When I bent down to get a closer look, I recognized the necklace as a rosary made of rosewood beads with a silver crucifix attached. So, Fredricks was Catholic. I wouldn't have figured a man of his great prowess to be religious, let alone Catholic. I wondered how many Hail Marys he had to say to atone for his sins.

My next stop was the washstand, where a cream-colored pitcher with blue floral designs stood inside a matching bowl. Alongside it sat a straight razor, tiny scissors, a tiny comb, a small tin of D. R. Harris wax, a silk snood, and an ornately handled silver rod with a lever and clip, which I can only assume was for straightening the ends of his pencil mustache. Each of these items was placed as precisely as if on a surgeon's tray.

Examining Fredrick's mustache paraphernalia, I recalled one of Kipling's women saying being kissed by a man who didn't wax his mustache was like eating an egg without salt. I didn't particularly like eggs, with or without salt.

I sat down at the table and read the spines of his books: May Sinclair's *A Journal of Impressions in Belgium* (I wonder if he knows she's a suffragette); a fat book in German, *Logische Untersuchungen,* by someone called Edmund Husserl; a slim German pamphlet entitled *Zeitschrift für Psychologie,* a book in French; *Matière et Mémoire* by someone called Henri Bergson; *Die Traumdeutung* by Sigmund Freud (I'd heard of him—an Austrian doctor who attributed all illness to sexual frustration); Teresa of Avila's *Conceptos del Amor de Dios,* a *Dictionnaire Larousse Français-Anglais; Field Guide to Poisonous Plants* (Could Fredricks be the murderer?); and on the very top of the stack, a well-worn copy of *The Handy Black Cat English-French Dictionary.*

There were certainly enough German books to make me wonder whether he was a German spy. I took a mental note of all the titles, planning to research them later. Sometimes a photographic memory came in handy.

I took my gloves from the pocket of my apron, slipped them on, and carefully opened Fredricks's notebook. Each page was dated, and in a tight cursive written straight across the page was line after line of French. *Blast!* I should have paid more attention in my French classes at North London Collegiate. I could make out a few words, and given the dates, it seems he was making notes on the Wilkinson case. *Why is he writing in French? Could this somehow mean he is a German spy? Was the French actually some kind of code?*

I glanced up at the clock on the mantel. If he had set out for Colchester directly after breakfast—say about nine—then he had been gone for just over three hours. I figured he would need at least four hours to get there and back. Still, I had to dust the rest of the rooms and get out of the house before he returned. I didn't want to risk running into the eagle-eyed man. He might notice a certain freckle or mole that would give me away.

Still wearing my gloves, I opened the armoire. *Golly.* He had a lot of clothes for a man. Jackets, waistcoats, and trousers were segregated and arranged by color. Three feet tall leather boots stood at attention on the floor of the wardrobe, and three Slouch hats were lined up on the top shelf. An assortment of bow ties hung from special hooks on the inside of the armoire door, again arranged by color and also by length. A clothes brush hung from a hook on the inside of the door. A tidier wardrobe I'd never seen. I gently closed the door so as not to disturb anything, and then checked to make sure I hadn't moved the books or notebook. I straightened the notebook so it was exactly aligned with the pen.

Why was this man so obsessed with order? Had his childhood been so chaotic he had to overcompensate now with military precision? Or was order his penance for a misspent youth?

I stood in the center of the room and slowly turned, surveying every nook to see if I had missed anything of interest. I knelt down and, on hands and knees, peeked under the bed. *Aha!* A small leather case sat atop a large suitcase. I carefully slid them out from under the bed. I sat cross-legged on the floor and opened the small case. It contained several corked lab tubes, a pair of tweezers, a magnifying glass, a pen, and a pad of paper. Given every item had its own slot or leather restraint, it looked as though the case had been specially made. I closed the latch on the newsman's tool case and set it to one side. His greatest tool was not in this case. On more than one occasion, I'd overheard him say he didn't need any special equipment to solve a case, only his animal instincts housed deep inside his lizard brain.

Listening to make sure no one was stirring downstairs, I depressed the latches on either side of the large suitcase. To my surprise, it was unlocked. The case was empty except for an album book and a small box. I picked up the box and suppressed a chuckle. The vain man used coal hair dye. I shook the box. Sure enough, there was a bottle inside containing the liquid dye. I replaced the box, removed the album, and opened its heavy embossed leather cover. Inside the album, photographs were skillfully glued to each black page. The first was of a beautiful woman holding two babies. *Did the reporter have a wife and children waiting for him somewhere?* Were they still in Africa or America? Or perhaps he had lost them in the war. That would explain a good deal.

The album was full of photographs of the same dark beauty and two boys who grew with each turn of the page. About four years in, a baby joined the family. A couple of pages later, she was a gorgeous curly-headed little girl of probably four years old. Then she disappeared from the rest of the pictures. By the end, the boys—who looked to be identical twins—must have been around nine years of age. They both had strong noses like their father and dark features like their mother, and both were wearing matching Knickerbocker suits and captain's hats. I wondered where they were now and why Fredricks never spoke of them.

As I lifted the album from my lap to replace it in the case, something fell out. At first, I thought it was an insect. I jumped up and the wretched thing tumbled off my apron onto the floor. *What in the world?* It was a false mustache. Why would Fredricks have a false mustache? Wasn't his mustache real? It looked real enough. Then again, I'd been sporting a false beard and so far—touch wood—no one was the wiser. Could Fredricks be wearing a disguise? His fancy hunting kit did look more like a costume than anyone's regular attire. If he were a German spy, of course he'd be incognito. The sly fox.

I picked up the caterpillar mustache, returned it to the album, and put the book back in the suitcase. Closing the latches, I sat the smaller case on top, and glided them back under the bed. Then I wiped the floor where they had slid just in case they'd made any marks.

Finally, I was getting somewhere. I wasn't the only one living a double life. The Great White Hunter, it seemed, had secrets of his own.

I brushed myself off and had just reached the chamber door when the handle turned and in strode Mr. Fredrick Fredricks himself. You could have knocked me down with a feather. I felt the blood drain from my face until I'm sure my complexion matched my apron.

"I was just cleaning your room, sir," I said, my voice cracking.

"Mademoiselle," he said, tipping his hat. "And now you're finished, *n'est-ce pas?*"

"Yes, sir." I curtsied.

"Too bad." He stood in the doorway and wouldn't let me pass. "Might I ask your name?"

Blimey! What was my name?

"Teresa, sir," I blurted out.

"Mademoiselle Teresa..." He held an arm across the entrance, blocking my way. "And your family name?"

I felt like a trapped animal. Had he recognized me and now he was toying with me like a cat with a mouse?

"Baldasarré." I lowered my eyes and focused on the buckles on my shoes. "Teresa Baldasarré."

"That's a familiar name," he said. "Where have I heard it before?" He lifted my chin with one of his large fingers.

What cheek! If I weren't in disguise and trying not to call attention to myself, I might have slapped his face.

"And your eyes..." he said, staring into my face.

As I closed my eyes tight, I had the strangest sensation in the region of my stomach.

"You're not the regular domestic. You're much prettier."

My eyes flashed open in indignation.

He patted his heart. "Have we met elsewhere? Perhaps in the village?"

I shook my head.

"Teresa Baldasarré," he repeated. "Such a beautiful name for such a beautiful girl." A wolfish grin spread across his face.

I had the strongest urge to bolt.

"Would you like some brandy, Mademoiselle Teresa?" With one finger, he lightly stroked my sleeve.

I stifled a gasp.

He smiled and bowed his head. "Papa Fredricks won't bite, you know."

Aha! Papa Fredricks. He has children then.

"Unless you prefer it that way." He flashed a devilish grin.

My hand flew to my mouth. "No thank you, sir." I ducked under his arm and resisted the urge to run. "I'd best get back to work."

I barely escaped a pat on the bottom on my way out. I hurried up the hall and down the stairs before he realized Teresa and Baldasarré were the two leads of *The Maid of the Mountains*.

Chapter Eight: The Encounter

The next morning was the dowager's funeral. It was a glorious Sunday with only a few puffy clouds, and the entire village turned out to honor one of its prime benefactors. Many of the mourners were deeply indebted to the countess, including the Great White Hunter and the Belgian refugees. With his slicked-back mane, the big game hunting reporter looked like a zebra in his black suit, white shirt, and dark glasses. He was accompanied by the irritating Lieutenant Douglas, also dressed in black. As usual, the lieutenant snubbed me as I passed him going into the church.

The quaint medieval church was round with a thatched roof upon which a turret was perched like a biretta atop the head of a bishop. We entered by a massive wooden door tucked into a stone archway. Inside, the church was built in stone blocks, and contained a circular nave. Between the ambulatory and nave were eight massive Norman columns and round arches decorated with dogtooth ornamentation and carved human heads. Except for the light streaming through colorful stained-glass windows, the church was almost dark. An appropriate ambiance for a funeral.

Packed with mourners dressed in black, which contrasted with the light gray of the stone walls, the pews looked to be inundated by a flock of crows surging against a concrete sky. When Derek Wilkinson entered the sanctuary and took a place in the front pew, the crows clucked their tongues. His face remained impassive—if anything, he seemed to look down his nose at the other parishioners. Why hadn't those chaps from Scotland Yard arrested him yet?

I positioned myself in the rear and off to one side of the chapel, which gave me an unobstructed view of Fredricks. So Papa Zebra had foals. But why had he never mentioned them? And what of his wife, the dark beauty in the photograph? Why had he left her behind? And what about that fake mustache? I wished I could get a closer look at his mustache. To do so, however, would put him much too close to my own false facial hair. I stared at the altar without seeing, and the voice of the minister became background noise for my own nagging thoughts.

The heat in the church was stifling. I instinctively looked for something to fan myself with, and then remembered I was a man, and men don't fan themselves. Beads of sweat were forming under my beard. I patted it to make sure it was still in place. The last thing I needed was my beard sliding off during the dowager's funeral.

As the minister droned on about the countess's good works and her importance to the community, I admired the arched ceiling and vibrant stained-glass windows, which depicted the last temptation of Christ—the morning sun was at the perfect angle to enliven the deathly scene with rich blood-soaked hues.

After the service, the mourners followed the pallbearers into the graveyard just outside the church. Centuries-old headstones sat at odd angles, giving the churchyard a whimsical feel. The dowager's freshly carved headstone stood out straight and tall amongst its ancestors.

During the burial, I hung back from the flock of mourners and planted myself under the shade of an oak tree to escape the beastly unseasonable heat. At least a skirt allowed for air circulation and some modest relief, though nothing a man had to endure in the way of clothing could compare to the dreaded corset. As a man, I could finally take a deep breath without feeling I was going to burst out of my stays.

A nightingale whistled a mournful lament overhead. I looked up and spotted the little caramel-colored creature bobbing up and down on a branch, its feathers soft with dappled sunshine filtering through the leaves. It seemed the whole world, even the birds, were mourning the dead. The dowager's death was criminal, but she was an old woman after all.

At the hospital, I'd seen boys no more than fourteen for whom the loss of innocence meant the loss of limbs. Boys who would never whirl their sweetheart around a dance floor. Boys who would grow into men haunted for the rest of their lives by the atrocities of war. Men who would never truly find comfort in their lovers' arms, men who cowered whenever an airplane roared across the sky.

Instead of masquerading as a doctor, I should be helping in the hospital. Not for the war effort, but for all the boys and men who sacrificed everything to answer a call for help from our neighbors across the channel.

My tawny feathered friend raised her voice in a final twittered song and then flew away. Goodbye, Florence Nightingale, the lady with the lamp. Guide our boys home safely.

"*Excusez-moi.*"

My hand flew to my heart. "You startled me, Mr. Fredricks." *Blast!* In my surprise, I'd forgotten to properly lower my voice.

He gave me an appraising look. "Might I ask you a few questions, *s'il vous plaît.*"

Why was he always speaking French? Was it because, like me, he was leading a double life? Or was it just to impress the ladies?

"Of course," I said in the deepest tenor I could muster. "I'm at your service." Trying not to stare, I examined his mustache, looking for any signs of spirit glue.

"You were there when the countess died, *n'est-ce pas?*"

"Yes, but you don't think—"

"No, no, ma—monsieur." He gave me a reassuring smile. "Can you describe what you saw from the time you arrived at the house early that morning?"

"When I arrived, the family was gathered upstairs in the countess, ah, Mrs. Wilkinson's room. She was in bed, gasping and writhing violently. With ghastly terror in her eyes, she stared straight at me and called out something in German and then collapsed. I attempted resuscitation but it was too late. She was dead."

"And you proposed strychnine poisoning?"

"Actually, I proposed poisoning by mercury bichloride. I recognized the symptoms. The tremors and violent spasms. It's very easy to procure because...of the epidemic." For some reason, I couldn't bring myself to say syphilis, as if saying it risked infection. "But I was wrong, it seems. It was strychnine, or so they say." I still suspected the strychnine was a red herring.

"And you are an expert on poisons, Doctor?"

"Yes, poisons and female maladies are my specialties." I didn't mention that in my opinion most female maladies might be best cured by administering a lethal dose of poison to an unfaithful lover. I doubted the War Office made this connection when they came up with the cover story for the good Dr. Vogel.

"So, it was you who insisted on an autopsy, and rightly so."

"Yes. Dr. Booth and her son Ian thought it was her heart, but I knew otherwise."

"Very correct, too. Did you notice anything strange in her boudoir?"

What could I say? *You mean, dear Fredricks, did I notice anything strange other than the ripped will in the fire grate, the nearly empty tincture bottle, the* Ryno's Remedy *cocaine snuff, and an ornate cordial bottle and incriminating letter in her handbag?* I wiped my brow with a handkerchief.

"In the commotion, I didn't notice anything except the dowager's distress." The nosy journalist didn't need to know about my mission to retrieve the letter implicating Lord Elliott, a letter still held hostage in a hatband in the dowager's room, or the cordial bottle, which was at this very moment being analyzed by Daisy Nelson at Charing Cross dispensary, at least I hoped that's where it was. Although, I was beginning to wonder since I hadn't heard back from Daisy. I hope she didn't get it into her mind to report me to the War Office, or worse, to Scotland Yard.

"Perhaps you glanced at her medicine bottle or the little box of powders in her drawer?" When he smiled, his mustache turned up even more.

I stroked my beard. I wouldn't let this clever fellow unnerve me. "The medicine bottle was nearly empty but for one last dose at the bottom. The powder was Ryno's Remedy, a snuff made of cocaine used to treat various ailments, including allergies. "

He nodded encouragingly. "And is it safe to take the tincture containing strychnine along with cocaine powder?"

"They're both stimulants, so I suppose—"

"May I?" he asked and picked a speck off the shoulder of my jacket with his gloved fingers. He looked at the tiny ball on the end of his glove and then sniffed it. "Spirit gum, I think."

Crikey! He was on to me. "I really should be going now."

He brushed his hands together. "You were saying, they're both stimulants."

Perhaps if I laid my cards on the table, he'd overlook the spirit gum on my jacket and any suspicions he had about my glued-on beard. "Strychnine is a stimulant, and in very small doses it is prescribed for heart ailments, especially in cases of slow heart rates. But in larger doses, as you know, it's toxic. Dr. Booth swears his prescription couldn't have been lethal unless she'd swallowed the entire bottle at once. The maid swore under oath there was only one dose left. But what if someone added the cocaine powder to the full bottle of heart medicine? Cocaine is also a potent stimulant." I remembered now where I'd read about a similar case. That's exactly what happened. An addled patient thought she could combine them and take just one dose per night instead of two.

"What would happen? Pray tell me, good Doctor."

"An overdose of stimulants could cause cardiac arrest." *And that's exactly what happened*, I thought. *A very clever person who knew chemistry had added cocaine to the tincture...and yet, perhaps their efforts were in vain.*

"*My God!*" Fredricks grabbed my sleeve. "And the *pauvre* Countess would have taken an overdose without knowing it. My friend, you're a genius!"

"But she didn't take the—" I started to say. If someone did add Ryno's Remedy to the tincture, as the crystals at the bottom of the bottle suggested, then they were still waiting. For the countess had not yet taken the last dose.

Fredricks tipped his hat and started in the direction of the manor house.

Thank goodness. I was perspiring like a farmhand. I'd best contact the War Office and tell them the jig was up. I needed to find a telephone and tell them to extract me before Fredricks ripped off my beard and exposed me.

"Just one more question, *wenn es dir nichts ausmacht.*"

Blimey! What did he want now? Fredricks's baritone voice caught me off guard.

"*Mein Freund.*" His disarming smile seemed rehearsed. "What were you doing out walking before dawn on the night of the murder? An odd time to be out for a stroll, *n'est-ce pas?*"

Was he speaking German and French? I'd read he was multilingual, but he should make up his mind.

"You don't think *I* poisoned the countess, do you?"

"Did you?"

"Of course not."

"So why don't you answer my question?" he asked with that annoying white-fanged grin of his.

"I couldn't sleep. Insomnia." I forced myself to make eye contact and speak with conviction. "I went out for a walk."

"Why don't you just take sleeping powders?"

"I like to keep a clear head."

"You prescribe them but you don't take them yourself?"

"They are better for the ladies."

"I see. And what doesn't let you sleep, Doctor? You're troubled perhaps?"

"Nightmares. The blasted war has given everyone nightmares."

"Not me." He tapped his swagger stick on the ground for emphasis.

I narrowed my fake bushy brows. *How odd. Why wasn't the war giving Fredricks nightmares?* "Then you, sir, are a lucky man."

"My clear conscience has nothing to do with luck, good Doctor."

"And you think I have a guilty conscience?"

"Do you?" he asked, giving me an unnerving stare.

"No more than any other man," I replied with more confidence than I felt. Of course, I was not any other man.

The huntsman gave me a smug smile and then turned on his heels. "Fredrick Fredricks always learns the truth," he called over his shoulder as he marched away, his back as stiff as a windup toy.

I leaned against the oak tree and removed my hat. That little interrogation had taken my breath away. I removed a handkerchief from my breast pocket, dabbed at my forehead, and longed for a glass of cool lemonade. I hadn't seen a lemon in two years. The war had taken so much away from us, even the simplest of pleasures.

I closed my eyes and inhaled the scent of May in the countryside, damp grass and freesia so sweet it hinted at rotting fruit. I was going to have to leave the pleasures of the country and return to London without having fulfilled my assignment. I hadn't discovered the truth about Fredricks. I had no proof he was working for the Germans…or the French. After all, reading German philosophy didn't make him a spy.

He had a wife and children tucked away, hopefully someplace safe. But where? The only certainty from my excursion into his room was his fastidiousness with his mustache, which was obvious to anyone who met him. The surgical precision of his paraphernalia suggested a mind obsessed with order and deeply troubled by the chaos of life. What had this man suffered in his life to make him so dependent upon symmetry? Was orderliness another symptom of shell shock? Was it from his years in military service? Or maybe in prison? If he truly were a war hero, he must have seen atrocities unimaginable to those who have never looked war in the face. I thought of the hospital and all those broken men.

For their sakes, I had been sent here to sniff out Fredricks's real reason for being in England. For their sakes, I was part of the effort to stop the Germans. But I'd failed. I'd failed them. My marriage had been a failure. My assignment had been a failure. I was a failure. The only thing I was good for was filing. I should be locked away in a musty library, filing documents no one wanted to read. *What good was I, anyway?* Andrew saw the truth. And now Fredricks would learn the truth. Then where would I be? I'd be sacked for sure…no husband, no job…worthless. I'd failed everyone, especially myself.

I wiped a tear from my eye with the back of my hand and stood up straight. Enough of feeling sorry for myself. Time to face the music and telephone the War Office.

"Doctor, are you ill?"

I opened my eyes to see Lady Mary standing before me, as lovely as a white lily in a black vase.

"Are you crying?" She touched my arm. "I didn't realize you were so fond of Edith, after all you barely knew her."

I pointed at the yellow and orange freesia blossoms surrounding the tree. "Hay fever. I get it every spring." I blew my nose on my handkerchief for effect and stuffed the rag back into my pocket.

"You should try Ryno's Remedy. It worked wonders for Edith, poor dear."

Wonders indeed. I shook my head. I could hear my father's voice in my head, "Stiff upper lip, my girl, that's the English way." Wouldn't he be surprised to see a mustache sprouting from mine?

"Doctor, can we talk?" Lady Mary asked with fear in her eyes.

"I have to walk to the village." I brushed the back of my trousers where I'd been leaning against the tree. "Perhaps you could come by my cottage later this afternoon?"

"Can I walk with you?" There was a pleading tone in her voice. "Something dreadful has happened."

Chapter Nine: The Smoking Gun

Lady Mary insisted on accompanying me into the village. We walked by the churchyard in silence. I shuddered when we passed the fresh grave of Edith Wilkinson.

"Before the funeral, Ernest and I had the most awful row," Lady Mary said finally, her forlorn countenance adding ten years to her face.

As we walked up the path to the village, she recounted the quarrel. The trees and grasses were in the height of their greenery and the pastoral scene made me realize how much I would miss the countryside. I inhaled the smell of spring, and wished I hadn't when hay fever made me sneeze so violently I worried I might eject my beard.

Lady Mary continued reporting every detail of her quarrel with Ernest as the path met the main road. I glanced at the white houses with their high-pitched thatch roofs on both sides of the road, wondering what the village ladies would say about a married woman on the arm of a man who wasn't her husband. Assuming Lady Mary would have the decorum not to follow me into a public house, I headed for the Lamb and Three Kings. Although, the way she grasped my arm made me wonder about her propriety.

A few ladies tightened their lips when we passed, while some of the gentlemen gave us knowing smiles. I didn't want to cultivate the reputation of a philanderer, even if it would increase my believability as a man.

By the time we reached the pub, Lady Mary was breathless from talking a mile a minute, relating every aspect of her row with Ernest.

"He accused me of being in love with you!" she said indignantly.

"What?" I stopped in my tracks and turned to face her. "Impossible. Why would he say that?"

"Is it so impossible?"

When she looked up at me with those lovely emerald eyes, I had the strangest sensation in my chest. "Impossible," I repeated under my breath. I was tempted to rip off my beard and show her why.

"He said I was the talk of the village, gadding about with you while his mother, poor thing, was lying dead." She pulled her hand from my elbow and stared at her muddy shoes. "I told him he cared more about what other people thought than about me."

Her lower lip trembled, and I thought she might start crying.

"Oh dear," I said. "The last thing I want is to cause trouble between you and Ernest."

"It's not your fault." There was fire in her cheeks and ice in her voice. "It's his. He's carrying on with Mrs. Roland, so he has no right to dictate my friends." The way she said *friends* gave me that queer feeling again.

"Look, Lady Mary," I said, adjusting the bottom of my waistcoat. "I'm leaving Wickham Bishops."

"You're leaving?" A shadow fell over her face. "When?"

"Soon. Very soon." I patted her hand. "Now I really must be going. I have to make a telephone call."

"Why didn't you say so? You could have come up to the house."

"It's a private matter."

"A secret wife or lover?" She laughed.

"Something like that."

The shadow returned to her face, and with a dollop of remorse, I turned to go. "It's a matter of some urgency," I said over my shoulder.

Without looking back, I strode to the door of the pub. A hardened heart was the best way—make a clean break of it and all that.

"Wait," she called after me.

I didn't wait. I went inside.

Blimey! She followed me into the public house. She was a pertinacious woman, I'd give her that.

Three old farmers wearing sack coats and soft felt hats sat at the counter drinking beer and talking in loud voices. They went quiet and stared at us as we walked past. I felt their eyes follow us to the back of the pub.

"I have to warn you," Lady Mary said in a low voice.

Warn me? My heart sped up, and I stopped in my tracks. *Had Fredricks told her I wasn't what I seemed? Was he planning to expose me?*

"Lieutenant Douglas is convinced you killed Edith," she said. "And he's going to the police."

"Clifford Douglas is the most ridiculous man I've ever met." I started walking again and lengthened my stride.

Lady Mary followed me to a small table in the back of the pub away from the prying eyes—and ears—of the farmers.

"Yes, but Mr. Fredricks thinks you did it too," Lady Mary said as she caught up to me.

"What?" I dropped into a wooden chair.

"When Mr. Fredricks found out you'd been at the abbey on the fatal night before Edith went up to her room, he said that altered everything." She grimaced. "That's what Lieutenant Douglas told Ernest. He said you either dropped something into Edith's tea or sneaked upstairs and poisoned the warm milk and then lied about the analysis."

"But I wasn't even there when the warm milk was brought up."

"According to Ernest, Lieutenant Douglas thinks you could have substituted some ordinary milk for the sample you sent to be tested and that's why they found no strychnine." She sat down across from me at the table. "And that's why Mr. Fredricks is taking another sample to be tested."

"Fredricks actually suspects I did it?" Worse than being exposed, I'd be executed. "What about the bitter taste of the strychnine? The warm milk wouldn't disguise it."

"Since you're one of the world's greatest toxicologists, they think you've found a way to make the poison tasteless or used some obscure poison no one has ever heard of that produces the same symptoms."

One of the world's greatest frauds more like. "But I never had access to the blasted milk!" I blurted out. "Sorry."

The men at the counter all turned around and stared at us.

Lady Mary's face was flushed. "Lieutenant Douglas hinted I might have been your accomplice and poisoned Edith's milk because she found out about us."

"Us?" I lowered my voice to a whisper.

"Apparently Lieutenant Douglas thinks Edith discovered *we* were having an affair—preposterous, I know—and threatened to tell Ernest, and that's why we supposedly killed her. It's all too ghastly for words." Her voice broke.

"It's absurd. Lieutenant Douglas is a fool. Surely Fredricks doesn't believe any of this." I hoped to heavens he didn't. "If he does, he's not a very good detective."

"Mr. Fredricks was asking why you were wandering around the estate fully clothed before dawn."

"Yes, he asked me point blank. But I can't very well tell the truth about that, can I?"

"It's all my fault." She glanced around the pub and then whispered, "If only I hadn't asked you to help me retrieve the letter."

I'd almost forgotten about the blasted letter. In my rush to take it from the handbag and hide it in the hatband, I hadn't had time to read more than the salutation, which just this moment flashed before my mind as if I were reading it for the first time. *Sehr geehrte Dame.* Not the English, Dear Madam or Dear Countess, but the German, *Sehr geehrte Dame.*

"The letter is not what you think," I said, surprising even myself.

"That's what Edith said when I confronted her about it. Those were her exact words."

"She was telling the truth. The letter is not about Ernest." *It was addressed to the countess in German, but who sent it?* I had a feeling in the pit of my stomach that finding out was the key to the dowager's murder, and probably much more too. A chill passed through my bones as I realized the possible import of a letter in German so distressing to the countess that she locked it in her handbag and became ill from worry.

"How do you know?"

"I saw it."

She gasped and put her hand to her mouth.

"I took it from her handbag as you asked, but Dr. Booth almost caught me in the act, so I disposed of the letter."

"You destroyed it!"

"No, I hid it, and in a jolly clever place too."

"Why didn't you tell me?" She was adamant. "Where is it? I must see for myself."

"I wanted to read it first to make sure we were both prepared for its contents. After all, you entrusted me to help you. And I didn't want to see you hurt."

"Where is it?" she demanded again. "I want to see that letter."

"Why don't we have some tea and discuss this calmly." I sounded just like a man, telling a woman not to be so hysterical. I remembered Andrew chastising me when I found him in the arms of that tart, as if he were the one who'd been wronged.

A couple of old gents came in, took a seat at a table, and ordered brandies. Hard to believe this was the same place where I'd given testimony just two days ago. Lady Mary blushed and averted her eyes when the men stared at us. No doubt she was self-conscious about being the only woman in the place, except for me, of course.

When I went to the counter and ordered a pot of tea, the barkeep gave me a sly look. He probably wasn't used to tea drinkers in his establishment. Hopefully he didn't think there was some intrigue between Lady Mary and me. Now I blushed.

"Where is the letter?" Lady Mary repeated once I'd returned to the table. "Don't you see, I must read it. Otherwise I'll go mad."

"The letter is locked away in the dowager's bedroom." As I said it, I realized it was also locked away in my photographic memory. I just hadn't taken the time to access it.

"Please, Doctor. I need to know."

We both went quiet when the barmaid appeared with our tea. I nodded as she put the pot down in the middle of the table, along with a chipped milk pitcher and a mismatched sugar bowl.

"Give me a minute, Mary," I said, putting my head into my hands. "I need to think." The smell of stale beer and cigarette smoke made it difficult to concentrate.

While I pondered, Mary poured us each a cup of tea.

My memory for documents is unlike other fleeting memories flowing by like a stream or flashing like a picture show in my mind. Books, papers, letters, documents of any kind, come back to me fully formed, as if I were looking directly at them, only sometimes they are just out of focus. I had to work to pull them closer and then miraculously they would appear before my mind as if I were actually seeing them anew. Mr. Fredricks may have his lizard brain, but I have my mental photographs. Dark marks on light pages become stamped onto my brain like ink from a printing press.

Maybe a nice cuppa would help me focus. I dropped a sugar cube into my cup, added just a splash of milk, and then stirred until the tea turned a rich caramel color. I took a sip. Not bad for a pub. I dabbed my mustache with a serviette. It was blasted difficult to drink tea with a hairy caterpillar on your upper lip.

"Did the letter mention Ernest and Mrs. Roland?" Lady Mary asked. "I overheard Ernest arguing with his mother on the day she died. I just know she was berating him for gadding about with the shepherd's widow. I clearly heard her say marital discord. What else could she have meant?"

I couldn't help but smile. "Maybe she thought we were causing the discord. Maybe she was referring to our gadding about."

The clouds lifted from her countenance. "What's good for the gander is good for the goose," she said with a sly smile.

"Is that what you're up to? Trying to make Ernest jealous?" As I said it, I felt a pang. All this while, I'd thought she enjoyed my company.

"Of course not. Although it would serve him right."

I couldn't agree more. If he was cheating on her, then he deserved a dose of poison himself.

Her face grew serious. "I saw Edith holding the letter, and she was agitated to no end. I think she made a new will to cut Ernest out entirely."

"That's the bit of paper the reporter found in her fire grate?" I didn't tell her I had found it first.

"Yes." Her hand trembled as she sipped her tea. "You see why I absolutely must read that letter, don't you, Doctor?"

"You don't think Ernest could have poisoned her, do you?"

She bit her lip.

"And then thrown the new will in the fireplace..." my voice trailed off. "Why would she make a new will and then destroy it the same day?" I scratched my beard.

"She was angry with Ernest for his liaison with Mrs. Roland, but then changed her mind and couldn't bring herself to cut him out entirely. The manor house has been in the Elliott family for generations. It wouldn't be right, no matter what Ernest had done."

"True." Being cut from a will wasn't the only cutting I thought appropriate for philandering husbands.

"You must tell me the whereabouts of the letter." Mary's features hardened. "Mr. Fredricks examined Edith's handbag and knows you forced the lock."

"I told you before, I didn't!" I put down my teacup with too much force, and it nearly cracked the saucer. Heads turned and stared. I continued in a whisper, "The key was in the lock when I found the handbag. I merely unlocked the handbag, took the letter, and hid it before Dr. Booth found me out. I left the bag with the key in the lock."

"Then why was the lock forced?"

"Why indeed." The letter must have implicated the murderer in some way, and he wanted it back. He must have been desperate when he found it missing. The cordial bottle could also be important evidence, but I was convinced the killer was after that letter. "The letter is the key," I said and then closed my eyes, took several deep breaths, and tried yet again to conjure the letter.

I'd been trying to reconstruct it, but for the life of me, I couldn't get a clear picture. What a time for my photographic memory to fail me. I put all my mental energy into recalling the letter. *I was holding it in my hand...I glanced down at it before Dr. Booth called my name.* In those few seconds, somewhere, my brain had registered its contents. I just needed to access them now. With my mind's eye, again I stared down at the mental image of the page.

What I saw startled me. I didn't dare tell Lady Mary. I needed to get back to the manor house and retrieve that letter myself. If I was right, it was the smoking gun that would hang the murderer.

Chapter Ten: The Wrong Man

Once I explained to Mr. Montgomery my fears about Fredricks exposing me, he insisted on extracting me immediately. Even if I could figure out how to retrieve the damning letter, I couldn't ask Mr. Montgomery to give me more time. He was adamant about getting me out of Wickham Bishop as soon as possible. He didn't want me to compromise the mission. I tried not to be too contrite or admit failure just yet. After all, if my memory wasn't playing tricks on me, I could be instrumental in bringing a killer to justice. But how?

I couldn't tell the War Office I'd stolen a letter from the dowager's handbag and hidden it at the behest of a jealous wife who fancied me her savior. And until I could confirm the contents of the letter, I dared not make accusations that might turn out to be complete figments of my imagination. What was a bearded lady to do?

I was packing up my meager belongings: the maid's outfit, the one suit I wasn't wearing, and my notebook, when there was a knock at the door. Luckily, I was still undercover as Doctor Vogel. I went to the cottage door and wasn't surprised to see Lady Mary, as she was a regular visitor. I was going to miss our daily walks and sharing in her confidences.

"Lady Mary, what a nice surprise!" For fear of rousing more gossip, I didn't invited her in.

"Doctor, you've got to help me!" She was quivering like a half-baked treacle pudding.

"Whatever is the matter?"

"They've arrested Ernest!"

"Ernest? Why?"

"They found a poison vial in his room. The police took him away to Scotland Yard. They've charged him with murder." She broke down and threw her head upon my shoulder. "They're keeping him in jail in London until the trial," she said in a muffled voice into my jacket.

I put my arm around her. "There, there. Don't worry. We'll sort it out. Isn't Mr. Fredricks still on the case?"

A muffled "yes" came from the vicinity of my armpit.

"He's a brilliant investigator. I'm certain he can exonerate Ernest and catch the true killer." Perhaps Ernest *was* the true killer. If he had quarreled with his mother, and he was having an affair with Mrs. Roland, and the countess threatened to tell Lady Mary and cut him out of her will, then he had a motive. And he certainly had the means. But did he have the character? Mr. Fredricks says anyone is capable of murder in the right circumstances. I disagree. Only a degenerate character is capable of murder under any circumstances. Although as far as I'm concerned, most men are degenerates. All the lives wasted and lost to wars, not to mention sons poisoning their mothers. If women ran the world, things would be decidedly different.

"Isn't there something you can do?" she pleaded.

"I'm a doctor, not a detective." I patted her shoulder. "Anyway, I'm afraid I have to get back to London. I have a sick patient desperately in need of my care. She refuses to see any other doctor." I was pleased with myself for thinking that up on the spot.

"Oh, you can't leave me now!" she cried.

"I'm afraid I must." I went back to my packing, careful to cover my underthings and the maid's costume with more manly attire.

"Perhaps I could see you in London. Ian has found us a house in Paddington where we can be near Ernest and await the trial."

"Good plan." I folded my socks and patted them into the corner of my case.

"They say it could be weeks, even months. Lieutenant Douglas and Mr. Fredricks are coming too. Why don't you join us? After you check on your patient, of course."

"Lieutenant Douglas?" I shuddered at the thought of sharing a house with that rude man.

"He's taken a job at the War Office. Since he was wounded, he doesn't have to go back to the Front."

"At the War Office!" I couldn't help but blurt out.

"What's the matter with that? Don't you think he's done enough already? He's served his country. Anyway, he says he might make a regular career of the army. He figures if he sticks it out, he may even be promoted to captain."

Captain Douglas. *Horsefeathers!* I doubted he could make the grade.

"Won't you join us at the house in Paddington? We've got plenty of room. I need you now more than ever. My nerves are ruined. Please, Doctor."

"I'm afraid that's impossible. But I will promise to visit you when I can."

"I imagine you'll be called on to testify again at Ernest's trial."

I hadn't considered I would be called as a witness in London. I'd planned on discarding Doctor Vogel as soon as I reached a safe distance from Wickham Bishops. I'd better keep the two suits and the beard and brow set just in case. "Could be." I didn't relish the idea of reprising my role as Dr. Vogel on the London stage, even if that stage was a courtroom.

"Oh, I almost forgot to tell you. They also found a false beard hidden behind his socks, and those fellows from Scotland Yard accused Ernest of using it to impersonate Derek to purchase the strychnine."

"Good heavens!" My voice raised an octave. "I mean, bloody hell!" I corrected myself in my most manly register. "They can't really have a case against Ernest."

"I'm afraid they might, Doctor." Lady Mary's face fell. "He doesn't have an alibi for the time someone dressed as Derek bought the poison. What can we do? We can't let Ernest—" She didn't finish the sentence.

"No, we can't," I agreed. I needed to get that letter back. *But how?* The War Office expected me back in London tonight. I was to leave immediately. Furthermore, the diligent maid was keeping the room under lock and key on strict instructions from Scotland Yard. I doubted even Lady Mary could get into the bedroom. Given Lady Mary's role in the whole affair, she was not in the best position to find such a letter in any case. Luckily, Ernest's trial was weeks off, so I had time to devise a plan to retrieve the letter. Most likely, I was imagining its damning contents. Maybe Lady Mary was right, and it was about a marital discord. I couldn't be certain it wasn't from some busybody speculating about Lady Mary and me.

By the time I got back to London, the results from the cordial bottle analysis should be ready. Perhaps they would resolve everything. Of course, they may not resolve it in Lord Elliott's favor, especially if he was a man of many dalliances and had contracted "the French disease." He could have laced the cordial with mercury bichloride and offered it to his mother. I remembered the tiny card attached to the bottle. "To E with all my love, J." E for Edith…But who was J?

"What can we do to save Ernest?" Lady Mary seemed to shrink in stature. "Poor Ernest, spending the next few weeks in prison."

"Don't worry. We have time. We'll think of something." I hoped I was right. I didn't feel as certain as I sounded. Anyway, what if Ernest really were the murderer?

"Thank you, Doctor." Mary gave me a sad smile. "Until we meet in London." She held out her hand.

I took it, bent toward it and kissed the air in its general direction like I'd seen other gentleman doing.

Once Mary left, I rushed about to finish packing my one suitcase and tidy up the cottage. I double-checked the nightstand and the chest of drawers. I didn't want to leave behind some telltale sign of my disguise. For a second time, I passed a rag over the counter of the kitchenette. I'd say it was even cleaner than when I arrived. I gathered my toiletries and spirit gum and tucked them into a corner of my suitcase, closed it, and sat on the small wooden chair, at the ready. A driver from the War Office would be fetching me in less than ten minutes, and I didn't want to keep him waiting.

A brusque knock on the door signaled his arrival. Although I would miss Lady Mary and the sweet country air, I was eager to get back to my flat in London and take off my disguise. Suitcase in hand, I opened the door, ready to depart this place for good.

To my surprise, a uniformed officer was standing on my stoop. I had expected someone undercover or at least wearing plain clothes, someone who wouldn't call attention to my departure. Instead, there was a police car with another uniformed officer waiting in the driver's seat—hardly a discrete send-off. The whole village would be talking.

"Dr. Vogel?" the officer asked. Wearing the standard issue navy-blue overcoat and custodian helmet fastened under the chin, the poor fellow was sweating like a cold beverage on a hot day. "The expert on poisons?"

"Yes." I played along.

"Come with me." The constable put his hand on my arm. "You're under arrest."

What? Had that blasted Lieutenant Douglas actually persuaded the police I killed the countess? "There must be some mistake."

"Come along." The officer took my suitcase from me and dropped it on the stoop.

"Why? What's going on?"

"You'll find out soon 'nuff." He slapped metal ratcheted bracelets around my wrists, picked up my case, and then gestured toward the car.

I had no choice but to comply. With its front fenders suspended above large white tires, its long shiny snout, two round lamps for eyes, and license plate mustache, the car looked like a menacing cartoon dog. The levered front window only added to the effect.

The constable opened the passenger door and roughly deposited me, along with my luggage, in the backseat. I'd never been in a police car before. In fact, having grown up in London, except for family holidays to the seaside, I'd only been in an automobile a few times in my life, the most memorable had been my wedding day when Andrew hired a car to take us to Torquay where we spent our honeymoon at The Grand Hotel. Andrew had tried to carry me over the threshold but tripped, and we both went crashing to the floor, his elbow jamming into my eye socket on the way down. I had a great shiner for the rest of the week. Those had been the happiest days of my life.

Strangely enough, even after his infidelity and the divorce, I didn't regret having given my whole heart to Andrew. Yet, I already regretted coming to Wickham Bishops, which could prove to be my last regret, if I end up hanging for a crime I didn't commit.

The backseat of the Arrol-Ernestston—as a tiny plaque on the bonnet announced—was cramped and claustrophobic, especially with my case on my lap. At least the top was up, hiding my shame. I'd hate to have to ride through town with the top down, everyone gawking at me. They already thought I was carrying on an intrigue with a married woman.

As we drove past, several refugees from the cottages were standing on their stoops, smoking and watching the scene. A couple of others peered down from their first-floor windows. My arrest was the most exciting thing to happen in the village for months, next to the dowager's murder, and the arrest of Lord Elliott, of course. I was glad when the police car had left the village behind and we were driving along deserted country roads.

I hadn't realized Wickham Bishops was so close to the coast until I saw a giant concrete "ear" in the far distance across a green field, a large dot against a gray-blue horizon. I recognized the large dome as one of the new sound mirrors the War Office had installed along the coast to amplify the sounds of approaching enemy aircraft. The car continued along the coast, passing more fields of various grasses and an occasional stand of black poplars or other hardwood trees.

I was happy to see the green spire of Chelmsford Cathedral. I recognized it from when I was a child, and my mother and I would take the train from London to Chelmsford to visit my aunt. The police station couldn't be far away, and finally I could get out of this deuced uncomfortable automobile. Give me a train over a car any day.

Wait! What? We passed right by the Essex Constabulary. "Where are we going?" I asked. We'd already been driving on this bumpy horse path long enough for my back to hurt. *Where were they taking me?* Now I was getting nervous.

"London," the driver said. "Keep your shirt on."

They would be in for a surprise if I took it off!

"Might you at least tell me the charge against me?" I asked as politely as I could manage under the circumstances. *Had they released Lord Elliott and I was now to take his place in a London prison?* My mind was racing.

"All in good time," the arresting officer said. "All in good time."

It was not a good time. Not by a long shot. But one didn't argue with bobbies armed with Billy clubs.

Surely the War Office would help me sort this out once we got to the London police station. As my father used to say, "The day's not over till the cows come home." I just hope I'm not said cow heading for the slaughter.

On the outskirts of town, we passed an abandoned farm. The once bucolic landscape of rural England was haunted by what it lacked—able-bodied men.

I must have nodded off for quite a while because I awoke when the car stopped in front of the Essex Regiment Depot at Warley, or so the sign said. The depot was a big square brick building surrounded by scrubby lawns and dirt. Across the road, by the looks of it, the chapel had become the regiment's home church, and a group of men in uniform stood huddled in the churchyard, no doubt at another funeral for a fallen friend. Lorries carrying wounded soldiers pulled up in front of a makeshift hospital. And a group of men—some in wheelchairs and others on crutches, stood smoking near the entrance.

When the acrid smell of cigarette smoke reached my nostrils, it transformed into the familiar penetrating spirits smell of ether and brought the war back in all its vivid gore. I could practically feel the soldier's cold flesh under my palpating fingertips.

"Out you go," the driver said. "A break to use the lav."

"Don't let him out of your sight," his partner said.

I desperately needed to use the facilities, but I couldn't bloody well do so within his sight. Although, if I revealed my true identity perhaps the case against me would be dropped. Then again, I might appear even more suspicious for wearing a costume and posing as a doctor. In fact, they might think the whole ruse was devised in order to murder the countess.

I'd never traveled from Warley to London by car, but it must be at least another two hours. I didn't know if my bladder could hold out against these blasted bumpy roads. Under the circumstances, I had no choice but to risk it.

"I'm fine," I lied.

"Alrighty then." The driver reached over the backseat and unlocked my hands.

Were they dumping me off in Warley? Or worse, enlisting me in the army? I was passing myself off as an able-bodied man, and a doctor no less. And the Warley Depot included a hospital central to the war effort. I'd seen the effects of war, and I could stomach the sight of bloody and severed limbs, but I definitely couldn't amputate one.

"Cuff him to the car," the driver said to his mate. He stretched out my right arm and handcuffed my wrist to the car's metal frame, while his partner took my left hand and cuffed my left wrist to the opposite side of the car frame. I was stretched out like Christ on the cross. What in blazes did they have planned for me? Was I to be horsewhipped while chained to this vehicle?

"Now see here," I said.

"Let's get us a pint," the driver said heading for the depot with his partner in tow.

"You can't just leave me!" I called after them.

The driver called back, "We'll see about that, ya dodgy berk." Then they both laughed.

I didn't know what a berk was, but it didn't sound good.

An hour later, the pair returned in good spirits, smelling of beer. I, on the other hand, was more than a bit miffed and planned to report them to the War Office as soon as I got the chance. My arms were aching and the cuffs bit into my wrists.

"Enjoy the view?" the driver asked as he uncuffed my right hand and then reached across to my left. He pocketed the extra cuffs and locked my wrists together again with the remaining set.

I scowled at him but said nothing. I didn't want to be conked on the head with a truncheon, or worse.

After thirty minutes on the road, the sky turned as dark as my mood. A crow sitting atop a dead tree alongside the road gave me an eerie feeling. Dotted with drooping thatched roofs and an occasional dilapidated farmhouse, the landscape spoke to me in a shadow language full of foreboding.

By the time we reached the outskirts of London, I was convinced there was apocalypse amid the hedgerows.

"Where we supposed to drop this dirty Hun spy?" the driver asked his partner.

"Spy!" I exclaimed. Truth be told, I was a spy but not for the Germans.

"That's right," his partner said. "And you'll hang for it. Unless you gets the firing squad."

The driver snorted. "Hangin' or shootin's too good for the likes of him. He outta be drawn and quartered or burnt alive."

Burnt alive! I shuddered.

"We should string him up by his ugly black beard," his partner chimed in.

As much as I'd been looking forward to losing the beard, that's not exactly how I'd imagined doing it.

Chapter Eleven: Back in London

I was greatly relieved when we turned onto Whitehall Street and then pulled up in front of the Old Admiralty Building. If I could just talk to Mr. Montgomery or someone from Room 40, I could get this mess straightened out.

One of the constables grabbed my suitcase, dropped it on the curb, and then grabbed me. I stumbled as he pulled me out of the car. After five hours folded into the back of that car, I could barely walk...and my need for the facilities was dire.

"Might I talk to someone in Room 40?" I asked, with as much deference as I could muster. "Please, I know people there. They can vouch for me."

The driver pulled a piece of crumpled paper from his pocket and read it. "Says we're to take him to some bloke called Captain Hall."

I'd heard that name, but I'd never met him. Captain Reginald Hall, or "Blinker" as the lads called him, was the director of British Intelligence. Thank goodness. There was hope for me yet. Surely he would let me speak to Mr. Montgomery, or Mr. Grey, or even Mr. Knox.

The bobbies deposited me in the reception area outside Captain Hall's office. His secretary gave me an appraising look and reluctantly offered me a seat. When I made for an overstuffed upholstered chair near a low coffee table, she shook her head and pointed to a high-backed wooden chair in the corner. She pushed a button on a squat box, announced me to a man on the other end, and then escorted me inside to the interior office.

Captain Hall's office was spacious and contained only the bare essentials—a desk and chair, which gave it a forsaken appearance. Unlike Room

40, his office had big windows facing Whitehall Street. The sound of cars and carriages created ambient background noise for our meeting. The captain was sitting at his desk. He was a slight man with a band of white hair encircling a bald head, sharp eyes, and a pleasant if tight-lipped smile. He was wearing a dark uniform decorated with the multicolored stripes of an officer, a stiff white collar, and a neat black necktie. He greeted me with a smile, stood up from his desk, and held out his hand.

I dropped my suitcase and reached out to take it, but he'd already withdrawn it with a chuckle.

"Brilliant disguise, Miss Figg," he said. "I nearly fell for it myself."

"Thank you, sir," I said with relief.

"But, if you don't mind me saying, you look at bit worse for wear." His eyes twitched and flashed like a Navy signal lamp. No wonder they called him Blinker.

"It was a long ride from Wickham Bishops, and those officers were convinced I'm a German spy. Needless to say, they weren't happy with me."

"Sorry about that, old boy—Miss Figg. We had to maintain your cover throughout the extraction. Standard procedure. Apologies if it was uncomfortable, but it's safer that way." He gestured to another high-backed wooden chair, the only other piece of furniture in the room besides his desk and chair.

"Perhaps I could freshen up before our interview?" My bladder was full to bursting.

"Of course. The gents'—ladies'," he corrected himself, "is just downstairs. I'm afraid there's not a ladies' on every floor." He cleared his throat. "Although I'm not sure you should visit the ladies dressed like that."

"Good point." A man in the powder room, and one in my disheveled state, would surely cause a panic. "Is there a place where I can change?" I pointed to my suitcase.

"Mrs. Reynolds will take care of you. After you've freshened up, tell her to bring us a couple of coffees, will you? Unless of course you prefer tea? I'm a coffee man myself." He chuckled. "You really are very convincing, Miss Figg.

It's uncanny." He shook his head, and his eyes flashed their Morse code.

"Thank you, sir," I said, wondering if it was flattering that I could so easily pass as a man.

It took a while to persuade Mrs. Reynolds I didn't want to change my clothes in the men's lavatory. What would the Navy men think if I went in as a man and emerged as a maid?

Mrs. Reynolds buzzed the captain again and asked if she could escort me to his private lavatory. She gave me a scornful look as she did so.

Besides my second suit, the maid's kit was my only option. I pulled off my trousers, jacket, waistcoat, and shirtwaist, and slipped into the black dress. I decided to do without the apron. I was on my way out the door when I caught my reflection in the glass. *Good heavens!*

I'd forgotten to remove my beard and bushy brows. When I ripped off the beard, at least one layer of skin went with it. I peeled the brows off more slowly, and then adjusted my maid's cap to cover my shorn hair. First thing tomorrow, I'd have to shop for a new hat to wear until my hair was long enough for a fingerwave. Nothing like buying a new hat to lift the spirits.

I returned to Captain Hall's office. He looked up from his desk and stared at me with astonishment. "Uncanny." He gestured to the wooden chair. "Take a seat, Miss Figg."

I smoothed the skirt of my dress and sat down. I felt self-conscious about my legs. In my haste, I'd forgotten to put on my stockings. I tugged the dress down over my knees. A few minutes ago, I'd sat in the same chair with all the confidence of a man, and now here I was as fidgety as a schoolgirl called before the headmistress. It was amazing the difference wearing trousers made to one's confidence. If women wore trousers, we'd rule the world.

"I'd like a full report on this supposed American newspaperman, Fredrick Fredricks." He blinked. "Can you type it up and have it to me by next week? Handy you're a secretary too." When he chuckled, his eyelids fluttered. "You can do your own typing."

"Just so," I said with a forced smile.

"In a nutshell, what did you find out about the blighter? Is he spying for the Germans?"

I didn't want to admit what'd I'd found out could actually fit inside a nutshell. "He's very secretive. Based on my investigation, I suspect he has a family somewhere, a family he never mentions."

"Did you find evidence of espionage?"

"He had several books in German."

"Books? What kind of books?" Captain Hall's mustache framed his scowl.

"From what I could tell, German psychology and philosophy."

"No coded messages or secret telegrams?"

I shook my head.

"Well, type up everything. Even the smallest detail could be relevant."

The captain sounded just like Fredricks. Anything, even the smallest detail, could be a clue.

I hesitated for a moment, wondering whether or not I should bring it up, as I was expressly told in no uncertain terms to stay out of local intrigues unless they were directly connected to the suspicious newspaperman. "Remember I mentioned the murder investigation at Ravenswick Abbey?"

"Yes, and I told you to stay out of it."

"But what if Fredrick Fredricks is involved?"

The captain blinked a few times and furrowed his brows. "Involved? How?"

I cleared my throat. "He had a *Field Guide to Poisonous Plants* in his room. And I suspect the countess was not poisoned with strychnine as Scotland Yard proposed." I tugged on the hem of my maid's uniform. "I found a suspicious little cordial bottle—"

"Stay out of it, Miss Figg, and let Scotland Yard to their job. They don't interfere with our business, and we don't interfere with theirs. Is that clear?"

"But, sir—"

"The War Office can't get involved in local criminal cases. You're assigned to get information on our potential spy. Keep after..." He stuttered over Fredrick Fredricks and gave up. "The suspicious newspaperman. Unless you can prove the murder is connected to espionage and Fredricks is the murderer, leave it alone. Stick to your mission."

I nodded and took my leave. Tomorrow, I would follow up with Daisy

Nelson and swear her to secrecy. In the meantime, I was eager to get home.

It was good to be back in my flat after so many weeks away. Motes billowed into great clouds as I pulled open the drapes in the drawing room. In spite of the fetid premature summer smells wafting up from the sweltering street below, I opened the windows to air out the place. London was malodorous and my flat was stuffy, but it was home. And I thought the cottage was oppressive. I'd have to start the ice delivery service again as soon as possible. If only I could get my hands on some lemons. I was dying for a glass of cold lemonade. With the war, icemen were replaced by ice girls, who delivered only once a week, and my beverage choices were limited to water or beer.

I'd say one thing for Dr. Vogel, he'd taught me how to hold my liquor. Before my assignment, I'd been a teetotaler. Now I enjoyed the occasional pint as much as the next bloke.

I surveyed the drawing room. Except for a layer of dust, it looked just as I had left it, and yet it felt different. Something had changed. The furniture was the same—four ornate chairs in crimson velvet inherited from my grandmother, a Charles II oak court cupboard, and a pink and blue Donegal carpet. The silver candelabra on the round oak table and my grandfather's cuckoo clock on the fireplace mantle were exactly where I'd left them. *So, what is different? Is something missing?* I walked around the room, touching my favorite pieces, the smooth wood of the cupboard, the soft plush of the velvet. Then it dawned on me. *Incredible!* I swirled around taking in the entire room. *That's it!* The overwhelming absence of Andrew, it had vanished.

I flew about the flat like a bird just released from its cage. I threw open the drapes. I sorted my mail. I put on the kettle. It was reassuring to sit at my own kitchen table and listen to the crescendo of the kettle reaching a boil. I poured the boiling water into my favorite teapot and waited for the reviving beverage to steep. I never imagined cobalt-blue and-white porcelain could bring such joy.

After my cuppa, I took a long hot bath, which made me sleepy. Sleep won out over food, and I went to bed without supper, which was just as well since my icebox was empty. When I lay in bed, looking up at the familiar wallpaper, a hint of the absence of Andrew was barely perceptible in the curve of a particular paisley or that faded patch near the chandelier. I closed my eyes to blot it out, but the presence of his absence spread from the wallpaper to my walled-in heart.

I thought of the evening at the Royal Caledonian Ball when my second cousin, who'd been at Eton with Andrew, dared him to dance with me. Apparently, I had a reputation for being prickly, and at the ripe old age of twenty was already considered a hopeless spinster. Andrew was a beautiful dancer, so graceful I felt like I was flying. Unlike other boys, he laughed at my zingers and quips instead of running away. To the chagrin of my mother, I scratched out the rest of my dance card and he abandoned his other partners. We danced together for the rest of the night. We were married three weeks later on Christmas Eve.

Where is he now? I could almost feel his arms around me. Brushing tears from my cheeks, I closed my eyes and said a prayer for him. Then, completely knackered, I fell into a deathlike sleep.

The next morning, I awoke, disturbed by nightmares about Andrew and a terrible sense of foreboding. I was tempted to track down Nancy, the husband-stealing tart, and ask if he was all right. But first, I had do something about my hair. Even if I wore a hat, I couldn't completely cover the black bristles sticking out of my head like a valet's brush. And I wasn't about to let her see me looking like a love-sick porcupine.

Famished, I searched my kitchen cupboards for something to eat. I had to settle for a couple of stale biscuits and a tin of beans. I made a cup of tea, dunked the biscuits, and resolved to restock my pantry as soon as possible.

After breakfast, such as it was, I picked out a flowered spring frock, my nicest silk stockings, a pair of low-heeled but stylish strappy pumps, and laid them out on the bed. Then I went to find a hat. Before the war—and the divorce—deciding on a hat to wear was the most difficult decision of my day. Now, I might find myself decoding a German telegram that could change the course of history or trailing a suspicious refugee.

I grabbed my fancy pink garden hat off the shelf. It was loaded with silk flowers and lace and looked like a great blooming meringue. I hurried to my dressing table and placed it atop my shorn head. *Blast!* I didn't have enough hair to pin it into and it kept sliding off. Mourning my auburn locks, I went back to my wardrobe to fetch my old stand-by, a beige bucket-shaped felt number. It wasn't as pretty, but at least it stayed on. I would have to leave the flat early enough to stop at Raoul's Wig Shop and find a suitable wig. I couldn't wear this ugly hat for the next six months waiting for my hair to grow back.

I may have overdone the lipstick and rouge just a tad. But it was so nice to be able to paint my face again. The reflection in the mirror didn't seem to belong to me, but to some long-lost twin, who looked like me but lived a parallel life more exciting than my own. I held the bottle of Atkinsons Lavender at arm's length, spritzed the air in front of my face, and walked through the fragrant mist. Ah, to smell like a woman again instead of a sweaty farm hand.

It was a rare fogless morning, and early enough that the early summer sun was still pleasant, so I decided to walk the mile to Raoul's. Excited to be back in the hubbub of the city, I enjoyed the bustle of women on their way to work. Before the war, the walkways would have been thick with the hard browns, grays, and whites of men's suits, but now they'd been replaced by the soft yellows, pinks, baby blues of tunics and skirts...and of course uniforms. It was easy to distinguish the shop girls from the munitions workers.

Oh, bother! Raoul's wouldn't open for another twenty minutes. I might as well continue on to the Italian Garden, one of my favorite spots. Every Sunday before the war, Andrew and I would walk arm in arm through Hyde Park and stop in the Italian Garden for tea. I hadn't visited the garden since before the divorce. My life, it seems, had been divided into BD and AD, before-divorce and after-divorce.

Sadly, the fountains in the Italian Garden were off and the water lilies, flag iris, flowering rush, and purple loosestrife, were dead—just like my life with Andrew. I plunked down on a bench and wondered what it would be like to have an everlasting love like Prince Albert and Queen Victoria. Albert made this garden for her, his one true love, as a token of his undying devotion.

Look at it now. The war may have destroyed the earthly tokens of undying love, but I had faith it couldn't destroy what they represented. Even now, after everything, as hard as I tried, I couldn't squelch my love for Andrew.

With my spirits as brittle as the dried rush stalks, I headed back toward Raoul's.

The clerk seemed put out when she unlocked the door for me. Luckily, I didn't need her to direct me to the wigs. I knew the shop by heart since my mother was an avid wearer of wigs. I glanced around before taking off my hat. Anyone who saw my shorn head would think I suffered from some nasty tropical disease or contagious fungus. I selected a wig closest to my natural auburn hair color. It wasn't in the finger curl style I preferred, but it would have to do. I tugged my felt bucket back over my brush of dyed hair, paid for the wig, and hurried to catch the train to Whitehall.

Parcel under my arm, I disembarked at Whitehall station. I'd have to run to make it to work on time.

Oh no! Not him! The station was crowded, but I would recognize that gray fedora, long neck, and languid posture anywhere.

Flustered, I faced the other direction so he wouldn't see me. What was Lieutenant Clifford Douglas doing getting off the train at my stop? And why was he heading up Whitehall Street? I ducked under the awning of the teashop next door to the Old Admiralty and watched him enter the building. *Blimey! That's right.* Lady Mary had told me he was working here now. *Perhaps he is being recommissioned to the Front,* I thought hopefully. Although I wouldn't wish the Front on my worst enemy, I would be pleased never to see the narky chap again.

I gave him a couple of minutes head start and then headed into the building myself. I arrived at Room 40 a good five minutes late thanks to blasted Lieutenant Douglas.

I hurried to my desk, which was exactly as I left it, neat and tidy.

"Miss Figg." Mr. Grey greeted me with a big smile. "Or should I say Dr. Vogel?" He turned to the table where the rest of the team was working. "Look who's here!"

"The prodigal daughter returns." Mr. Montgomery waved me over. "Tell us all about your adventure at Ravenswick Abbey. Did you catch the little Frenchie in the act?"

I was so used to people confusing the Great White Hunter for a Frenchman I didn't bother correcting him.

"I'm afraid I wasn't much of a success," I said. "In fact, I think I rather corked it up."

"No." Mr. Knox held out his hand. "You could never do that, my dear."

When I didn't extend my hand in return, he grasped my bare arm. Cheeky devil. Some things never changed.

"Why don't you make us some tea and tell us all about it," Mr. Montgomery said.

Yes, some things never changed. I'd been commissioned by the War Office as a spy and was still expected to make the tea.

The fellows seemed so genuinely glad to see me, I was happy to make tea as long as I didn't have to do it wearing a beard. If only they could have seen me in my disguise. Amused by the thought of serving them tea in a beard, I turned the corner into the kitchenette.

"I say!" a familiar voice said. "You should be more careful."

I'd run smack into Lieutenant Clifford Douglas.

"Excuse me," I said, my face hot. I stared at the floor as I passed him.

"Have we met before?" he asked, following me to the sink.

"I'm sure we haven't."

"You look awfully familiar."

"I have one of those faces, I guess."

"I'm sure I've seen you before. Didn't I meet you at a supper party..."

I shook my head and busied myself with the kettle, but he wouldn't go away. He just stood there watching me. I could feel his eyes on the back of my head. He was on to me. I knew it. Now I was in the soup.

When I turned around, I caught him staring at my ankles. He certainly hadn't seen my ankles before!

"I say," he repeated. "Would you like to have lunch with me this afternoon? I know a nice tea shop next door."

"I'm afraid I'm busy during lunch. Anyway, I don't know you."

"Oh, so sorry. Captain Douglas, but why don't you call me Clifford."

Captain! Had he been promoted or was he promoting himself?

"Glad to meet you, *Captain*." I sat four cups on a tray, poured the boiling water into the cleanest teapot I could find, and turned to go. "Excuse me, the men are waiting."

"But you haven't introduced yourself," Captain Douglas said in that whiny tone of his.

"Miss Figg. Now, I really must get the men their tea before it gets cold."

"Miss Figg," he repeated. "As in my favorite sweet fruit?"

I rolled my eyes. "Figs are not actually fruit, but flowers pollinated by wasps that die in the process." I pushed past him with the tea tray, half tempted to pour it down his front.

Chapter Twelve: Lunch with Captain Douglas

D istracted by my encounter with the newly minted Captain Douglas, for the rest of the morning I found it difficult to concentrate on my report. With my luck, he'd been reassigned to the War Office permanently. The only way to find out was to accept his lunch invitation. As much as I despised the man, he could be helpful in getting more information on Fredricks. And I still had another six days before my report was due to Captain Hall. Instead of shunning him, I should try to befriend him. He was such a windbag, he was bound to spill the beans if I let him rabbit on long enough. Yes, I would try my best to get along with *Captain* Douglas for the sake of my investigation.

Throughout the morning, I'd made several trips to the lavatory to check my appearance. I'd reapplied my lipstick, pinched my cheeks, and adjusted my hat so it covered my spiky black hair. As much as I'd relished reclaiming a dress, I felt quite vulnerable with so much of my body exposed.

Between my self-consciousness about my hair and the men's boisterous discussion of the value of the Playfair cipher—a manual encryption technique—I couldn't concentrate on my report.

"It's absolute rubbish," Mr. Knox said. "Schoolboys could break it—"

"Funny you should say that," Mr. Montgomery interrupted. "When the Foreign Office rejected it as too complicated, Wheatstone offered to demonstrate with a few schoolboys." He chuckled. "The Foreign Office responded, 'schoolboys yes, but you could never teach it to attachés!'"

"You could never teach it to attachés," Mr. Grey repeated and burst out laughing.

It was good to hear the men laughing. Since the war had begun, there hadn't been much laughter in Room 40.

I glanced at my watch. Golly, it was almost noon. I slid the paper sack out from under my desk, tucked it under my arm, and headed for the lavatory. I'd intended to wait until tomorrow, when I'd have proper hair pins to attach my wig, but if I were going to lunch with Captain Douglas, I didn't want to wear this frumpy hat all afternoon.

The wig was styled in short loose curls and reminded me of Lady Mary Pickford in *Poor Little Peppina*. I pulled it over my cropped mess and tugged it down onto my scalp. The transformation was startling. The color was a shade darker than my own, more auburn than flax, and the curls were unrulier than the ones I favored. But at least I didn't look like a freshly shorn sheep.

Unfortunately, I didn't look like Lady Mary Pickford either. I touched up my makeup, re-tied the bow on my blouse, secured my stockings, and straightened my skirt. When I'd done all I could to improve my appearance, I returned to my desk, uncertain as to whether or not the captain would turn up.

At half past, I realized he wasn't coming, which, to my surprise, was a bit disappointing. I had been looking forward to pumping him for information about Fredricks. At one o'clock, I gave up on him completely and went into the kitchenette to fetch my ham and margarine sandwich from the icebox. I put on the kettle to make a cup of tea to wash it down. Waiting for the water to boil, I unwrapped the sandwich and took a bite. With stale bread and watery ham, it was hardly the best sandwich in London. I'd ordered it from Paul Rothe's sandwich shop to treat myself since I hadn't eaten a proper meal since yesterday's breakfast, which consisted of toast sans marmalade and tepid tea.

I devoured the sandwich standing at the counter, washing down the hard bread with sips of strong tea between each bite. I was just finishing up in the kitchenette, washing my cup and everyone else's, when Captain Douglas rounded the corner.

"I say, I've been looking for you," he said with a smile.

"You've found me."

"So I have. Lucky me."

The way he said it made me snort.

"Are we on for lunch then?" he asked.

I swallowed, blinked, and then looked at my watch. Technically, my lunch break was over. "Let me ask my boss," I said finally. "If you'll excuse me a moment, Captain Douglas."

"Clifford, please."

I left *Clifford* cooling his heels at a small table in the kitchenette and went to find Mr. Montgomery. I explained my plan—using Captain Clifford Douglas to find out more about the "Frenchie" before I turned in my report to the upper brass.

"Take as much time as you need." He nodded his approval and went back to his paperwork.

I returned to the kitchenette. "I'm free."

"So old Monty let you go, did he? Splendid." Captain Douglas grinned like an alley cat that just spotted a tasty rodent. He took my elbow and led me into the hall, down the stairs, and out onto the street. If I hadn't been on a mission for information, I would have objected to such familiarity. I must say, I didn't appreciate the snide grin Mr. Knox gave me on the way out the door.

An easterly breeze mitigated the late-May warmth. As we walked up Whitehall Street, Captain Douglas pointed to an ornate building.

"Too bad I can't take you to the Constitution Club in the Old Metropole. Best lunch in London. But I'm afraid it's men only."

Too bad I'm not wearing trousers and a beard or I could sample the best lunch in London.

"And I'm not dressed for Strand Palace," he said, glancing down at *my* attire. "Would you mind terribly taking lunch at Old Shades?" He waved in the direction of an amber stone building topped with a crown shaped like an ornate perfume bottle.

"It looks lovely," I said.

Old Shades turned out to be more public house than restaurant. Given I was on an assignment, I couldn't complain. With its dark mahogany paneling, beveled glass windows, and electric pendant lamps, it was most inviting. Between two large dining rooms sat a long wooden counter with siding in green, blue, and gold tiles, which gave it a festive feel. The floor was dotted with magnificent black-and-white mosaic tiles.

Captain Douglas took my elbow again and led me to a table in the snug, an area where women could eat and drink in private. The wait staff greeted him by name. I supposed this was meant to impress me.

I looked around the place. So, this was a regular haunt of Clifford Douglas. I doubted his friend Fredricks would be caught dead in a place like this...too plebeian for his aristocratic tastes. But it suited me just fine.

"With the damned—sorry—Defense of the Realm," Captain Douglas said, "we have less than an hour before closing. It's my fault for being so late, I'm afraid. You see, I was just promoted to captain—which is jolly nice—but mostly means I have to sit through insufferably boring meetings."

"A quick lunch suits me fine," I said. "I need to be getting back to the office soon anyway."

"The mussels are quite good here," said Captain Douglas. "That's what I usually order."

"Make it two orders of mussels." They couldn't be any worse than my stale sandwich.

"I say, you're a jolly good sport." Captain Douglas grinned.

The shape of his face, accentuated by a receding hairline, put me in mind of a horse, and his lips were a bit too thin. But at least he didn't have a blasted mustache like so many men nowadays. And with his pale-blue eyes and aquiline nose, he really wasn't a bad-looking sort.

"Your hair is a lovely shade of auburn, if you don't mind me saying," he said, almost apologetically. "You look like an exotic film star."

I blushed. No one had ever said that before. Perhaps I should forget about growing my hair out and keep wearing the wig.

"How long have you been back from the Front?" I asked, changing the subject. I'd seen Clifford Douglas in action back at Ravenswick Abbey, flirting with Lady Mary and Lilian Mandrake, oblivious to the fact Lady Mary was married and Lilian was obviously smitten with Ian.

"Yes, I suppose every soldier you've met has been to the Front." He smiled wistfully and stared into space. "I was wounded in France six months ago. I was recuperating in a rather depressing convalescent home when I ran into my old friend Ernest Elliott." He glanced over at me as if he'd suddenly remembered he wasn't alone. "You've probably heard of the affair at Ravenswick? Poor Ernest. He's been wrongfully accused of murder, you see."

"I read about it in the newspaper. That poor man." As far as I knew, the poor man just might be guilty of cold-blooded murder.

"Yes, his poor wife, too."

"Must be dreadful for her." I thought of poor Lady Mary, bearing up so well under pressure. If she'd had any designs on Dr. Vogel, they'd completely evaporated in the heat of defending her "dearest Ernest."

"I'm sure we'll be able to clear Ernest's good name. I'm helping investigate, along with my good friend the great newsman—"

"You're a journalist too?" I asked with feigned excitement.

"Well, you know, I dabble a bit." He tilted his head in false modesty. "I've been known to help my friend from time to time."

"And who is this great reporter friend of yours?" Given I knew Captain Douglas hadn't seen his friend for years before their reunion at Ravenswick, I doubted they were the great pals he made them out to be.

"Oh, that is an interesting story. We met in South Africa before the war. I helped him solve the case of a big game poacher. He was a suspect. Can you imagine?"

Yes, I could. I knew there was something sneaky about the Great White Hunter. I wasn't surprised he was a poacher. I nodded encouragingly.

Captain Douglas waffled on nonstop throughout lunch and coffee afterward, clearly exaggerating his relationship with the "world famous hunter and great newsman."

"He taught me his method, you see," Captain Douglas nattered on. "We don't go in for footprints and cigarette butts and all that rot. We use animal psychology to solve crime. All animals act according to their species. It's instinctual. And Fredricks is frightfully concerned with the order of the animal kingdom."

"Psychology, well that is interesting." I said. That would explain why Fredricks had those German psychology books. "You mean like that Austrian chap Sigmund Freud?" Since discovering *The Interpretation of Dreams* amongst Fredricks's possessions, I'd done some research and learned quite a bit about Mr. Freud and his outlandish theories.

"Well, yes." Captain Douglas seemed to warm to the idea. "I suppose so."

"Do you think crime is related to sexual repression then?" I asked innocently.

"Good Lord! Sexual repression," he stammered. "Well, I never—"

I smiled sweetly at him from across the table. "You know, Mr. Freud attributes all neuroses, criminal and otherwise, to the Oedipal complex and one's repressed sexual feelings for one's parents. He says humans are different from animals precisely because we suppress our incestuous instincts while other animals don't."

"I say!" He blushed. "What an idea."

"What do you know of Mr. Fredricks's parents? Perhaps his frightful concern with the order of things can be attributed to them?"

"I guess I've never asked about his family." Captain Douglas took a sip of beer. "I suppose he must have had parents though."

"Unless he sprouted on a mushroom in the Australia outback or was found under a Weeping Wattle in South Africa."

"Yes, silly of me." The captain shook his head. "Of course, he had parents. I assume they're dead. He's never mentioned them."

"Where is he from?"

The captain looked confused. "Well, South Africa, of course. But he's traveled the world. He's a brilliant newsman and everyone in New York—"

"What about a wife and children?" I interrupted. "Does he have a family?" I nibbled on a crust of bread as nonchalantly as I could, given my sense of anticipation.

"Why now that you mention it, I'm not sure. I just assumed he was a bachelor. Yes, he must be. The way he travels the world. He couldn't have a wife, you see." Captain Douglas took a bite of bread. "Anyway, I can't see as any woman would put up with him always ordering everyone about and demanding things be put just so."

"He sounds like what Mr. Freud would call an anal personality."

"Good Lord!" His face turned beet red, and I thought he might choke on his bread.

I stifled a giggle.

When he'd regained his composure, he said, "I've never met a woman quite like you, Miss Figg. You're full of surprises."

Why Clifford, you don't know by halves.

After lunch, Captain Douglas walked me back to Room 40, where we awkwardly said goodbye. I was just turning the doorknob to go inside when he asked, "Would you like to have lunch again tomorrow?"

He had an apologetic look on his face, like he was sorry to impose by asking me to join him for lunch. "You do have to eat, you know," he added before I had time to accept.

"I'd be delighted." *Provided you tip the wink on your* great friend *Fredrick Fredricks.*

Chapter Thirteen: More Brilliant than the Sun

On the way home from the War Office, I stopped by Charing Cross Hospital. I had to find out the results of Daisy's analysis of the cordial bottle. At this point, I hoped it contained nothing more than a delightful sloe-berry liquor, coincidentally enjoyed by the countess a few hours before her death. For, if I discovered it contained the fatal poison, how could I ever present the evidence, and to whom? To do so would be to reveal my true identity and ruin my investigation of Fredrick Fredricks. Moreover, Captain Hall had made it painfully clear I was not to meddle in domestic criminal matters, especially those involving Scotland Yard.

When I reached the dispensary, I was met by Daisy Nelson's scrawny backside as she bent over a microscope, completely absorbed by the infinitesimal world it revealed. I hoped it was the secret world of my mysterious J's sloe-berry liquor.

My heels tapped on the hardwood floor as I approached, and Daisy spun around, her hand on her chest and her mouth agape. Her nest of mousy hair was piled atop her head with a tiny white cap perched in the middle.

"Gor! Don't sneak up on me like that." She gasped, and then her face relaxed into a smile. "Blimey, Fiona. I haven't seen you for yonks. Did the countryside calm your nerves?"

The cover story for my absence at the hospital was a nervous condition that required a restful stay in the country. "Yes, very calming," I fibbed. Wearing a disguise, spying on a deuced clever and unnecessarily handsome big game hunter, and becoming involved in a murder trial were far from calming. Indeed, my nerves had never been so stimulated in my life.

"Did you receive the parcel I sent?" I gestured toward the microscope. "May I?"

"Tickety-boo." She moved aside. "I hope you sent *Oenothera biennis*. My rheumatism's been acting up something terrible."

"No, sorry, not evening primrose." I peered at the squiggly threads swimming through an obstacle course of blistering blobs. "Actually, I sent you the remnants of a homemade liquor in the hopes you could test it for plant poison."

"Stone the crows! *Heracleum Mantegazzianum* or *Digitalis purpurea*?" Daisy rubbed her calloused hands together.

"I doubt it contains hogweed or foxglove. I'm thinking more along the lines of Gyromitra esculenta or Amanita phalloides." I gave up trying to discern what I was looking at in the microscope and leaned against the counter.

"Poisonous mushrooms!" Daisy's horse face lit up.

"Exactly."

"I never got it. The post is rubbish."

I thought a minute. Living at Ravenswick, I'd lost track of time. "I sent it the day of the inquest," I said more to myself than to Daisy. "That was Friday. I left Wickham Bishops on Monday, so four days ago."

When she shook her head, her tiny white cap wagged at me. "So what's this about poison?"

"Just a hunch."

"As a wise woman, I might be able to conjure the poisoner without it."

I narrowed my brows. "What do you mean?"

"Bring me something belonging to the dodgy rascal, and I'll tell you if he—or she—used the poison."

I must have looked as confused as I felt.

Daisy scoffed. "You think it's a bunch of hocus-pocus, but it ain't." She went back to her microscope. "If you want my help, you know where to find me."

"Thanks. So, you'll test the bottle in the parcel when it arrives?"

"Of course."

"Thanks, Daisy." I turned to go.

"Toodle pip," she said without looking up.

"Can we keep this our little secret?"

"My lips are sealed."

"Brilliant. Thanks, Daisy."

As I walked home, I cursed the British postal service. I shouldn't have let the bottle out of my sight. It could be vital evidence. *Fiona Figg, sometimes you're such a dimwit.*

The next morning, my mind was abuzz as I went about my ablutions and prepared my toilette. I sat at my dressing table, mindlessly rearranging my boar's bristle brushes, pin trays, talcum bottles, handkerchief box, and cuticle scissors. When I got to my swans-down powder puff, I picked it up and gently stroked my cheek.

Only five days left until my report was due. I really must get something useful out of Clifford Douglas. I must say, I was doing better as Miss Figg than I had as Dr. Vogel. I still don't understand why Captain—then Lieutenant—Douglas took such a disliking to me as Dr. Vogel, unless he truly believed I killed the countess...silly man.

So far, I'd learned Fredricks was a bit of a fashion plate—in an outdoor magazine sort of way, and a ladies' man, which was obvious to anyone who'd met him—at least to any lady who'd met him. He was Catholic, and had a wife, a daughter, and twin boys he kept hidden somewhere. I had to find out more about them. Why did he keep them secret? Even Captain Douglas didn't seem to know about them.

Then there were his books. I suppose the German books on psychology and philosophy might be explained by his interest in the human mind. While revolutionary thinkers, Freud and Husserl were hardly the stuff of politics, let alone espionage. Perhaps I'd missed something and the books contained coded messages. Teresa of Avila claimed to have received coded messages from God, but that's another story...perhaps one worth investigating. Mr. Fredricks's Catholicism just didn't jibe with all that nonsense about lizard brains, animal instincts, and his love of killing large beasts in cold blood...Then again, the history of Catholicism wasn't exactly a cakewalk. For all of the captain's talk of clues as rubbish and the importance of human instinct, from what I'd seen, Mr. Fredricks was as interested in old-fashioned pawprints as the next investigator cum hunter.

And what about the *Field Guide to Poisonous Plants*? Was that for his investigation, or was he planning to poison someone? Perhaps the strangest clue I had found was the false mustache. Why would Fredricks have a false mustache? His clothes certainly looked like a costume, but not one designed to be inconspicuous. Jodhpurs? Starched white shirts. That oversized Slouch hat and showy swagger stick? Come on, men only dressed like that in American films. I had to find a way to ask Captain Douglas about that mustache.

If I were to get more information out of Captain Douglas, I needed to look my best. I went to my wardrobe and examined my choice of dresses. Although not as beastly as last month—when I was wearing trousers—it was still warm, so I concentrated on my summer wardrobe. I flipped through my dresses, but nothing seemed right. They were either too proper or not suitable for work. I settled on a pretty plum two-piece frock with three-quarter length sleeves. The skirt fell just below my knees. The sheath was low-waisted and the outer layer had a delightful lavender border.

I'd been a man for so long, I was still struggling with the blasted corset. I wished I could just burn the damnable thing and be done with it. There was so little of me to push up or squeeze in, I didn't see the point. But who was I to buck convention? I'd seen others do it at their own peril. After lacing my corset, I slipped into the silky sheath, and then sat at my dressing table and carefully rolled on my stockings. I applied a bit of face paint and stared at my reflection in my hand mirror. With my spiky black hair and deep-red rouge, I looked like one of Drury Lane's pantomime dames.

On my dressing table, the wig was draped across a hair receiver like the pelt of some animal. Too bad I couldn't pull a rat out of my hair receiver and attach it to my bristled head. Oh well, I never was a fan of pulling hair from my brushes, collecting it in my receivers, and then stuffing it into nets to use as coiffure fillers. I twirled a hatpin in its holder. I'd missed my rose china dresser set with its matching jewelry boxes, hatpin holder, and hair receivers.

I tugged the wig onto my head and maneuvered it into place. I wondered if I could give my furry friend a fingerwave. I needed to do something to tame the beast. One of my turban hats would be perfect, except those were strictly for evening wear. But a pretty felt bowler might do nicely for the office. I knew just the one, my purple felt hat with the lovely lavender bow and just a touch of lace. I grabbed it off the top shelf, returned to my dressing table, held the hat in one hand and the mirror in the other, and with much effort, pinned the hat into my wig. Yes, that would do.

I pulled on matching gloves and selected an appropriate handbag, transferred my necessaries into it, and off I went. It felt so good to wear colors again. Men's clothes were more comfortable to be sure but deadly boring.

My commute to the office went like clockwork, and I arrived before the team, which gave me time to tidy the kitchenette and the men's desks and the large working table. I didn't dare move any papers though, since they each had their own system, or in the case of Mr. Dilly Knox, a royal mess. Working around the important documents, I removed old coffee cups and sandwich wrappers, and straightened as best I could.

A newspaper clipping with a photograph of three shepherd children was lying amongst the muddle on Mr. Knox's desk. Two girls wearing heavy headscarves and thick skirts stared out at me with haunting seriousness. In between them stood a boy who wore something like a loose dark turban and held a walking stick. The smallest girl's scowl was accompanied by a defiant hand on her hip. *No wonder! Poor things.* They'd just been released from jail.

I removed an abandoned necktie from Mr. Knox's chair and sat down to continue reading the article. For the last year, nine-year-old Lúcia dos Santos and her two cousins had repeatedly seen apparitions of the Angel of Peace and the Virgin Mary. The Virgin appeared "more brilliant than the sun," and told them to pray using their rosaries daily to bring peace and end the war. *Good Heavens!* She also told them that on October 13th she would reveal her identity and perform a miracle, ending the Great War "so that all may believe." It would be a miracle if the war ended by October. If only I could have the faith of these children.

I sat back in the chair, marveling at the devotion of those so young, and wondering if this article was of interest to the War Office or if Dilly Knox was just passing the time. The article did say the children were arrested because "these events were politically disruptive." Perhaps Catholicism was more revolutionary than I had realized. I thought of Fredricks and his rosary. *What was the origin of his devotion? Was he as serious and devoted as these children when he was a boy? Had he heard the voice of the Virgin?*

Apparently, my focus on the photograph had tuned out the rest of the world, because I was startled when Mr. Knox's booming baritone interrupted my meditations.

"Moving in, are we?" he asked with a chuckle.

Flustered, I dropped the clipping back on his desk and popped up out of his chair. "Sorry, Mr. Knox. I didn't mean—"

"No worries, Fiona," he said with a wink. "What's mine is yours." His use of my Christian name and his impertinent wink sent me skittering off to my own desk behind the partition a few feet away. I suppose I was lucky the mischief-loving Dilly Knox had found me and not the somber Mr. Grey, or worse, the boss, Mr. Montgomery.

As the morning went on, I found myself checking my watch every half hour to see if it was lunchtime yet. I was eager to get on with my investigation. I'd typed up my notes from Ravenswick Abbey, peppering them with the tidbits I'd learned from Captain Douglas. Still, it wasn't much. If I didn't come up with more in the next five days, I'd surely be taken off the case. I had the Great White Hunter in my sights now and I wasn't about to let him slip away.

I looked at my watch again. It was half past eleven, my usual lunchtime. I liked an early luncheon so I wouldn't be too full to enjoy my afternoon tea, but if yesterday was any indication, Captain Douglas preferred a late lunch. Having had breakfast this morning, I wasn't going to eat two lunches again today. My stomach growled as I went on typing.

I continued typing and checking my watch for another hour before Captain Douglas finally poked his head around the partition.

"Are you ready for lunch?" He held up two umbrellas. "It's pouring buckets outside."

"Why don't we just go down to the canteen then?"

"Jolly good idea, if you don't mind." He leaned the brollies against the partition. "Is it all right to leave these here?"

I nodded.

The canteen was a vast room with marble pillars and wooden beams crisscrossing the high ceiling. Groups of military men, file clerks, office girls, and code breakers sat at rows of long rectangular tables dressed with white tablecloths. Since the officers had their own dining hall next door, Captain Douglas was the only officer of the lot.

We stood in line to get our lunch, which consisted of fish and potato pie and baked raisin pudding.

"Save the wheat, defend the fleet," I said, wishing our motto were "defend the fleet and still eat meat."

"Damn sight better than what we ate in the trenches." Captain Douglas led me to the end of the closest table. "It was almost worth getting shot to get away from bully beef and biscuits. Dreadful stuff."

Of course, the boys in the trenches got so little to eat. I felt wretched for complaining.

"When your wound is fully healed, will you be going back?"

"To the Front? I hope the damned war is over by then." Captain Douglas got that far away look he got whenever we talked about the war.

I suspected in his own genteel way, he, too, suffered from shell shock.

I thought of Andrew, wounded and home six months, only to leave me for his secretary. Now, like so many women, she was alone with their baby. Not that I felt sorry for her after what she did to me. *And what about what Andrew did to me?* I'd taken three weeks off work to nurse him back to health after the training accident. Amazing that after the plane crash, he'd only had a broken hand. But it's deuced difficult to do anything with just one hand, especially if it was shaking constantly in terror. I thought of his beautiful hands and wanted to weep.

"Although, I must say…" Captain Douglas's voice brought me back. "I don't fancy pushing papers at a desk all day." He tucked into his lunch. "Decent fish pie."

It tasted like seaweed mixed with dirt. I swallowed the bite in my mouth and nodded politely.

"Will you continue to work with Mr. Fredricks after the war?" I asked, hoping to steer the conversation toward my prey.

"We do make a jolly good team."

"He's the brains and you're the brawn?" I raised one eyebrow. Of course I was joking. Whatever his intellect, there was no denying "Apollo" Fredricks had a physique to rival some of those I'd seen in Eugen Sandow's bodybuilding book.

"Well, I'd like to think I have some smarts of my own." He pointed his fork at his plate. "Fredricks says fish is good for the brain."

"Didn't you tell me Fredricks uses only his instincts and doesn't collect evidence or examine clues?" Of course, I'd already heard everything from Lady Mary, but I hoped Captain Douglas might be able to add some important details that might give me a clue as to the reporter's modus operandi.

"Well, yes. Yes, he did. I was with him of course, helping search and collect clues."

"Of course," I said with a knowing smile. "And what did you find, if you don't mind me asking?"

"Oh no, I don't mind. I rather enjoy talking about our work." He laid his fork on the table and then wiped his mouth with his serviette. "Let's see. We found the corner of a will in the fireplace grate. That was an important piece of evidence, indeed. Fredricks made a fuss over some candle grease on the floor next to a tea stain, but I don't really see the importance of those. Then there was the warm milk. Fredricks insisted on sending it out for testing even though Dr. Vogel had already had it tested—"

"Dr. Vogel. I've heard of him. He's that recently arrested German spy." *Who, in reality, is a very clever spy for the War Office, on a mission to trap a suspicious Boer infiltrator.*

"Yes, that's right. I knew he was sinister from the moment I met him." Captain Douglas scowled. "I never did like him. Some say I'm an excellent judge of character."

"I'm sure you are, Captain Douglas." I repressed a giggle.

"I'm still half-convinced it was that evil man who killed the countess."

"Why would a German spy kill the countess?" *Yes, indeed. Why would a spy for the Germans kill the countess?* Fredricks was studying poisonous plants. Now it seemed Edith Wilkinson may have been poisoned with mushrooms. Perhaps the wronged lover was not to blame after all. But if the Great White Hunter was a German spy and did away with the countess, what in the world could be his motive? Was Edith Wilkinson important to the war effort? Were her good works and support for refugees somehow more than they seemed? Were they a cover for part of the war effort? Or perhaps they were a cover for something else, something so dreadful I didn't even want to consider the possibility. Maybe that's why the War Office had been so keen to send me to Ravenswick Abbey.

Captain Douglas thought for a moment. "You've got me there, but I knew that Vogel chap was trouble."

Ah, good captain, if you only knew. "You're so astute. I'm impressed with the evidence you found. Most people wouldn't have noticed such things as candle grease and fireplace grates."

"Oh, that's not all. I'm the one who noticed the powder on the serving tray."

"Powder?"

"Someone drugged the tea. The evidence was there on the tea tray."

Had the pesky reporter somehow discovered Lady Mary had put sleeping powders in the dowager's tea and then snuck into her bedroom to steal the letter? "Who do you suspect?" I asked innocently.

"I'm not sure. Fredricks has his hypotheses, but he's not sharing them with me. It's rather frustrating. How can I help him if he doesn't confide in me?"

"Perhaps you should tell him how frustrating it is for you. If he knew how you felt, maybe he'd take you into his confidence." From what I'd seen at

Ravenswick Abbey, the "famous newsman" used Clifford Douglas something terrible. In fact, Fredricks treated Captain Douglas more like a nagging wife than a sleuthing partner. Or was Fredricks the nagging wife, and Clifford Douglas the put-upon husband? In any case, they made an odd couple indeed.

"I'm afraid he thinks I talk too much." Captain Douglas took a sip of coffee.

I'm counting on it! "I find it all fascinating, Captain Douglas." I smiled in as coy a fashion as I was able given my allergy to flirting.

"Do you?" He looked pleased.

"Tell me, Captain, is Mr. Fredricks a religious man?"

"Religious? Not really." He stared down at his raisin pudding. "Well, now that you mention it, he does go to church from time to time." He glanced up at me from across the table. "He was raised Catholic, you see. But I'd say he's what you'd call a lapsed Catholic."

"So his parents were Catholic?"

"Come to think of it, I remember now, he once mentioned his mother was devout. He rarely talks of her, but when he does, you'd think she was a saint."

His mother is a saint. And is her son also a saint? Or is he hiding an evil secret?

"Does Mr. Fredricks have siblings?"

"You know, I've never asked him. He might have mentioned a sister or brother, but I can't recall. You certainly are fascinated by my friend."

"He sounds like a very mysterious fellow."

"I say, would you like to meet him?" A broad smile lit up his face. "Fredricks loves attention. He's not what you'd call modest. I'm sure he'd be very pleased to meet you. We could all go out for supper. Or better yet, you could come to Paddington. We are all staying there with Lady Mary Elliott until after Ernest's trial."

"That's very kind of you, but I couldn't impose—"

"Nonsense! You'd like Lady Mary. She's a lovely woman. And she would absolutely adore you."

I wondered if Lady Mary would adore me as much as she had Dr. Vogel. In any case, I didn't dare find out. If anyone would recognize me—with or without a beard—it would be Lady Mary Elliott.

Chapter Fourteen: The Bloodbath

Today was toad-in-the hole and suet pudding, which at least meant a bit of sausage in the thick gluey pastry, and some mutton fat in the pudding. For the last two weeks, Captain Douglas and I had lunched together, taking whatever the canteen had on offer: Mondays and Tuesdays it was bean soup and treacle pudding; Wednesdays and Thursdays it was toad-in-the-hole and suet pudding, and on Fridays it was fish and potato pie and baked raisin pudding. The food was warm if not particularly appetizing.

Captain Douglas didn't seem to mind. He'd happily eat just about anything. In fact, he grumbled more about Saturday night meals in Paddington when Fredricks insisted on cooking fancy French food, which didn't sit well with the captain. The way Captain Douglas complained about Fredricks once again reminded me of an old married man complaining about his nagging wife.

I didn't learn much more about Fredricks or the murder of the countess, but it was nice to have someone to talk with, even if Captain Douglas did most of the talking. And so far, I'd managed to put off the question of my going to supper at the Elliott house in Paddington. Furthermore, we'd compromised on the time of lunch, and I'd trained Captain Douglas to fetch me at noon on the dot...or thereabouts.

This afternoon, instead of poking his head around the partition and asking, "Are you ready for lunch?" he stomped right up to my desk and dropped a white feather on top of my typewriter.

"The nerve," he said. "I'm going to start wearing my uniform again." He narrowed his eyes. "Horrible woman."

"I hope you don't mean me, Captain Douglas," I said playfully as I stood up from my desk.

"Good heavens, no." He was positively fuming. "There's a band of those horrible suffragettes on Whitehall handing out white feathers. I may have been injured, but I'm no coward."

"I know," I said, patting his hand. "You have the courage of a lion."

He got the strangest look on his face, like a little boy who'd just been given a sweetie. I withdrew my hand before he got any improper ideas about our relationship. My report was already finished and sent up to Blinker Hall, but my investigation of the Great White Hunter was far from over. And Captain Douglas was my best informant. I needed to keep him close, but not too close.

"Please call me Clifford." When he gazed down at me, I got a most uncomfortable sensation in my abdominal region.

I nodded.

Clifford and I sat at our usual table in the canteen and dutifully ate our meager lunch.

Searching for the bits of sausage in my Yorkshire pudding, I asked, "Do you disapprove of the suffragettes generally or only their misplaced white feathers?"

"Why do women want to be bothered with votes and politics and war and all that rot?" He asked, already finished with half of his toad-in-the-hole.

"Because *all that rot* affects their lives as much as it does a man's." I washed down the gluey pudding with my lukewarm tea. If it wasn't raining the day after tomorrow, I'd suggest we lunch at Old Shades. Tomorrow was my day off and I'd be taking lunch alone at the hospital.

"I suppose you're right," he conceded. "But women are too sensitive and fragile—"

"I don't think you'll make a good reporter thinking like that," I stopped him before he could go on with such drivel.

"Why ever not?" He looked hurt.

"You're underestimating half the population."

"Underestimating!" His lips tightened. "No, I think women are too good for all that rot. They're the fair sex—"

"Keep wearing those rose-colored glasses, and on your watch, women will get away with murder."

"What do you mean?"

"Don't you think women are just as capable of lying and cheating and stealing as men?"

"I don't know."

"They're just as capable, Captain. They're just not as foolish."

"You think men are foolish?"

"Men started this war and all wars. If women were in charge, war wouldn't exist, and the world would be orderly and tidy." Certainly suffragettes can also be pacifists.

"You mean if *you* were in charge." Clifford laughed. "I rather like the chaos of life. You never know what's going to happen."

"Give me a good filing system over the chaos of life any day."

"I really should introduce you to Fredricks. You two are birds of a feather."

"From his photograph, I'd say he's more of a peacock, and I'm just a common sparrow."

"You're far from common, Miss Figg." Clifford gazed at me from across the plank table. "I think you're a smashing girl."

I suddenly felt warm and took a drink of water. Maybe Clifford Douglas wasn't such a bad sort after all.

The next morning on the way to the train station, I bought a newspaper to catch up on news of the war. We'd been at it for three years, but it seemed a lifetime.

The train was packed with women on their way to work in factories and offices, women who'd taken over men's jobs while they were away fighting. It was as if most of the young men had just disappeared one day and we were now a society of girls, women, old men and little boys. When an oversized middle-aged woman got up to get off, I took her seat. I settled in and opened my newspaper and read the front page.

Yet another peace proposal had come from the Vatican. Pope Benedict had called the Great War the "suicide of Europe," but Germany wasn't convinced the Pope was neutral, especially after he'd publicly said he wished he'd been born a Frenchman. I wondered what Mr. Fredricks would make of his Holy Father calling the war a "useless massacre."

Volunteering at the hospital, seeing so many young men's lives cut short so brutally, and witnessing the fractured lives of those who survived, made me inclined to agree with Pope Benedict. How much longer could it go on? How many more boys would be lost?

I was starting to think like a pacifist. I heard Suffragist Millicent Fawcett's chastising voice in my head. "It's akin to treason to talk of peace." Although I was as patriotic as the next woman, after the misery I'd seen at the hospital, I was in favor of peace, whatever it took—short of surrender, of course. The only thing worse than a steady diet of fish pies and suet pudding would be a steady diet of blutwurst and gingerbread.

I exited the Charing Cross station with a sense of foreboding. As if in response, the sky opened and rain poured down on me. Of course, I'd forgotten my brolly, so I took off running toward the hospital. Outside the entrance was a caravan of covered lorries, no doubt loaded with wounded soldiers. I dashed inside, brushing off my wet trench coat as I went. At least I'd worn a sturdy hat and lace-up leather boots.

There was a great commotion in the hall as the wounded were brought in on stretchers. I didn't need to read the newspaper to know this wasn't a good sign. Whenever we'd lost a battle, bleeding and broken soldiers poured into the hospital.

I rushed into the staff room, removed my coat and hat, replaced them with my nurse's apron and cap, washed my hands, and went to the hallway to help with the triage. A shock of sandy hair and full lips seeming to mouth my name made my pulse quicken. I ran to the soldier's side, afraid to look at his distorted countenance.

"Andrew?" I muttered, saying a silent prayer. *Please God, no, not Andrew.*

I inhaled sharply and looked into his face. To my relief, it wasn't Andrew. Hands trembling, I prepared to irrigate the long, deep inflamed gash that threatened to take his leg. I prepared a weak solution of sodium hypochlorite, fixed a glass container to the head of the gurney, and proceeded with the ghastly business of packing a small rubber hose into the wound. The man cried out each time I touched the wound, but this was the only chance he had to keep his leg.

Amidst the pandemonium of screaming and groaning, wounded men called out for "mummy," doctors barked orders, and nurses darted back and forth consoling the men and assisting the doctors. There weren't enough operating rooms, so men lay on gurneys in the hallway. Some were unconscious and others writhed in agony.

It was my business to sort out the wounded as they were brought in from the ambulances and to keep them from dying before they got to the operating rooms. I had to distinguish the nearly dying from the dying. Life was leaking away, but with some it would take hours or days and with others it would be only a matter of minutes. My hands could tell all on their own one kind of cold from another. All the wounded were cold, but the chill of icy flesh was not the same as the cold that gripped their insides when life was almost extinguished. My hands could tell the difference between the natural cold of night and the stealthy cold of death. I didn't think about it, my fingers simply felt it. As if in a dream, my hands did things and knew things I didn't have time to think about.

I administered morphia to the hopeless cases and left them there to die with the names of sweethearts on their lips. Others got morphia to get them through the painful hours until their injuries could be treated. Breathless, I dashed about, cleaning wounds, applying dressings, twisting tourniquets, administering morphia, and rigging up Thomas splints, while the strongest nurses transported the soldiers hemorrhaging life from the emergency ward to the hallway outside the operating rooms. Every minute counted. Skill and reaction time determined whether a soldier would make it to the surgeons alive.

Everything happened quickly and yet as if in slow motion. As I focused on saving bits from the wreckage, the whole world disappeared. I saw only fragments of men—legs, arms, heads, a cheek, an eye, a finger. I heard only sounds, some of them phrases that sent me into action, while others sent me into a panic. The pungent smells of unwashed bodies, blood, iodine, and carbolic acid mixed with adrenaline and fear. This overload of brute sensation kept the unutterable anguish from completely destroying my spirit. It was as if time stood still and I lived an eternity in those hours of single-minded focus on saving as many men as I could.

I glanced at my watch. It was past midnight. We'd been working in the dark with only meager candlelight for hours. My eyes hurt and my hands were trembling.

When we'd done our best for the wounded and prayed for the dead, we were faced with the gruesome task of cleaning the operating theater. Along with an orderly, I began washing sheets and bedding in a big bathtub. Soon I was swimming in a sea of blood. When the lights were allowed on, we stared at one another, drenched in blood as if we'd come from a slaughterhouse. In a sense, we had.

I washed myself off as best I could and took a break for a cup of tea. As I sat in the staff room, I stared into the void, an empty shell. The warm cup and hot liquid couldn't penetrate the depths of my icy soul. What I'd seen here tonight had become so quotidian as to be cliché, and yet it would haunt me for the rest of my life.

Still running on adrenaline, I decided to stay the night at the hospital and help out. Many poor souls were still fighting for their very lives. What were a few hours of lost sleep to me, when these men had given so much?

After another hour of attending to agony, my spirits needed lifting, so I visited the convalescent wing of the hospital where, after having been put back together again, the men were on their way to discharge. The corridor was dimly lit, and only the sound of coughing or snoring broke the silence of the night. I walked softly to keep the heels of my boots from clicking on the tile floor. The peace of knowing men were sleeping and healing and on their way home was a palliative balm on my frayed nerves.

I stopped at an open door where a light shone from the bedside table of one of the men. The room held six cots, but his was the only one occupied. How we could have used those cots in the emergency wing. I'd have to suggest moving them.

I peeked in to see if he needed anything, a cup of tea or a snack perhaps—something simple, the basic needs or the pleasures of everyday life when it wasn't thrown into the teeth of war. He beckoned me to his bedside.

When I stepped inside the room, I had the strangest sensation of déjà vu. *I didn't know you were going to be here.* What an odd thought to pass through my mind. I'd never met this man before in my life. I tiptoed to his bedside and introduced myself.

"I'm Miss Figg, one of the volunteer nurses."

A lock of wavy chestnut hair falling across his forehead practically dared me to reach out and sweep it out of his face. I held my hands behind my back to restrain myself.

"You're a sight for sore eyes," he said with a playful grin.

"Can I bring you something?" I asked. "Some biscuits and tea?"

He held up his bandaged right hand. "I've been trying to write a letter to my mum, but it's deuced difficult with my left hand. I wonder if you might help me write to her? She's probably worried because she hasn't heard from me."

"I'd be delighted." Finally, a task I could do with confidence and calm. I took up a blank piece of paper and pencil from the nightstand. "What should I write?"

He stared at me for a few seconds, and then asked, "What would you write to your mother?"

"My mother is dead," I said, and then regretted my abruptness.

"Oh, I am sorry." He adjusted the sheet draped over his torso, which I couldn't help but notice was lean and fit. "Do you happen to have a cigarette?"

"I'm afraid I don't smoke. Shall I try to find you one?" I set the paper and pencil back on the nightstand and made to stand up.

"No, don't leave. Just sit with me for a while." He leaned back into his pillow. "Now that I'm on the mend, it's deuced boring waiting to get out of this lockup."

I was struck by the elegance of his posture. In the light from the oil lamp on the nightstand, he looked like a nineteenth-century portrait. His soft features made me want to reach out and caress his cheek.

"Let's write to your mother, shall we?" I picked up the pencil again. *"Dear Mum*, to start, right?"

He nodded and then brushed the provocative curl away from his face.

Together we composed a fine letter reassuring his mother he had been wounded but was safe... for now.

"I want to post this letter before I go back to South Africa," he said proudly.

"South Africa?"

"I'm working for British Intelligence. We're trying to stop another Boer uprising."

"You're a spy!"

"If I tell you, I'm afraid I'll have to kill you." When he laughed, his angelic cheeks took on devilishly handsome dimples. "I have many secrets, Miss Figg. If I divulge all of them now, what mystery will bring you back to see me tomorrow?"

"I would come back even if you were as dull as ditch water."

His smile alone was enough to inspire another trip across the hospital. And those sea-green eyes framed by dark lashes definitely warranted another look during daylight.

"Are you well acquainted with much ditch water, then?" His eyes danced mischievously, and his laughter was contagious.

I straighten my skirt and patted my wig. It wouldn't do to be giggling like a schoolgirl with a soldier I'd just met.

"Since you've been working in South Africa, have you by any chance heard of a famous big game hunter named Fredrick Fredricks? I met him recently." I shouldn't have said I'd met him since it was only Dr. Vogel who had met the Great White Hunter. Of course, the chance of this soldier finding out about my alter ego was slim, even if he was a spy.

"Apollo Fredricks?" he asked and narrowed his perfectly symmetrical brows. "You've met him?"

Blast it all! Why did I say I'd met him? "Well, I haven't actually met him. I've seen him. He's in town investigating a murder case. Some country gentleman who supposedly poisoned his mother."

"Blimey! Matricide amongst the aristocracy." He sat up in bed and ran his fingers through his thick hair.

"Yes, indeed," I said. "I understand Mr. Fredricks doesn't think this gentleman committed the crime."

"If his reputation is anything to go on, he'll find out who did."

"So you've heard of him?"

"He's a person of interest."

"What do you mean?"

"Let's just say both his hunting methods and journalistic techniques are bizarre, and he is as arrogant and commanding as Napoleon." With his good hand, he reached for a glass of water on the side table. "What's your interest in Fredricks, if you don't mind me asking?"

"If I tell you, I'm afraid I'll have to kill you," I said with a wink.

"If the bloody Germans don't do it first." He replaced the glass on the table and then held out his left hand. "I'm Archie, by the way. Archie Somersby."

When I took his hand, I felt a warm current pass between us. Perhaps it was just the contrast with the icy flesh in the emergency wing. Still, I could swear there was an electric connection. A spark of delight ignited in my chest. Suddenly, I wanted to impress this mysterious soldier.

"We have something in common," I said.

"Something besides wishing we were out of this bloody hospital?"

"That, and I work for British Intelligence, too. Room 40."

"Room 40. Impressive. Are you a code breaker?"

"You know I can't tell you."

"Good girl. I was just testing you."

"Figures British Intelligence is interested in Fredricks." He raised his eyebrows. "Of course all those bloody journalists are suspect. Anyone of them could be a spy." When he crossed his bare arms over his chest, the sheet slipped and I had to avert my eyes…well, I tried not to look, but couldn't help myself.

His arms were smooth and tanned. I wished Archie Somersby would put on his shirt. Flustered, I said, "I'd better be getting back. There was a frightful onslaught of casualties earlier, and I'll be needed back in emergency."

"I'm being discharged the day after tomorrow. If you promise to come back before then, I promise to find out what I can about Fredricks."

He held out his hand. As I put my hand in his, I admired his long, straight fingers. We shook on it, and again I felt a warm pulse of energy that cheered me up considerably.

"Pleasure to meet you, Archie Somersby."

"The pleasure is all mine, Miss Figg."

I fairly skipped back to the triage unit.

My joy was short-lived. Another caravan of injured had arrived, even worse than the first. They'd been the targets of a new hell invented by the Germans called mustard gas.

I remembered a line from a gruesome poem about the horrors of gas: "You would not tell with such high zest, to children ardent for some desperate glory, the old Lie: *Dulce et decorum est Pro patria mori,*" how sweet and proper it is to die for your country.

Chapter Fifteen: My Worst Nightmare

I was accustomed to soldiers dying, but not to being impotent to ease their agony before they died. Even morphia was no match for the excruciating pain of skin, lungs, and eyes burned by mustard gas. The men being carried into the hospital were delirious with pain, not from gaping wounds or shrapnel, but from raw exposed nerves. Dozens of men lay on cots in the hallway, gasping for breath. Even I had to look away when a patient whose body was covered with third-degree burns also had his eyes and face marred beyond recognition. Many were so badly burned we couldn't touch them. There was nothing we could do for them but pray.

The smell of gas emanated from the men, and proximity to them caused respiratory problems for nurses too. I stood at the sink, lathering my hands over and over. Burns could easily become infected. Staring down at the white suds, my hands scalding under the hot water, I wanted to cry. But now was no time to break down. These poor brave soldiers were suffering, and many would die. Those who didn't would suffer the effects for the rest of their lives. I wiped my hands on a clean towel, took a deep breath, and headed for the trenches.

I started my labors of assessing the men and dividing them into two groups: those who would die within the day and those who would die within the week. Of the latter group, a few lucky ones might survive—if you could call them lucky. I couldn't rely on the knowledge in my hands and fingers because I didn't dare touch most of the men. It came down to whether or not they could speak their names and answer my questions. Those who could answer might live through the day, those who could only cry out would not.

One young man—a boy really—had burns on his arms, scorched eyes, and was coughing. But through gritted teeth, he told me his name, "Bobby Miles," and then described how the Germans had ambushed his unit. Something about Bobby's voice reminded me of Ian Elliott, and I wondered why neither Ian nor Ernest had joined the war effort. After all, their wealth was the result of the labor of boys like Bobby.

"Try to rest. Save your strength." I called an orderly to help me rig up a croup tent around the young patient.

Weary and beaten down, but intent on easing the dying into the afterlife if we couldn't keep them alive, I went to the next cot. The man was lying on his side facing the wall. I could see why. His right shoulder was badly burned, along with his neck and the side of his head. I asked another orderly to help me turn him around so I could try to talk to him. It took four women to lift the man, cot and all, and turn the whole thing around away from the wall.

The man's eyes were closed in a tight grimace.

I knelt down next to the cot to speak to him. "What is your name?"

His eyes flew open and met mine with a jolt of recognition.

No, no, no! It couldn't be.

"Andrew?" I whispered.

"Fio, is it really you?" he asked in a weak voice.

"It's me. I'm here." I fought back tears. *Andrew, dear Andrew, please don't die.* "Everything will be okay. I'll take care of you."

"Where am I?"

"You're in the hospital. In London."

"Shot down near Calais." He groaned. "Parachuted out just in time. Lucky to catch up with the Royal Field Artillery." He wheezed. "Bad luck to worse." He sucked in breath and then fell into a coughing fit.

"Try to rest." I quickly made up a syringe of morphia, but with him lying on his good arm, I couldn't find a place to inject it. I asked an orderly to run to the dispensary and get morphia tablets. They weren't as effective, but they were better than nothing. The orderly returned with the bottle and I tapped a double dose into my palm.

"Chew these. They will be bitter, but chewing them will make them act more quickly." I knelt down and slipped the tablets into his open mouth.

After several minutes that seemed like an eternity, he appeared more relaxed. Still, every time he coughed, he flinched in pain.

I asked another nurse to help me rig up a croup tent so I could administer steam to help ease his coughing. On a small burner, I boiled water in a pan, and then held it close to his face so he could breathe in the steam. It was tiring on my arm, but it was the only way to sooth his burnt lungs. I should be seeing to the other men, but I didn't want to leave Andrew. The other nurses would have to cover for me.

I left him only long enough to find a doctor to help me save him. Although I knew it was hopeless, I ran from one operating theater to the next looking for a doctor to perform a miracle. Every doctor I saw was busy operating or treating another patient. I waited outside the operating room where Dr. Armstrong had just finished an amputation. Although only forty, he looked haggard and old as he exited the operating room.

"Dr. Armstrong, can you please help me?" I heard the desperation in my voice. "It's my husband. He's been gassed."

"There's not much we can do for gas," he said.

"Please, just come. We have to try to save him."

"I'll see what I can do," he said and followed me back to the emergency ward.

I led him to Andrew's cot, where an orderly had taken over administering steam. I lifted the croup tent and Andrew stared up at us with red, glazed eyes. I had already cut away Andrew's shirt—what was left of it—and applied oil to the burns.

Dr. Armstrong took one look at Andrew and his countenance turned grave. He glanced over at me and shook his head. "Make him comfortable. That's all we can do."

The doctor's words shattered my illusions of hope. Andrew was going to die. It was only a matter of time. I vowed to stay with him however long he had left. The trauma of the night before, combined with lack of sleep and very little food, made it harder than ever to hold myself together. I felt I might break down at any minute. I had to be strong for Andrew's sake.

As I sat on a stool next to his cot holding the croup pan, it occurred to me I should get word to Nancy. No, even though she'd wrecked my marriage, I couldn't allow her to see him like this. Her last memory of Andrew should be a happy one. And, truth be told, I didn't want to share him with her. For these last precious hours, Andrew belonged to me.

"Fio." Andrew's voice interrupted my thoughts. "Tell me a story. I always loved your stories."

I smiled and pulled my stool closer to his cot. "A story. Let's see." I narrowed my brow in concentration. "Once upon a time..." It was difficult to be creative in the midst of the awful smell of mustard gas and death. "Once upon a time, there was a Great White Hunter named Apollo Fredricks. Apollo, who was not a modest man, thought himself the best investigative reporter in all of Europe. He dressed in fine clothes and enjoyed fine food and was generally considered a dandy of the first order." I gazed at Andrew, who seemed to be resting easier now. I could see that the sound of my voice was reassuring to him, which pleased me.

"One day," I continued, "the arrogant huntsman met his match in the fearless Miss Fiona Figg."

Andrew's laughter caused a paroxysm of coughing.

"Oh dear," I said and refilled the croup pan with water, added a drop of eucalyptus, and heated it on the little stove.

"Mrs. Andrew Cunningham," he said when the coughing subsided.

Was he delirious? Did he still think we were married?

"Former," I corrected.

"First," he replied with a grimace.

Each contortion was a like a dagger through my heart. I couldn't stand to see him suffer. I checked my watch to see if I could give him another morphia tablet. Technically, we had another two hours to wait. Given the circumstances, I didn't think it would hurt to give him the tablet early. Thank God for morphia. Within half an hour after chewing another double dose, his rigid form melted into the cot. Between the steam and the drug, his cough weakened too.

Morphia. *Good heavens.* At that moment I realized why toxic stimulants used to poison the countess had had a delayed affect. The depressant effect of the sleeping powders Lady Mary stirred into the dowager's coffee slowed the effects of the poison.

I glanced down at Andrew. I would have to file that bit of information away. I couldn't think of the dowager's murder right now.

My arm began to hurt from holding the croup pan. My back smarted from leaning over beneath the croup tent. Yet more than anything, my heart ached from the intimacy of huddling so close to the love of my life. I wiped a tear from my cheek. I'd never love anyone else the way I loved Andrew. He was my first love and no one else could take his place. *Dear, beautiful Andrew.*

I regarded his face, now partially disfigured by gas. *Oh, Andrew, don't die. Please, don't die.*

"I'm sorry," Andrew whispered. "I'm so sorry, Fio." His whole body convulsed with a sob. "I treated you terribly," he said through his tears.

"Don't say that." I gently touched his hair. "You gave me the best years of my life."

"I'm so sorry," he repeated.

I slid off the stool, sat the croup pan on the floor, and stared into his bloodshot eyes. "Look at me." I took his good hand in mine. "We loved each other with all our hearts. Who could ask for more than that?" I squeezed his hand.

"I never stopped loving you," he whispered.

"I love you, my dearest Andrew." I couldn't help it. I started crying. I tried not to make a sound as the tears rolled down my cheeks. I didn't want to let go of his hand, even to wipe away my tears. I let them run.

His eyes widened and his mouth moved but no words came out.

"Georgie," he finally muttered. "Help her, Fio. Please help her," he said in hoarse desperation.

"I will." *Who was Georgie?* Then it dawned on me. Georgie must be his son.

"Promise me," he pleaded.

"I promise."

He held my gaze. "I love you, Fiona," he whispered and then gasped, taking his last breath.

"I love you too, dearest."

His hand went limp and his eyes glazed over. The love of my life was gone forever.

I broke down sobbing. All the pent-up emotion from the last twenty-four hours, from the last year, from our entire marriage, exploded through my wracked body. The croup tent shook as I sobbed myself dry.

"Are you okay?" an orderly asked.

I nodded.

"Did you know him?"

I nodded again.

"Come on, love, let me get you a cuppa." She took me by the elbow and led me to the break room. She put a kettle on to boil.

Unable to speak, I sat at the table and waited. *Waited for what?* The war to end? The grief to pass? The water to boil? Nothing mattered anymore. Nothing made sense. He'd asked me to help her take care of Georgie.

The orderly slid a cup of tea across the table. "Come on then, drink up, love. A nice cuppa will lift your spirits."

I took a sip and closed my eyes.

I don't know how long the orderly watched me from across the table. After a while, she said, "Sorry, love, but me little ones need tending. I'm going home now. Will you be all right, then?"

"I'll be all right."

She patted my hand. "Cheer up, love. You'll meet another fella. Don't seem like it now. But you's young yet."

I sat in the dark canteen sipping my tea until I'd drained the cup. As if sleepwalking, I wandered the corridors until I found myself at the entrance to Archie Somersby's room.

"You've come back," he called from his bed.

I leaned against the doorframe and stared across the room.

"What's wrong?" he asked, getting out of bed.

Warm tears rolled down my cheeks.

"Oh dear," he said, taking my hand. "You look as though you've had a shock. Damned war is taking its toll." He led me into the room, and still holding my hand, sat on the edge of the bed. He patted a spot next to him.

I perched beside him, and he put his arm around my shoulders.

"There, there," he said softly. "It will be all right, you'll see."

I buried my head in his shoulder and wept.

Chapter Sixteen: The Funeral

I awoke in Archie's arms, curled up next to him on his hospital bed. I didn't know how long I'd been asleep. Enclosed in his warmth, I didn't want to open my eyes. I longed to stay in this cozy dream and not face the harsh reality awaiting me. His body...

HIS BODY!

My eyes flew open, and I leapt out of bed. What if an orderly had seen me? I blushed all the way to my toes.

"Good afternoon," he said with a laugh. "Are you feeling a bit better?"

Flustered, I scanned the floor for my boots. Unable to put them on standing up, I moved to one of the empty cots, sat, and slipped them on. "Yes, better," I said, avoiding his gaze.

"I don't know about you, but I'm starving." When he sat up in bed, the sheet slipped, revealing his bare chest. "I could do with a full English." He got out of bed. He was wearing pajama bottoms and nothing more.

I'd never been in a bed with a man before...except Andrew. I was mortified.

"I'll settle for anything other than another hospital breakfast." Archie went to a small cupboard, opened a drawer, and removed his uniform, which was as neatly folded as a flag. "Can I take you out for a proper breakfast? I've had enough hospital food."

"What time is it?" I glanced at my watch. "Good heavens!" It was three in the afternoon. "I need to get to work."

"After what you went through last night, work can wait. A hearty breakfast is just what the doctor ordered. Then you can vanish like Cinderella."

"No, I can't. I really must be going." I headed toward the hallway without looking back.

Archie ran around me and slid to a stop in the doorway. "Are you sure you'll be all right?" He put his hand on my shoulder.

I nodded.

"Please take care of yourself." His gentle countenance almost melted my resolve. "And come back to see me tomorrow before they send me back to Africa."

"I will."

"Promise?" He gently lifted my chin so I was gazing into his endless green eyes.

"I promise," I said, fighting the urge to kiss him. I ducked under his arm and made my escape.

I dashed across the hospital, and back to the staff room, where I gathered my clothes, purse, and coat. I quickly changed my clothes and dropped my soiled nurse's dress and apron in the laundry basket. I dreaded looking in the mirror. I must be quite a sight. I braved the glass and immediately regretted it. Good heavens! My eyes were swollen to the size of walnuts, my complexion was wan, my wig was crooked, and I had black rings under my eyes like a raccoon where my kohl had run. I looked like a ghoul. I was embarrassed Archie had seen me at my worst. Now I'd *have* to visit him tomorrow…just to show him that even if I wasn't pretty, I wasn't hideous either.

I fixed my face as best I could and decided to just head home. It didn't make sense to go into work since by the time I got there it would be nearly four in the afternoon. Anyway, I wasn't up to it. I needed time to be alone with my sorrow. I thought of Nancy and little Georgie, who probably wouldn't even remember his father.

In a daze, I pushed open the heavy front door to the hospital and found myself on Charing Street somehow confused about which direction to go. I'd come and gone from here so many times, yet nothing seemed familiar. My world had gone, and an impostor had taken its place.

"Miss Figg, is that you?" A tenor voice jolted me out of my stupor. "I say, what happened to you? You look terrible, as if you've just come from the trenches." Captain Clifford Douglas stood in front of me, staring me up and down.

"I feel even worse." My trench coat hung off my shoulders. *Could I have shrunk in the last twenty-four hours?*

"Come on. Let's get you some coffee." He took my elbow and led me to a coffee shop across the street from the hospital.

"When you didn't show up for lunch, I set out to find you," he said as he pulled me along.

"It was an awful night. First victims from a bloodbath and then mustard gas."

"Damned war!" He shook his head. "Women shouldn't have to see such horrors."

Men make the messes, and women clean them up.

The coffee shop was too loud, and the lights too bright. My head hurt and I wanted to be left alone, but I allowed Clifford to lead me to a booth in the back, where it was dimmer and less busy.

"Can we get two coffees?" Clifford asked the waitress. "And say, can you add some brandy." After the waitress left, he said, "Some brandy will do you good."

I leaned my elbows on the table and put my head in my hands.

"I say, cheer up, old girl."

"Andrew died last night." I looked across the table at him through my fingers.

"Oh dear. I am sorry. How did it happen?"

The waitress delivered two cups of coffee with brandy and cream. I'd never drunk brandy in coffee before. Once I got used to the bite, it was quite soothing. After my second cup, I told Clifford every detail of the nightmare hell of my last twenty-four hours. My dry eyes burned when I described the effects of the mustard gas and seeing Andrew's beautiful face burned. I had cried so much already, I was out of tears.

"At least as a divorcée, he was only gone from my life. As a war widow, he's gone forever." I pulled a handkerchief out of my purse and dabbed at my swollen eyes.

147

Clifford reached across the table and took my hand. "Marry me, Fiona."

I was speechless.

"Marry me," he repeated.

"Are you mad?"

"Why it is mad to ask you to do me the honor of becoming my wife?"

"Because you don't want to marry me."

"I do—"

He looked so sincere and ridiculous that I laughed.

"What's so funny? I'm asking you to marry me."

"And it's perfectly sweet of you. But you don't want to marry me, and I don't want to marry you."

"Oh, well," he said stiffly. "In that case—" His cheeks reddened and he withdrew his hand. "It's settled." He twisted around in his chair, trying to get the waitress's attention.

"You're a wonderful man, Clifford. You know, you shouldn't go around asking girls to marry you. One of them might say yes!"

"Why do you say that?" he asked haughtily. "You didn't."

"Not today, anyway." I smiled weakly. "But you've cheered me up a great deal. Thank you, dear friend."

"My word." He returned my smile.

By the time I got home, I was so knackered I went straight to bed. Before losing consciousness, I marveled at the past twenty-four hours, during which I'd lost my husband forever, slept in bed with a strange man, and received a marriage proposal. What bittersweet wonders would tomorrow bring?

The next morning, I was searching my wardrobe for a black dress for Andrew's funeral, which had already been planned for Monday. The dowager's funeral was the first I'd attended as an adult, and there I was dressed as a man. To my surprise, my fully stocked closet didn't contain a single suitable black dress, which meant I'd have to go shopping. Thankfully, when I telephoned earlier, Mr. Montgomery had given me a few days off from work.

Shopping always lifted my spirits. The depth of my despair could be measured by the store's degree of posh. My usual, Liberty's, wouldn't do today. A trip to Knightsbridge was in order. There I could choose between Debenhams, Harvey Nicks, and Harrods, which—given the price tags—I reserved for especially bad days.

Today was an especially bad day.

An hour later, I arrived at Harrods. Harrods's art nouveau windows and giant dome gave the regal appearance of a Parliament building. At Harrods, one might spot luminaries, such as cinema stars Eve Balfour and Chrissie White, or members of the royal family—who wisely changed their family name from the unwieldy Saxe-Coburg-Gotha to the less German-sounding Windsor.

Engraved over the entrance of the posh store were the words *Omnia Omnibus Ubique* (All Things for All People Everywhere). They should have added, *Praestare Possunt Provism* (Provided They Can Afford It). Harrods really did have everything. In the exotic-pets department, one could buy lemurs, and even lions, on special order. Luckily, I was only in the market for a dress and matching accessories.

Strolling through the perfume department, intoxicated by the heady scents of jasmine, bergamot, lemon, lavender, and rose, I wondered if I shouldn't splurge on a bottle. I stopped at a particularly beautiful bottle called Hammam Bouquet. The death of a husband warranted an extravagance. When I saw the price—a full month's pay—I turned on my heels and headed for ladies' wear. He was, after all, an ex-husband.

The moving staircase always unnerved me. I wished they still offered brandies after the journey like they did in the old days.

On the first floor, I took my time browsing. With time off from work, for once, I wasn't in a hurry. I liked touching the garments, even if I didn't try them on. Smooth silk, rough wool, crinkled gabardine—the textures of shopping delighted my fingertips as I flipped through dresses hanging on racks. For amusement, I held up a low-cut pale-blue lampshade tunic with a long silk skirt. *Who would wear such a thing?* I lingered on a gorgeous deep-purple tube sheath with a beaded bodice. *How lovely!* The price tag reminded me of my more practical mission. As uplifting as it was, this shopping trip wasn't just a diversion.

I gave up my research on the newest fashions and went directly to a long rack of black dresses. I chose a black crepe with full sleeves and skirt. I found a graceful crepe-trimmed Marie Stuart coif hat with a heavy veil, and black suede gloves. As a divorced woman, I wouldn't be expected to wear widow's weeds, so I didn't need more than the funeral attire.

I gulped when I added up the cost. But I wanted to look smart, especially since I was bound to see *her* there. I wiped the price tags from my mind and gathered up my plunder. Now all I needed was to find a small black handbag.

After searching through fancy beaded handbags, I chose a plain black clutch purse. With my wardrobe complete, it hit me that even this lovely funerary armor wouldn't protect me from the pain of seeing Andrew in a coffin or meeting his widow and little Georgie.

To take my mind off the dreadful image of Andrew on his deathbed, I decided to stop off at the hospital to visit Archie Somersby as I'd promised. I wanted to say goodbye to him before he was to be shipped back into action. Who knew if I'd ever see him again? A shiver ran down my spine. Or, if I did, would he too be gasping his last breath or lying in a coffin? It was all too beastly to bear.

Before hopping back on the train, I purchased a box of Cadbury Biscuits as a going away present for Archie.

When I exited the train station, it was pouring rain, and like an idiot, I'd forgotten my brolly yet again. By the time I reached the hospital, my shoes were soaked through and my parcels were soggy. I put my dripping coat and packages into my locker and sloshed my way to Archie's room. Luckily, the box of biscuits was only slightly damp.

The prospect of seeing Archie's beautiful smile cheered me considerably. The closer I got to his room, the more my excitement rose. As I knocked on his door, I felt I could practically take flight from the buzzing in my chest.

"I'm back as promised," I said, as I opened the door.

The set of eyes that stared back at me were not Archie's but those of a grizzled man, no doubt prematurely aged by the war. "Nurse, I'm glad you're here," he said blushing. "I need to use the…" His voice broke off and he nodded toward a bedpan.

Blast! I'd missed Archie. He must have been discharged already. Perhaps I'd never see him again.

"Nurse," the bedridden man repeated.

"Of course, soldier," I said, depositing the box of biscuits on the side-table, trading it for the required receptacle.

By Monday morning my stomach was in knots. I hadn't slept well and was dreading what lay ahead. Worried about keeping breakfast down, I only took plain tea and dry toast.

My hands shook as I drew the black veil over my face. Looking through the veil, my bedroom was blurry and dark, like looking through a sieve. Perhaps I could raise the veil until I reached the church.

The service was held at Holy Trinity Cathedral. The church's façade of bright-orange bricks and beige stone stood out amongst the drab grays on Sloane Street. The alternating colors created a striped effect, which suggested a festive layer cake rather than a somber church.

Inside, the stained glass was magnificent. The enormous east window presented saints in individual panels, topped by panels featuring Adam and Eve, and a crucified Christ. The throng of mourners created a black splash against a tapestry of the rich textures and colors in the lavish cathedral.

As I walked up the side aisle, I scanned the crowd for anyone I knew. A group of Andrew's friends wearing dark uniforms were seated to my right. Another bunch of men I recognized as coworkers from Imperial and Foreign Corporation sat together. There were many people I didn't know, and I imagined these must be Nancy's friends and family.

I took a seat at the end of a pew near the front of the chapel. When the minister appeared, the murmuring of the crowd faded into hushed silence. Wearing a long black robe and white sash, the minister began the service. He described Andrew as a hero who had given his life for his country. Next, several of Andrew's friends presented eulogies. One of his Royal Flying Corp buddies talked about his bravery and his passion for life.

I thought of our first year of marriage when Andrew was taking flying lessons and persuaded me to go with him. I was terrified, but he just laughed, his indigo eyes dancing with excitement as he loaded me in the passenger's seat. He loved adventure, and I loved him for it.

I wiped my eyes with my handkerchief and listened to funny and touching stories about Andrew from the friends who also loved him. By the end of the service, my handkerchief was sopping wet with tears of grief and regret. Andrew's disfigured face came back to haunt me.

"Help her, Fio. Please help her." Amidst the horrible memories of his final night, Andrew's words came back to me. With his last request in mind, I steeled myself to pay my respects to his widow.

Nancy was standing in the front of the chapel surrounded by people paying their respects. I hung back and waited. When the last of the mourners left, I made my way to the front. Even veiled, her grief was overwhelming. As she cradled the baby, the boy nuzzled his sandy-haired head into her shoulder.

"Nancy," I said. "I'm so sorry for your loss. If there's anything I can do—"

When little Georgie looked up at me with his father's indigo eyes, my heart leapt into my throat. He was a miniature version of Andrew. In that moment, I resolved to do anything I could to help the boy.

Chapter Seventeen: Lord Elliott's Trial

The next week was a blur. Haunted by Andrew's gruesome death, I almost forgot all about Ravenswick Abbey, Lady Mary and Lord Elliott, and the Great White Hunter. I hid whenever Captain Douglas came looking for me for lunch, and I buried myself in my filing system.

In early June, I was stunned when I was called on to reprise my disguise as Dr. Vogel and appear at the Old Alfred as a witness for the prosecution in the case against Lord Elliott. And to think, my hair had finally grown out just barely enough for a fingerwave. With remorse, I took my scissors and chopped off my best hope of femininity. Once again, I looked like a hedgehog with fur sticking out in every direction.

Standing over the sink in my bathroom, I applied the pungent coal-dye to my roots, and waited the requisite fifteen minutes for it to sink in before I rinsed it out. The smell of coal tar on one's head was so unpleasant, I wondered at women—and some vain men, including, no doubt, Fredricks—who did this regularly. I rinsed my hair several times and then applied a dab of Brilliantine, which at least helped camouflage the tar smell.

Next, I set about assembling the rest of my disguise. I retrieved the dark navy suit from the back of my closet and dug the beard and spirit gum out of my dresser drawer. The smell of the spirit gum burned my nostrils as I applied it to my upper lip. I pressed the beard and mustache into place, patted on the bushy eyebrows, and assessed the results in my hand mirror.

I was dreading the appearance in court even more than I had feared the inquest. For now, I'd become friends with Clifford Douglas, who was bound to be at the trial, and, as Dr. Vogel, I was friends with the wife of the accused, who was fighting for his life. How was I going to face either of my friends without them discerning my double identity? Keeping up this charade was becoming deuced difficult. I would be glad when I could be rid of Dr. Vogel forever.

Satisfied with my disguise, I grabbed my handbag and headed out the door. I was halfway down Warwick Avenue when I realized people were staring at me...not me exactly, but my handbag. Oh bother! I tucked the handbag under my arm, turned on my booted heels, and hurried back to my flat. I tossed the handbag onto the sofa and started my journey over again.

From the train station just outside the western wall of the city, I strode up Alfred Street enjoying the freedom of a man walking alone. As I passed by St. Paul's Cathedral, I whispered a prayer for Lady Mary Elliott...and one for little Georgie. I wished I could do more than pray, but I didn't know how else to help.

I stopped in front of the courthouse and steeled myself for the proceedings. Only a decade old and lavishly outfitted with symbolic reminders of its virtuous purpose, the courthouse building sported a gold-leaf statue of a lady of justice perched atop a seventy-foot dome. Arms outstretched, she was holding a sword in one hand and scales in the other. Eyes wide open, she wasn't subject to the usual blindfold of justice.

As I approached the front doors, the sky opened up and a rain squall drenched the three stone figures looking down from above the hall, the angels of fortitude, records, and truth. As a file clerk, I had an in with the angel of records, but as a spy, I could use help with fortitude and truth. I ducked into the doorway to get out of the rain. An inscription above the door read "Defend the children of the poor and punish the wrongdoer." Lord Elliott was hardly a child of the poor, but was he a wrongdoer?

It took all my strength to pull open the heavy steel door...I needed to get back to my bodybuilding exercises. The interior of the Old Alfred took my breath away. With its Sicilian marble floors and allegorical paintings, it was as impressive inside as out.

The trial was to take place in courtroom number one of four. The oak-paneled courtroom had a spacious dock, enclosed by low partitions, and then a staircase leading directly below, presumably to the holding cells. I thought of Lord Elliott down there and wondered how he would appear after almost a month in prison.

How difficult this must have been for Lady Mary, not knowing whether her husband would live or die. So many wives had endured the pain of waiting, of not knowing whether their husbands would return home. And even if they did come home, nothing would ever be the same again. At least Lord Elliott was physically whole, whatever else had been taken from him in the last few weeks—and for now at least, he was alive.

People were crowding into the courtroom, most of them jovial as if they were going to a party, an air of excitement in the room. I glanced around looking for Lady Mary. I recognized the black felt hat she'd worn at the dowager's funeral. She was sitting in the ladies' gallery, and I quickened my pace to join her. I was halfway to the ladies' gallery when I remembered that today I wasn't a lady, and did an about-face.

The judge called the proceedings to order. I hurried to take a seat near the front of the room. Lord Elliott appeared in the dock directly facing the witness box, opposite the judge. He looked a decade older than the last time I'd seen him at Ravenswick Abbey. *Poor man.* The jurors—who would decide his fate—sat to his right, and at a table below the judge sat the clerk, two barristers, and a woman wearing a smart skirt and matching blazer who was taking shorthand notes of the proceedings.

"Lord Ernest Gerald Elliott," the judge said with solemnity. "You are charged with the willful murder of your mother, Mrs. Edith Wilkinson. How do you plead?"

"Not guilty, Your Honor." Ernest looked haggard. He had dark circles under his eyes, and he needed a haircut. But his clothes were neatly pressed and he was clean-shaven.

Mr. Smith, a member of the King's Counsel, strode to the front of the room, and with much ceremony opened the case for the Crown. What he lacked in stature, he made up for in dramatic gestures.

"Gentlemen of the jury," Mr. Smith announced with great fanfare. "I

155

submit that Lord Ernest Elliott committed the premeditated and cold-blooded murder of his mother by means of poison." The barrister for the prosecution had an angular appearance, and when he waved his arms, it gave the impression of a knife slicing the air.

"Why would her own son commit such a heinous crime? I will tell you why." With his craggy face, short white wig, and long black robe, he looked like an eagle ready to swoop down on his prey.

"Lord Ernest Elliott had gotten himself into such financial difficulties he killed his mother, believing he would inherit her fortune. His financial problems are the result of his gambling at the race track and his liaison with a neighboring widow, Mrs. Roland."

Gasps and murmurs from the crowd signaled their disapproval. I glanced up at Lady Mary, who was staring straight ahead with a face of stone.

"The lady in question brought this liaison to the attention of the countess, Lord Elliott's mother," Smith continued, "and she threatened to cut him out of her will. Not coincidentally, by early the next morning, she was dead." Smith waved his hand dramatically.

Surely Mrs. Roland wouldn't have told the countess if she were having a liaison with Ernest. It just didn't make sense. Again I glanced at Lady Mary, who was worrying a lace handkerchief something terrible.

"The police found the empty vial of strychnine, the very poison used to murder the countess, in Lord Elliott's bedroom, hidden among his undergarments in a dresser drawer." Smith's voice rose an octave as he sliced the air with his arms.

If Ernest had killed his mother, he wouldn't have been so daft as to leave the poison lying about in his room. I thought of the cordial bottle, most likely lost in the post thanks to my stupidity. If it contained the fatal dose, I was as much a criminal as the murderer himself. I studied the accused, whose complexion had taken on a yellowish tint that made him look positively waxy.

"I put it to the good gentlemen of the jury, Lord Ernest Elliott murdered his mother to prevent her from making a new will." Smith's wig trembled with excitement. "That evening it was Lord Elliott who doctored the fatal tea and later destroyed the new will." He glanced over at the jury before concluding, "As reasonable men, in light of the damning evidence I will present to you today, it is unthinkable for you to render a verdict other than guilty as charged." Mr. Smith sat down and mopped his forehead with a handkerchief.

I was the first witness called to testify for the prosecution. My heart constricted in my chest as I approached the stand. I'd never spoken in front of such a large crowd, and I was mortified to be testifying for the prosecution. I didn't dare look up to the ladies' gallery where Lady Mary was sitting. Instead, I scanned the room for Captain Douglas and Fredrick Fredricks. I hadn't seen them in the crowd, but I knew they had to be in the room somewhere.

With his manly chin and distinctive mustache, Fredricks was easy to pick out of the assembly. He and Captain Douglas were sitting near the back of the room to my right. Once I'd located them, I avoided looking at that section of the courtroom for fear one or the other of them would find me out—Captain Douglas because I'd seen him nearly every day for the last month, and Fredrick Fredricks because of his blasted lizard brain.

Under the harsh lights in the courtroom, I broke out in a sweat. I patted my forehead with my handkerchief and hoped the spirit gum didn't melt in the heat. I touched my eyebrows to make sure they were still in place. The last thing I needed was my facial hair dripping down my face during my testimony.

I gave Lord Elliott an apologetic look as I stepped into the witness box across from the dock where he stood. He remained impassive, holding onto the rail and staring straight ahead, poor man.

I repeated my testimony from the inquest, telling the court how I came upon the countess in the throes of fatal poisoning, and how I tried, unsuccessfully, to revive her. I also spoke about how I recognized the symptoms of poisoning, which at the time I thought was the result of a fatal dose of mercury bichloride, but had since realized must have been strychnine, and that I was the one who insisted upon an autopsy since Dr. Booth assumed it was her heart. "A reasonable conclusion considering he had been treating her for a heart ailment," I said.

Mr. Smith turned me over to the barrister for the defense, Granville Cornelius. His name suited him, as he was a walrus of a man with a stormy countenance. The only sound in the courtroom was his heavy breathing as he heaved his massive body forward and approached the bench. He was nearly panting as he addressed me.

"If Mrs. Wilkinson's tea or milk were poisoned in the evening, why didn't it take effect until early the next morning?"

"I don't know."

"No more questions."

Stupefied at the brevity of the interrogation, I stepped down from the witness box, doubly relieved I hadn't said anything damning to Lord Elliott, and even more so that my facial hair hadn't betrayed me. My testimony in no way pointed the finger at anyone. All I was asked to do was identify the symptoms of poisoning.

Of course, I didn't mention the ornate cordial bottle I'd lost in the post, or the letter I'd folded into the hatband, which I was certain held the solution to the case. If the cordial bottle was key, then I'd made a real hash of it.

I took my seat in the audience and then attempted to block out the proceedings in order to recall the contents of that blasted letter. I recalled it to my mind again, and saw the handwriting scrawled across the page. The letter contained only the salutation and a few lines of text. In my mind's eye, I could see the lines but couldn't make out the words. Still, I had the feeling that whoever wrote it did so in haste and must have been interrupted for there was no signature. I had to find a way to get back to Ravenswick Abbey, get into the dowager's bedroom, and retrieve that letter.

Granville Cornelius's booming voice interrupted my thoughts. He was cross-examining the frail old maid, who was gallantly defending her master.

I was glad Lady Mary couldn't testify against her husband and wouldn't be subjected to the tyranny of Grandville Cornelius or the pompous little Mr. Smith. I turned and glanced up at the ladies' gallery, where Lady Mary sat staring out into space, a million miles away.

"It weren't him," the maid insisted.

Grandville shook his head, and moved his jowls in silent rage.

It was hard to believe he was the barrister for the defense as he seemed intent on proving his client's guilt. I felt sorry for the poor maid. She was just trying to protect her master.

"Did you see the accused enter the bedroom of his mother at any time the night she died?" The barrister asked.

The maid made a pitiful mewling sound.

"Did you or did you not?"

"Well, sir," she began, "I were in bed when I remembered I bolted the front door. Since Mr. Wilkinson were still out of the house and not come home, I gets up again to leave it on the latch." She glanced over at Ernest, her face red and blotchy. "I hears a noise and goes to the east wing. I sees master Ernest knocking on her door. Or it could have been master Ian—"

"After caring for your *masters* for their entire lives, certainly by now you can tell them apart."

"Yes, sir," she said, wringing her hands.

"So, it could have been Ian you saw?"

"Yes, sir."

At least Granville's strategy was becoming clear to me. He was trying to convince the jury that the murderer could just as well have been Ian or someone else besides his client.

With every contradiction and twist or turn of a witness, the courtroom erupted with gasps or giggles. The judge had to use his gavel several times to call the court to order. Grandville seemed to be taking a special delight in the pandemonium, for every time the judge banged his gavel, the rotund man gave a hearty snort.

Finally, just short of five in the afternoon, the judge adjourned the proceeding until the following morning.

Despite Granville's efforts at confusing the jurors, at the end of the day, one was left with the impression that it was indeed Lord Ernest Elliott who brought his mother her tea, and he who knocked on her bedroom door. Things were not looking good for Lord Elliott if confusion was the best his defense had to offer.

On the way out of the building, I caught up to Lady Mary. Her face was pale and her eyes were puffy.

"I hate this whole proceeding, Doctor," she said. "What a trap is being set for my poor Ernest."

"Perhaps tomorrow will be better," I said. *Tomorrow will be worse*, I thought, given the prosecution had barely begun.

Out of the corner of my eye, I spotted Derek Wilkinson in a heated conversation with Gwen Bentham. They stood side-by-side, their heads nearly touching, as they whispered conspiratorially and patted each other's arms. Judging by their smiles and blushes, I would say their passionate hatred had turned into something else altogether. Or perhaps they had been secret lovers all along and the marital discord so frequently mentioned by witnesses was indeed that of the late countess and her husband.

It occurred to me, the letter delivered to the countess on the day she died—the letter that caused her such distress, she'd locked it in her handbag and went to bed ill, the letter I hid in the hatband—could very well be proof of a liaison between Gwen Bentham and Derek Wilkinson. Had the countess discovered that "Derek darling" was having an affair? Is that why she made a new will? Not to cut out Ernest, but to cut out the husband who had betrayed her? Perhaps the plot went further and Gwen and Derek poisoned the countess to get her out of the way so they could inherit her fortune. Indeed, the blackguards could have been planning the deed from the very beginning.

In any case, the pair had a lot of nerve flaunting their intimacy so soon after the dowager's death.

Lady Mary touched my sleeve. "Doctor, did you hear me?"

"Apologies." I turned back to Mary. "What were you saying?"

"You don't think Ian did it, do you? Is Mr. Grandville trying to prove Ian did it?"

"I think Mr. Grandville is trying to confuse the jury so they aren't convinced beyond a doubt that Ernest did it. It's a clever strategy as far as it goes." I glimpsed Fredricks coming toward us. "I'd better be going. Stay strong, Lady Mary." I patted her hand. "Everything will be all right."

"I hope you're right, Doctor," she said with a melancholy smile.

"I'm sure of it," I said, although I was far from sure of anything. I tipped my hat and took off down the sidewalk at a brisk pace. For Lady Mary's sake, I had to find a way to save Ernest Elliott from the gallows.

Chapter Eighteen: The Gallows Await

The next morning, I was up early to don my Dr. Vogel persona. Suffering from nightmares about hanging, I hadn't slept well. At least the purple bags under my eyes contributed to the manliness of my countenance.

I made an extra-strong cup of tea, added an additional dollop of sweet marmalade to my toast, and steeled myself for the second day of the trial as best as I could.

I hoped this would be the last time I would have to apply spirit gum and pat my beard into place or part my hair down the middle and plaster it down with greasy Brilliantine. I longed for a good finger wave. If the trial lasted long enough, I'd need another L'Oreal midnight treatment to hide my already dawning auburn roots.

Examining my two suits, the brown one appeared slightly less wrinkled than the navy one, so I pulled on the trousers, wrapped my chest, and donned the rest of my Dr. Vogel disguise. I was so sick of him I could scream. But the show must go on. Dr. Vogel was legally obliged to return to court in case he was recalled to the witness stand. And it wouldn't do for Dr. Vogel to go missing in action and raise even more suspicions.

If I was lucky, I could use this opportunity to observe Fredricks. He had to act soon to save Ernest Elliott. If he had an ace up his sleeve, now was the time to play it. Either Fredricks was a fraud, or, if he was waiting until the eleventh hour, he certainly had a flare for the dramatic. If he waited much longer, it would be too late for Lord Elliott.

I almost wished I could have taken Captain Douglas up on his offer to stay with the party in Paddington. At least then I would have had the opportunity to observe the daily habits of the mysterious huntsman that I suspected was just posing as a famous reporter. Perhaps after the trial, I could pull Lady Mary aside and ask her about Fredricks's daily habits since she'd been living with him this past month. Surely, she'd learned something about the secretive swaggart. *Sigh.* I missed my daily conversations with Lady Mary and the tidbits of information she provided me. Captain Douglas waffled on but provided jolly little of use to my investigation.

I took one last look in my hand mirror to make sure I hadn't forgotten some part of Dr. Vogel, took a deep breath, and then headed out to catch the train.

Even though I left my flat early, by the time I got to the Old Alfred, the courtroom was packed. It appeared to be the same crowd from yesterday with the addition of more blasted journalists. I felt sorry that poor Lady Mary had to endure the scandal. Every day the papers were full of speculations about Lord Elliott's financial ruination and his liaison with Mrs. Roland. I didn't know how Lady Mary could endure it. My thoughts turned to Andrew and Nancy and little Georgie…*No, no, not today.* I blocked them out and continued full steam ahead to the front of the courtroom.

The set-up at the courtroom was the same as the day before, and as creatures of habit, everyone took their same seats. I found mine near the front and glanced up to see Lady Mary back in the ladies' gallery. When her gaze met mine, she waved and gave a tired little smile.

The first witness for the prosecution was a detective inspector from Scotland Yard. His blondish brush mustache formed a permanent frown, which accentuated his strong chin. Aside from a gold watch chain, his attire was the usual boring three-piece suit and tie. He was no nonsense and professional as he recounted finding the poison bottle in Lord Ernest Elliott's bedroom, stuffed under some clothes in the back of a dresser drawer. Apparently he'd received an anonymous tip.

Anonymous tip? How suspicious. Without the daily updates from Lady Mary I'd received when I resided at Ravenswick Abbey, I was reliant on reports from Clifford Douglas, who obviously didn't pay as much attention to detail as Lady Mary had. To be fair, he paid attention to details, just the wrong ones.

The vial, which had already been identified by the chemist's assistant, Mr. Sage, as the vial of strychnine purchased by the false Mr. Wilkinson, was exhibited again for the jury.

I sat on the edge of my seat as Mr. Smith continued questioning the police inspector, who reported that Lord Elliott had no alibi for the time the impostor purchased the poison. Mr. Smith took the opportunity to insist it was the defendant who posed as Mr. Wilkinson on that fateful Monday afternoon.

The evidence was stacking up against poor Ernest…a little too conveniently. Why would a murderer keep the evidence of his crime in his bedroom, the first place the police would search? Something wasn't right with this scenario. I suspected someone was trying to frame Ernest Elliott for the murder of his mother. I glanced over at Fredricks, hoping he'd make his move soon. Perhaps the clever newsman was satisfied Ernest Elliott was the true killer. Unless something miraculous happened, Ernest would hang even if he was innocent.

Over the course of the day, the case against poor Ernest went from bad to worse. The prosecution presented more evidence as to his financial difficulties and his liaison with Mrs. Roland. I cringed at the mention of her name. Poor Lady Mary. I don't know how she soldiered on in the face of public humiliation. At least Andrew's infidelity was merely local and not national news. The thought of Andrew, and the memory of his last excruciating night on earth, made my stomach sour.

As the day dragged on, I realized I must have an allergy to trials. Just as it had at the inquest, the room began to close in on me and I urgently needed to escape. Perhaps my empathy was too strong, either that or I had a terribly guilty conscience. With every witness, I felt myself on trial. I wiped my brow with a handkerchief. *Buck up, old girl. You've got to compose yourself!* I quickly stuffed the handkerchief back into my waistcoat pocket when I realized it was one of my flowered lacy numbers.

Next, Ian Elliott was called to the witness stand for the defense. He was even thinner than I remembered, and his wan complexion was paler than ever. He didn't look well. His brother's trial must have been weighing on him, either that or, like me, he had a guilty conscience. After all, with his mother out of the way, he was free to marry Lilian.

"Who would inherit Ravenswick Abbey if your brother is hanged?" The oversized barrister took a step closer to the witness box.

The crowd gasped as one.

Grandville really was too much. I wondered why Ernest had engaged such a pillock. Poor Ian. He was so mild-mannered and such a gentle lad, he didn't look like he could hurt a flea. What kind of game was Grandville playing at, sacrificing one brother for the sake of the other? Red-faced, Ernest Elliott was holding onto the rail of the dock. He looked like he might jump over it and attack his own barrister.

After humiliating poor Ian, the defense called the prisoner himself to the witness stand. I scanned the ladies' gallery looking for Lady Mary, but she wasn't there. I twisted around to scan the crowd behind me, and I saw her standing at the back of the courtroom near the exit. She was already dressed like a widow, in black from head to toe.

A hush fell over the audience as Lord Elliott was moved from the dock to the witness stand.

"Where were you at four o'clock when the poison was purchased?"

"As I told the police, I was called out of the house by an anonymous note."

"Convenient." Mr. Smith sniffed again. "Is this the note?" The clerk handed him a piece of paper. The accused glanced at the paper and nodded. Head bowed, he handed the paper back to the clerk, who read it aloud, "Meet me at the old barn at four p.m. or I will tell your wife about Mrs. Roland." The clerk then passed the note to the jurors.

I didn't dare turn around to look at Lady Mary. Instead I watched the jurors as they read the note. Whatever they thought of the note, it was clear from their expressions they didn't approve of Ernest's liaison with Mrs. Roland. And judging by the clucking of tongues, neither did the women in the gallery.

"Who wrote this note?"

"I don't know."

"Did anyone see you when you were out of the house?"

"No. I waited at the old barn. After thirty minutes, I gave up and went home."

"And why did you make the journey if you didn't know who'd called you out? Are you in the habit of responding to strange requests to meet in isolated woods?"

"The note was threatening, and I wanted to put a stop to it."

"Threatening? What did it threaten?"

Ernest cleared his throat. "As you heard, it threatened to tell my wife about Janet...Mrs. Roland, unless I appeared with a check for fifty pounds."

There were audible gasps from the ladies' gallery. And even the jurors shifted in their seats.

Good heavens! Janet. J for Janet. The sloe-berry cordial came from Janet Roland. Of course! I'd been such an idiot. Why didn't I think to find out Mrs. Roland's Christian name? And then it dawned on me...E wasn't Edith but Ernest. If the cordial was poisoned, it was intended for Ernest and not his mother. If only the little bottle hadn't been lost in the post. Didn't it have to turn up eventually? Hopefully, before Ernest Elliott was swinging from a rope.

"So you were being blackmailed?"

"It appears so. But I wasn't—"

Mr. Smith cut him off. "Is this perhaps why you found yourself in financial difficulties?"

Ernest lowered his head. "No. It's not like that—"

Obviously sensing weakness in his prey, Mr. Smith went in for the kill. "I say you wrote the note yourself. And you, Lord Elliott, purchased the poison. And you murdered your own mother to pay off a blackmailer to continue your liaison with Mrs. Janet Roland."

"No!" Ernest shouted and pounded his fist against the dock railing. "It's a lie! It's a lie. I didn't do it..." He broke down and buried his face in his hands.

His loss of composure did not serve him well.

Seeing Lord Elliott reduced to tears put me over the edge. My head began spinning and my vision became cloudy. I absolutely had to remove myself from the sweltering courtroom before I fainted. It wouldn't do for a London doctor—a specialist in female maladies no less—to be overcome by a case of the vapors. If I collapsed on the floor and had to be revived, the jig would be up.

Excusing myself as I went, I did my best not to step on well-clad toes as I made my escape from the courtroom.

Staggering outside onto Alfred Street, I must have looked a sight. Strangers stared as I leaned against the stone building, my hands on my knees, trying not to pass out. I closed my eyes and concentrated on my breathing. My eyes flashed open again when I overheard a group of newspapermen discussing how the forthcoming hanging of Lord Elliott would be the biggest news of the year...a wealthy landowner swinging from a rope. I shuddered.

It was true, things were not looking good for Ernest Elliott. The noose was tightening around his neck.

Should I confess to taking the letter and bottle from the dowager's handbag? Should I go to Fredricks and tell him everything? Or, better yet, reveal my assignment and true identity to Scotland Yard? I still didn't understand why the War Office couldn't intervene. If we were fighting a war for justice abroad, shouldn't we be just as concerned about justice at home?

I didn't want to lose my assignment. These last two months had been some of the most exciting in my life. But would I let an innocent man go to the gallows?

A spark ignited in my brain. I had an idea of how to save Lord Elliott. My thoughts were racing. A plan was forming in my mind. But would it work, and could I carry it out in time? I had to. Ernest Elliott's life depended on it.

Chapter Nineteen: The Letter

Once outside the courthouse, I ducked into the coffee shop next door, asked to borrow a piece of paper and fountain pen, and jotted a quick note. I paid a newspaper boy a florin to deliver it to "the tall man in uniform queuing for a hackney carriage."

At eight o'clock on the dot, Clifford Douglas was ringing my doorbell. I adjusted my wig, smoothed my skirt, and answered the door. He was looking rather sharp in his beige wools. Fredricks must be giving him advice on his clothes.

"Miss Figg, I got your note and came round this evening to discuss an urgent matter. Do you mind?" He pointed at my lip. "You have a bit of something just there."

I touched my upper lip and removed a tiny ball of...spirit gum. *The blasted beard.* "Lip balm," I said, trying to regain my composure. "Please come in." I invited him into my sitting room and offered him tea.

"Do you happen to have anything stronger? Whiskey or maybe some brandy?" he asked. "That trial has put my nerves on end."

"That's why I asked to see you."

"Were you there? I didn't see you?"

"No." In a way, it was true. Miss Figg hadn't been there. I gestured toward the couch and Clifford sat down.

"Let me see if I still have any of Andrew's liquor in the cabinet," I said, stalling. At the mention of my husband's name, a stabbing pain struck my heart. *Why did the last gruesome memory displace four years of happy ones?* I'd rather remember that fateful day at his office when I found him in Nancy's arms than think of his burned body fighting for breath in the hospital.

I went into the kitchen and checked the cupboard where I'd stored Andrew's alcohol. He had a bottle of scotch whiskey from before the war and a bottle of rough rum. I poured two glasses of scotch, one large and one small, and returned to the sitting room.

"Do you take soda or water with your whiskey?" I asked.

"Neat is perfect," he said with a smile.

I handed the large whiskey to Clifford.

"I'm deuced worried about my friend Ernest. The prosecution has a strong case against him. I know he didn't do it. Ernest's a topping sort and could never do a wicked thing like that." He sipped his whiskey. "I wish there were something I could do to help him."

"Perhaps there is," I said, glancing up over the lip of my glass. The smell of the strong drink was enough to bring tears to my eyes. I sipped it tentatively. At first the alcohol burned my tongue, but then the tingling gave way to pleasant flavors of smoky bergamot and a hint of citrus. Yes, to my surprise, I rather liked whiskey.

"Really?" His eyes brightened. "What?"

"Remember that fellow, Dr. Vogel, who you mentioned attended your friend's mother?"

"That blackguard!" The captain pounded his fist on his knee.

"Be that as it may." I was somewhat annoyed at this attitude toward my good doctor. "He revealed to me the most stunning bit of information last week."

"Good Lord! You know Dr. Vogel?"

"In a manner of speaking," I said coyly.

"How do you know that wretched fellow?" He put his glass down on the side table and gazed over at me expectantly. "Good heavens! Don't tell me he's a friend of yours."

"Not exactly."

"You don't fancy him, do you?" Flustered, he reached for his glass again.

"No, nothing like that." I sipped my whiskey.

"With that horrid black beard. I hope not."

"I hate that beard!" There I was telling the truth. I did hate that beard. "Anyway, he's not my type."

"Who is your type?" His blue eyes shone.

The image of Archie Somersby lying shirtless in bed popped into my mind. My cheeks grew hot. "Shall we get back to saving your friend?"

"If it will help Ernest, you must tell me what you learned from the blighter."

"He's really not that bad, you know," I said, defending my alter ego. "If you must know, he's my doctor."

"I say. Why didn't you tell me?" He looked relieved.

"It's jolly awkward, actually."

"You can tell me, I promise, I won't say a word to anyone." He looked so sincere I almost laughed. "I'm nothing if not discrete," he added.

I looked him straight in the eyes and said. "I see him for *utero errantia* during *fluores menstruada*."

Clifford blushed from ear to ear. "Oh dear," he whispered.

"Yes, well." I cleared my throat. "Now you see why I was reluctant to say anything to you about my association with Dr. Vogel."

"Indeed." He took a gulp of whiskey, nearly spilling his drink down his front.

I took secret delight in torturing poor Clifford. He was so easily embarrassed.

"Female maladies—"

"My word!" he interrupted, turning an even darker shade of crimson.

"Shall we get back to your friend's trial, then?" I asked, to his obvious relief.

"Please."

"You must swear none of what I tell you leaves this room," I said.

"I swear," he said solemnly. "You can trust me with your life."

"I'm sure I can, but I'm glad I don't have to." I leaned forward in my chair. "Dr. Vogel told me Lady Mary Elliott asked him to take an incriminating letter from the dowager's handbag."

"Good Lord!"

"Exactly." I adjusted my skirt. "Now you see why you mustn't under any circumstances tell anyone about this."

"Good heavens, no." He shook his head.

"After the family left the bedroom the night the countess died, the good doctor had the letter in his possession when Dr. Booth threatened to return to the room and find him out. Thinking quickly, the clever doctor folded the letter into the hatband of the dowager's gorgeous..." I stopped myself before I got carried away describing that delicious hat.

"No!"

"Yes, just so." I stood up and moved closer to the couch.

"I knew that Vogel character was up to no good. Poor Lady Mary. I don't know what she saw in him."

"I think he's rather a good egg. He didn't need to come forward with this information about the letter, you know."

"Yes, but why didn't he mention it at the trial?"

"How would it look for *poor Lady Mary,* as you say, if she instigated a scheme to steal a letter?"

"You have a point. Poor Ernest, his wife carrying on with that horrid doctor. I can hardly believe it's true. She's such a lovely creature."

"Dr. Vogel would never carry on with a married woman." *Even if I really were a man, I'm quite sure I would not be the kind of bloke to commit adultery.*

"How do you know what the man's capable of?"

"I know him well enough to be certain that he's not the sort of man to be unfaithful or carry on liaisons with other men's wives!" I said with an offended tone that threatened to betray me.

He pouted like a scolded schoolboy.

I regained my composure. "Retrieve the letter, Clifford, and save your friend." I finished my drink and sat the glass on the side table for emphasis.

"How can this letter save Ernest?" he asked.

"The letter, you see, is not a love letter as Lady Mary suspects. It's not about Ernest's liaison with Mrs. Roland."

"Not a love letter?"

"No. According to the doctor, Lady Mary thought it implicated her husband in a liaison with some shepherd's widow—"

"Mrs. Roland," he said thoughtfully.

"Yes, that sounds right. You see, Lady Mary was only using her friendship with Dr. Vogel to make her husband jealous."

"I knew Lady Mary was a wonderful sort of woman. I have a brilliant sense for women, you know." He smiled, pleased with himself.

"Yes, I'm sure." I tried not to laugh. "After reading about the trial, I'm convinced this letter was not about Mr. Elliott's infidelity." I went with my instinct. "Rather, it incriminates someone else entirely and he's the blackguard you should be worried about, my friend." I wished I knew who that someone else was. I had a hunch, but I dare not tell Clifford. He wouldn't believe me anyway.

"Good Lord. It's Wilkinson. I knew he was a bad sort. I told Fredricks from the beginning Wilkinson was no good."

I couldn't tell him my real suspicions. So I let him believe it was indeed Wilkinson. Anything to make him recover that letter. "Now you've got to prove it and save your friend."

"Right. I'll go straight away and fetch the letter. The hatband, you say." He arose from the couch.

"Clifford, you can't just go retrieve the letter and reveal it to the world. What will you say? How will you explain how you knew about it? Do you want to expose Lady Mary to vicious gossip, or worse, suspicions she had something to do with her mother-in-law's death? No, sit down please. I have a better idea."

"I suppose you're right." He sat down again.

"Would you like another whiskey?"

"Yes, I think I would." He held up his glass and I took it into the kitchen to refill.

When I returned, Clifford was pacing around my sitting room, looking pensive.

"What's troubling you?" I asked.

"Why would Dr. Vogel tell you all this?" He shook his head. "And how do we know he's telling the truth? I just don't trust the man."

"Do you trust me?"

"Yes, of course. What a silly question."

"Then quit pacing and sit down." I pointed at the couch and like a puppy, he obeyed. "Now finish your whiskey like a good boy while I tell you my plan."

He took a sip and then looked up at me expectantly. "Your plan—"

"Who is the most likely person in London to solve this case?"

"You?"

I rolled my eyes. "No, not me. Who are you always telling me is the greatest investigative reporter in the world?"

"Fredricks!"

"Yes, Fredricks. But you mustn't tell him a word about our conversation, or about Dr. Vogel and Lady Mary." I gave him a stern look. "Not one word."

"You can count on me."

"Good. You wouldn't want to embarrass your poor Lady Mary." Poor Lady Mary would be mortified if she knew I'd told Clifford. Still, it was the only way to save her husband.

"No, indeed not."

"Then you must lead Fredricks to the letter."

"And how can I do that without telling him the truth? He'll ask all kinds of questions and I'll be obliged to answer. He's not the sort of fellow who takes anything on faith."

"No, that's what I'm counting on. He will need to see for himself."

Clifford gave me a puzzled look. "What are you suggesting?"

"You've got to get Fredricks to go back to Ravenswick Abbey and make him examine the hat. It's on the hat stand on the dowager's dressing table. You've got to make him suspect someone tampered with that hat."

"Any how do I do that?"

"You say he's obsessed with the natural order of things and animal instincts?"

"Yes."

"And does he understand women's instincts?"

"Well, perhaps not as well as I do, but yes, I would say so."

I suppressed a smile.

"Dr. Vogel told me he forgot to put the hat back on the hat stand. Instead he left it lying on her dressing table. No self-respecting hat lover would toss their hat on a table when they have a perfectly good hat stand waiting at the ready."

"Why not?" I would."

"You, dear Captain, are not a woman."

He blushed.

"Its brim will become misshapen and flat. Don't you know to sit your hat on its crown and not on its brim? No doubt your friend Fredricks does."

"Well, yes. I suppose he would."

"In fact, I'm surprised he didn't notice the hat was not as it should be, given his obsession with order, as you say."

"Quite."

"So if Fredricks had reason to believe someone mislaid the hat, he might suspect an interloper had entered the bedroom after the murder to tamper with important evidence."

"I say, that's genius!" he exclaimed.

I raised my glass and laughed. "Yes, isn't it just."

"How do I make Fredricks think someone tampered with the hat? He's not an easy fellow to lead down the garden path, you know."

"I suppose not. So you'll have to be jolly clever."

"Yes, I suppose I will." He smiled. "You can count on me."

"Hadn't you best be going then?"

"Yes. Yes, of course. I'll go now. Thank you. You can count on me," he repeated, taking up his hat and overcoat.

"Hopefully, Lord Elliott can too." I picked up the empty glasses and walked him to the front door. "His life depends upon it."

After Clifford left, I was so agitated I could hardly sit still. I wondered whether or not he would be successful in luring Fredricks back out to Ravenswick Abbey to investigate the hatband. Even more, I wondered if my memory served me right and the letter was much more than an incriminating love letter.

Sitting at my kitchen table, distractedly eating a margarine sandwich, I let my mind wander back to the night of the dowager's death. The family was waiting downstairs. I was back in her bedroom, alone, looking for clues. I spotted the handbag, turned the key in the lock, and discovered the letter. I took the letter out and had just started to read it when Dr. Booth called out to me. I hastily folded the letter and tucked it into the hatband. I replayed the scene in my mind, pausing at the moment when I held the letter in my hands.

Yes. Finally. The words came into view before my mind's eye. At last I saw it as clearly as if I were holding it at this moment.

Good heavens. It was addressed to *Sehr geehrte Dame.* And it said something…in German.

I struggled to piece the words together. Unfortunately, I hadn't paid any more attention in my German classes than I had in my French classes.

I saw the words: *Geh Raus. Sie sind auf dich. Dien Leben ist in Gefar.* The rest was written in English. *Never fear. Victory will be ours. Soon we will get what we deserve.*

They would get what they deserved alright. If only I knew who *they* were. Gwen and Derek? Ernest and Janet Roland? Ian and Lilian? Or, was the plot even more sinister than love or money?

I winced. I only hoped my scheme worked and the Great White Hunter would find the damning letter—and learn the identity of the beastly murderers—in time to save Lord Elliott from the gallows.

Chapter Twenty: Out at the Farm

The next morning, distracted by the trial, and eager to learn whether Clifford succeeded, I missed my stop for Charing Cross Hospital. Rather than change platforms and take the train back to my stop, I decided to walk. I'd worn sensible shoes to go with my hospital uniform and—if the noxious fumes of the city streets didn't kill me—the exercise would do me good.

I'd only gone a couple of blocks when I regretted my decision. It was a real pea-souper, and the smells of filth and decay hung heavy in the fog. I missed the clean country air of Ravenswick Abbey. I thought of the American Jack London's harsh commentary upon visiting London Town: "The children grow up into rotten adults, without virility or stamina, a weak-kneed, narrow-chested, listless breed, that crumples up and goes down in the brute struggle for life with the invading hordes from the country." And to think, I was one of those rotten adults who'd lived here all my life. Perhaps the miasma of London had rotted the souls of traitors, who at this very moment, continued to plot against king and country to aid our enemies. I was beginning to suspect the dearly departed countess was among them.

As I turned the corner onto the Strand, I was shocked by the sight of lorries lined up in front of the hospital. You'd think I'd be used to it by now. But one never gets used to seeing young men broken in body and spirit, marked for the rest of their lives, however long they live. Perhaps there were some who could say, "Another Saturday, another line up of lorries." But to me, every visit to Charing Cross was a brand-new tragedy as raw and haunting as the first casualties I'd witnessed, only now compounded by the horrors of

Andrew's last ghastly night lying on a cot in the hallway of an overcrowded triage.

Whenever I approached those heavy entrance doors, I dreaded what awaited me on the other side.

Today, no sooner had I emerged from the locker room where I'd deposited my handbag, Daisy Nelson came straight at me, dashing up the hallway, waving her scarecrow arm above her head.

Breathless and panting, she managed to spit out the words, "death cap."

I nodded encouragingly. "Go on."

"Your bottle finally arrived." A horse-toothed smile cracked her long face. "You were bloody right. Traces of Hygrophoropsis aurantiaca *and* Amanita phalloides."

"False chanterelles and death caps, two of the deadliest mushrooms in England." I covered my mouth with my hand. "Do you know what this means?"

"Whoever drank your sloe-berry cordial had a fatal hangover." Daisy grabbed my arm. "Come on. I'll show you."

She led me down the hall and up the stairs to her laboratory behind the dispensary where the little ornate cordial bottle was standing at attention on her dissection table.

"What would happen to someone who drank this concoction?" I pointed to the bottle.

"Within one to three days of ingestion, possible nausea and vomiting, followed by seizures, and a few days later, death by kidney and liver failure." Daisy's hands whirled as she spoke. "And Bob's your uncle, no one's the wiser."

"A dish of mushrooms changed the destiny of Europe," I said, quoting Voltaire. Of course, he was talking about the Roman emperor Charles VI, whose death by mushroom poisoning led to the war of Austrian succession. Whose fortunes had the death of Edith Wilkinson changed?

If the will favored Derek Wilkinson, he and his plotting paramour, Gwen Bentham, would stand to benefit the most. If the adulterous pair had killed the countess, I hoped they got what they deserved. In that case, Ernest

Elliott would be next in line to inherit, which would solve the problem of his gambling debts. I doubted he was truly in love with Janet Roland. In fact, I still believed the whole thing nothing more than a rumor started by Derek Wilkinson to turn the countess against her son. Perhaps that horrible rumor was part of the murderous scheme.

In any case, both Ernest and Ian would benefit from their mother's death. Independent of the fortune at stake, Ian Elliott benefitted in that now he would be free to marry his true love, of whom his mother had most assuredly disapproved.

And yet, if it wasn't strychnine but poisonous mushrooms that killed the countess, then all bets were off. Even if a member of the family had planned to murder the countess with an overdose of stimulants, someone else had beat them to it with a more natural poison.

"The countess was sick when I arrived," I said more to myself than to Daisy. "Then within a few days, she was dead." I picked up the little bottle and examined it. "Mary told me Mrs. Roland delivered a basket of fresh-picked chanterelle mushrooms....I've got to get back out to Ravenswick Abbey."

I slid the bottle into the pocket of my apron and headed for the door.

"What's this about?" Daisy caught my arm. "I'm coming with you!"

"Impossible."

Daisy wedged her rangy body between me and the door. "I'm not letting you leave until you bloody well tell me where you got that bottle."

I stared into the brilliant eyes shining out of Daisy's leathery face and wondered whether she could be trusted. *Dare I tell her the truth? More to the point, what was the truth?* Had Janet Roland been the one to poison the countess? Or had she planned to poison her lover, Ernest Elliott, and instead the countess drank the fatal concoction? What was Fredrick Fredricks doing out at the farm with Mrs. Roland that afternoon when Mary and I were walking. What was the mysterious Fredricks up to? I had to get back out to the farm and find out.

"Please let me pass." I held my hands together as if in prayer.

Daisy stood with her arms wide blocking the door. "Not until you spill the beans, ducky."

What choice did I have, short of knocking her over and making a break for it? *Sigh.*

"No doubt you've heard about Lord Elliott standing trial for the murder of his mother, the dowager countess?"

"Who hasn't?"

"I found that bottle in her handbag the night she died."

"You nicked it?"

I nodded. "It's part of my job at the War Office. You mustn't tell anyone." I shook my finger for emphasis.

"Don't be daft. Who would I tell?" She raised an eyebrow. "So Miss Goody Two-Shoes Fiona Figg is actually a spy...why, I never." A wry smile spread across her face.

"Not a spy exactly. More like an undercover agent."

"You're like Nan the spy girl, from the moving pictures. Cor, I never..." She looked me up and down appraisingly.

"Please let me go. I have to get back to Ravenswick Abbey and find out who poisoned this liquor. Ernest Elliott's life is at stake."

"This cunning woman is bespoke for your investigation." She tapped her breastbone. "Let me fetch my bag." She eyed me for a moment. "You won't hop it without me, will you?"

"If you're so cunning, perhaps you can tell me whodunnit and save me a trip." Many of the cunning folk around London claimed they could solve crimes through their white magic. If that were the case, why were there so many unsolved crimes? Perhaps because there weren't enough gullible people willing to pay their fees.

"I need a hair or nail-clipping or tooth," Daisy said in all seriousness. "Then I can tell you if your suspects are guilty."

I rolled my eyes. "Can't you just use cards or dice or something?"

"We'd best quit faffing around." She opened the door. "If we're going to catch the murderer and save Lord Elliott."

"Unless Lord Elliott is the murderer." I stepped out into the hallway, and wondered if I could outrun her.

"You need me." She must have read my mind. "I know a lot more about poisonous plants than you do, ducky."

Maybe Daisy was right. With her knowledge of poisonous mushrooms, she could help locate their source.

"Could someone have used those mushrooms by accident?" I asked as we started to run.

"Only a daft 'apeth."

"You mean a daft half penny like me?"

"You didn't poison the old mutton."

I hurried to keep up with her.

"I'd like to take a butcher's at that farm." Her heels clattered as she dashed down the stairs. "I can find your poison mushrooms."

"Stop!" I called after her. "We need to formulate a plan. For one thing, how are we going to get out to the farm?"

Daisy paused on the landing and looked up at me. "We can take my sister's car."

"Your sister has a car?" I stammered in disbelief. "And petrol, too?"

Daisy nodded and blushed. "She's married to Viscount Falmouth."

"Your sister is Viscountess Falmouth?" You could have knocked me down with a feather!

"Close your gob. She was the prettiest parlor maid in Kent." Daisy turned on her heels. "Lucky for us, she's in town."

"Wait!" A plan was forming in my lizard brain. "We need to stop at Angels Fancy Dress first."

Two hours later, dressed as a police constable and a land girl, we arrived at Mrs. Janet Roland's farm. Just so there was no question about who was in charge of this operation, I'd made sure I was the policewoman.

Daisy's sister, the Viscountess Falmouth, had insisted we let her driver take us in their Wolseley, which seemed ostentatious in any circumstance, but especially during the war and for members of the police force, no less. On the way, sitting comfortably in the spacious backseat, I studied the Land Army Agricultural Handbook.

Now, stepping out of the vehicle—which I had the driver park a half mile from the farm—the only thing I could remember was the warning to young women: *You are doing a man's work and so you're dressed rather like a man, but remember just because you wear a smock and breeches you should take care to behave like a British girl who expects chivalry and respect from everyone she meets.*

At least land girls and policewomen didn't have to wear big scratchy beards and full masculine kit. I was relieved that on this trip to Ravenswick Abbey I was dressed only *rather like* a man and not exactly like one.

"We have to find out if Mrs. Roland intentionally or accidentally poisoned the countess," I whispered to Daisy as we approached the farmhouse. "Keep quiet and follow my lead."

"Cor, what do you think I am? A bleeding idiot?" Daisy's jacket and breeches were held up by a thick black belt, which was the best we could do given her lanky frame. She adjusted her cap, which rode uneasily on her tight saffron curls.

The farmhouse door opened. There stood the same curvaceous brunette whom Mary and I had seen riding past on that grand chestnut horse.

She arched her brows. "Can I help you?"

Her face was so open and pretty, I couldn't help but trust her.

"I'm Constable Brown, and this is Miss Clutterbuck." The names came out of my mouth before I could think. "We're scouting for wild edibles for the Land Army. Mushrooms, berries, hedgerow, medicinal herbs, anything we might be able to use to help the war effort."

"Of course. But you're too late for early spring bloomers like the morels and forsythia. And you've just missed the wild strawberries. But the pheasant berries and crab apples should be ripe." Mrs. Roland wiped her hands on her apron. "I can show you if you like."

"If it's not too much trouble." I glanced back at Daisy, who had picked a leaf off a bush and was sniffing it. "We're especially interested in mushrooms. You know how the boys like their mushrooms on toast."

Mrs. Roland nodded and then disappeared into the house. She reappeared a minute later with a basket. She'd removed her apron and had sturdy boots on under a full skirt. She was the kind of natural beauty who would be stunning no matter what she wore. No wonder Lady Mary had been worried.

"There may still be some chanterelles in those woods." Mrs. Roland gestured toward a stand of birch.

Daisy and I trudged through the pasture, following Mrs. Roland, who, in her flowing skirt, seemed to glide above the grass like an apparition in the dusky haze.

"Over here." Mrs. Roland pointed to several patches of golden fungus.

The sun was heading toward the horizon and a purplish mist descended on the forest. I inhaled the sweet smell of flowering aster and the spicy scent of moist earth. For a moment, I closed my eyes and tried to memorize the sound of birdsong and the soft touch of the warm summer breeze.

"Oh good, there's still some left." Mrs. Roland's voice brought me back to my mission.

Daisy had stepped out ahead where several golden clumps dotted the ground in the shade of an old birch. She bent down and examined the mushrooms. She picked one and held it up in the sunlight streaming through the trees. She nodded at Mrs. Roland, opened her mouth wide, and popped the whole fungus inside.

"No!" Mrs. Roland ran to Daisy's side. "Spit it out! It's poisonous. That's false chanterelle. Spit it out now!"

Daisy opened her mouth wide again and let the mushroom drop out onto the ground. She wiped her tongue on the sleeve of her uniform. "I'm a bloomin' idiot."

"Are you okay?" I asked, rushing to where she knelt. How could she make such a mistake? I thought she was an expert on poisonous plants.

Did Daisy just wink at me? *Wait! What a jolly clever girl.* Daisy had just established that Mrs. Roland wouldn't have poisoned anyone by accident. If Mrs. Roland had committed the murder, she'd done so intentionally. Even at a distance, she knew a true chanterelle from a false one.

"I have it on good account you make a cordial from sloe berries." Encouraged by Daisy's demonstration, I decided to go straight to the point.

"Yes, every year I make sloe-berry liquor." Mrs. Roland smiled. "It's very popular at the big house."

Indeed. I suspected her cordial wasn't the only thing popular at the big house.

"If you don't mind me asking, when was the last time you delivered sloe-berry cordial to the big house?" I removed my gloves and tucked them into my belt.

A melancholy cloud crossed her pretty countenance. "The week of the countess's death. God rest her soul." She crossed herself. Like the Great White Hunter, Mrs. Roland was Catholic. Merely a coincidence no doubt.

"Is there any chance false chanterelles could have gotten mixed into the cordial by accident?" I asked.

Mrs. Roland's pretty face paled. "No, Miss. I know my mushrooms. I dry chanterelles and grind them into a powder to add a certain sweet earthiness to the liquor. But I'm always very careful."

"What's this?" Daisy held up an ugly fungus shaped like a brain. She was testing Mrs. Roland.

"Why that's a morel. It's past season. I'm surprised—"

I interrupted. "Did anyone else have access to the cordial?"

"Why are you asking me these questions about the cordial?" Mrs. Roland said softly.

"Actually, I'm with the police." I straighten my jacket.

"I didn't know women could be policemen."

"Police women," I corrected. "With the war on, men are in short supply. I hope you don't mind answering my questions."

She nodded.

"We have reason to believe your cordial contained poisonous mushrooms."

Mrs. Roland gasped. "My word. You don't think..."

"Did you?"

"No. No. I would never." She shook her head. "I couldn't. You mean the countess? No, never."

"What about Ernest Elliott? Could you poison him?"

"Ernest? Lord Elliott?"

"He broke it off with you, didn't he?"

"I would never." She put her hand to her chest. "I'm...fond of Lord Elliott."

"Passion is a common motive for murder."

"I didn't put poisonous mushrooms in the cordial."

"Do you have any more bottles of sloe-berry liquor that we might examine?" I asked.

"I have two left from that same batch." Mrs. Roland gestured for us to follow her. "They're back at the house."

Inside, the farm house was modest but very clean and cozy, and it smelled wonderful of freshly baked bread. I wondered if I could be happy in a place like this. It was so peaceful.

Mrs. Roland opened a rough wooden cupboard in the kitchen and took out two small bottles. When she handed them to me, I realized someone had tampered with the bottle delivered to the countess. These bottles had thick red wax covering their tiny corks. The bottle I found in the dowager's handbag had no trace of wax. Although, come to think of it, the cork had a slight pinkish tint.

"May I keep these?"

She nodded.

I handed the bottles to Daisy. "Let's test them back at the hospital...laboratory."

"Sure thing." Daisy pocketed the bottles.

"Do you always use wax to seal the bottles?"

"Yes, ma'am. Otherwise they go off."

The one used to kill the countess had gone off, all right.

The warm yeasty smell was distracting. "Did anyone else have access to the cordial bottle before you sent it to the big house?" I asked, glancing around the humble kitchen looking for the source of the delicious aroma.

Mrs. Roland shook her head.

"So you were the only person to touch that bottle?" I spotted two loaves of golden brown bread resting on a cloth.

She thought a minute. "No. Mr. Fredricks hand-delivered it for me."

"The South African, er, American journalist?" I asked, distracted by my

184

growling stomach.

Mrs. Roland nodded. "He came here often with the refugees. The countess has…had them do odd jobs. Sometimes, she would come down herself and pour tea for them, especially the ones from Germany. Poor souls." Her eyes drifted to the horizon.

"You say Mr. Fredricks delivered the cordial for you." In my excitement, I nearly knocked off my cap. I adjusted it atop my bristly scalp least the shepherd's widow notice my shorn head. "What did he say, if you don't mind me asking?"

"He promised he'd help find Jimmy." A pained expression marred her beauty.

"Jimmy?"

"My brother. He was shot down over Northern France. The men in his battalion, the ones still alive, think he's in a German prison camp. Mr. Fredricks pledged he'd help get him out." Mrs. Roland dug in the pocket of her tunic. "And when Jimmy comes back, Mr. Fredricks told me to be sure to give him this." She held out a folded piece of thick paper.

I took it from her trembling hand and carefully unfolded it.

Now *my* hand was trembling. Written in tight cursive script was an address, an address is Paris: *Hôtel Grand, Champs Elysées.*

Chapter Twenty-One: The Trojan Horse

I spent my entire Sunday morning pacing back and forth in my flat, racking my lizard brain for what to do. I couldn't sit still long enough to eat. And, even now a bite of plain toast soured my stomach. I had to do something about my discovery at Mrs. Roland's farm, but what? If only I knew *what* I had discovered.

The countess had been poisoned by mushrooms and not strychnine or cocaine. For, as I'd already pointed out to the "great" investigative journalist, the countess had not yet consumed the fatal dose of her heart medicine. Even if Derek Wilkinson and his lover Gwen Bentham had added cocaine to the medicine in the hopes of killing the countess with the last deadly dose, someone had beat them to it using toxic sloe-berry liquor.

But who? Who had added the lethal mushrooms to the cordial? Mrs. Roland had the means. Did she also have the motive? Why would she want the countess dead? Of course, she may have intended the cordial for Ernest and wanted to kill him because he'd thrown her over. Or perhaps she thought with the countess out of the way, Ernest would inherit the fortune, leave Mary, and marry her. Although Ernest played the ponies, I don't think he played the field. No, something about Mrs. Roland's unguarded countenance and sincere manner made me trust her.

Blimey, I was starting to sound like Clifford Douglas, trusting women just because they were pretty…or the annoying huntsman, trusting my animal instincts. No, Fiona Figg was going to reason this out using logic and a dose of good common sense.

The thick red wax sealing the bottles was further evidence that Mrs.

Roland was not the murderer. The cordial that killed the countess was missing the red wax. Of course, the absence of the wax was not conclusive.

Tomorrow, Daisy would be back at the hospital. Then she could test the new bottles for any traces of poisonous mushrooms and could test the old bottle for any traces of red wax. I would know more then.

My thoughts turned to Fredricks. The Great White Hunter—if he truly was a hunter at all—was the last person to touch the poisonous cordial. He was the one who delivered it to the countess. He also had the means. He had access to the cordial and the false chanterelles. Why else would he have the *Field Guide to Poisonous Plants* in his room? Then there's the question of why he delivered the liquor to the countess instead of to Ernest Elliott, who was, after all, presumably the intended recipient? Why would Fredricks want to kill the countess, the woman who had shown him hospitality and taken in so many wounded war heroes and refugees?

Exhausted from dozens of turns around my living room, I headed for the kitchen to make a cup of tea. Hopefully a nice cuppa would help me concentrate. As I stood at the stove waiting for the kettle to boil, a lightning bolt electrified my lizard brain. *Of course, a Trojan horse!*

I loathed the idea, but it had to be done. I retrieved my Doctor Vogel disguise from the back of my wardrobe, and forced myself to don it again. Wouldn't Lady Mary be surprised to find me on her doorstep at the Paddington house? I only hoped she'd be at home...and she'd receive me. After all, I'd hardly spoken to her since I left Ravenswick Abbey, and she'd made it abundantly clear she'd been counting on my narrow shoulders to lean on for comfort and support. Surely I'd let her down. Poor Mary. I could only imagine what she was going through...like so many other women in our war-ravaged country, waiting to see if her husband would live or die.

It was no surprise that the houses on Harrow Road near Paddington Park were very posh. Elegant horse-drawn carriages, along with shiny motorcars, lined the street in front of a row of stately manors of white stone. How they kept the buildings so clean with all the soot in the air was a miracle. *Not a miracle at all*, I reminded myself, but the result of servants putting their already aching backs into it.

Number forty-four had arched columns adorned with flowers carved into the stone. Each floor of the three-story building had a balcony surrounded by wrought-iron. Lovely lilac heliotropes waved in the breeze from their window-box planters. I walked up the four marble steps to the front porch and gave the brass knocker a tap.

Annabelle, one of the parlor maids from Ravenswick Abbey, answered the door. "Why Doctor, you've come. Thank goodness. My lady's in such a state."

She led me into the morning room and went to fetch "my lady." I took the opportunity to investigate the contents of the drawers of the writing desk. I was just shutting a drawer containing thick stationary when I heard footfalls clacking on the marble floor. Startled, I whirled around, certain guilt was written in bold letters all over my bearded face.

"My lady says to bring you upstairs." Annabelle circled around the writing desk, making sure all of the drawers were shut. "My lady's not feeling well enough to come down. If you'll follow me, Doctor."

I was shocked to see Lady Mary languishing in bed, her hair loose and uncombed, her complexion wan, and her usually bright eyes swollen and dull.

"Doctor, how good of you to come." When Lady Mary sat up in bed, the maid plumped "my lady's" pillows.

"My dear Mary," I said, forgetting to lower my voice. I cleared my throat and started again. "Are you ill?"

"You tell me, good Doctor." Her teeth chattered as she spoke.

I reached down and held the back of my hand against her forehead. "You're burning up." I may not be a real doctor, but I knew a fever this high was bad business.

"I'm worried sick about Ernest." Her lips trembled.

"That's why I'm here." I glanced at Annabelle, who was fussing around the side table, eavesdropping. On my way to fetch a chair from the dressing table, I asked the maid to go down and make us some tea. What I had to ask was not for her ears.

Once Annabelle was gone and out of earshot, and I removed my hat and sat beside the bed. I smiled down at Mary and asked in a whisper, "This may be a sensitive question, but I need to know, were any of the dowager's refugees German?"

"Why yes, doctor." Mary's eyes brightened. "My mother-in-law took a special interest in refugees from Germany, people who wanted to escape war rather than make it."

I nodded encouragingly.

"Why, didn't you know?" Mary smiled weakly. "Edith's grandfather was a Saxe-Coburg. Her great-uncle was Léopold, the first king of Belgium."

My heart skipped a beat. The countess was German by blood. Was she also a German sympathizer?

"What does this have to do with Ernest?" Mary asked. "Aren't you here to help with the trial?"

She held out her hand. I took it in both of mine and patted it gently.

"Trust me. I am." I let go of her hand and stood up. "But now I must go."

"But, Doctor," she pleaded, her eyes damp.

"Do you trust me?"

She nodded.

"Then, I must make haste if I'm to save Ernest from the…" My voice broke off. "Save your husband." I replaced my hat on my head and left the room.

I heard Mary's small voice call after me, "God bless you, Doctor Vogel."

My mind was abuzz as I stepped back out into the miasma that was the premature start of a London summer. Disoriented, I scanned the street in both directions, trying to locate the omnibus stop from whence I'd arrived.

I boarded the motorbus back to town without the foggiest notion of where to disembark. What now? I had learned that the countess was German and favored German refugees. I also knew the countess had served them tea at the farm, which could be a sign of her generosity or something much more sinister.

The countess was poisoned, perhaps at the hand of one of her refugees. And, now her son was fighting for his life, possibly framed for her murder.

Framed by Derek Wilkinson and Gwen Bentham, who may have tried to kill the old woman themselves? Or framed by the real poisoner—whoever he or she may be—who had discovered the dowager's connection to the Germans was not just in her past.

I thought of her last word, *derspitzel*. What did it mean? If it was German, it could be Der Spitzel. But what was Spitzel? I seem to recall a Christmas cookie called a spitzel. And, spaetzle was a German dumpling. Perhaps it was a pet name for Derek? He was rather doughy.

Swimming in questions, and moving by habit, I exited the bus on Whitehall Street. As I made my way through the crowded walkway toward the Old Admiralty, I became more convinced that my hunch was spot-on. The countess was smuggling in German spies disguised as refugees in a kind of Trojan-horse operation. Either someone had found her out—the astute Fredrick Fredricks perhaps—or she had a change of heart after her marriage to Derek Wilkinson. In either case, I'd wager she'd stopped working for the Germans, and possibly become a double agent. It occurred to me, the countess herself could have been working for the War Office.

As if conjured by my meditations, I found myself standing in front of the heavy metal doors of the Old Admiralty building. It was unlikely I'd find Mr. Montgomery or Mr. Grey working on a Sunday, but I didn't know what else to do. With the war still running full tilt, undoubtedly someone was working, evidenced by the unlocked front entrance.

In a confused sort of trance, I ascended the stairs to Room 40. I tried the doorknob, but the door was locked. I knocked and was about to give up, when Mr. Knox opened the door.

"Can I help you?" he asked, looking me up and down. "If you're looking for some action, you've come to the right place." He winked.

Cheeky devil. I felt like slapping his wicked face...until I remembered the great black beard on my own. I touched the offending bushy beast.

"Mr. Knox, it's me!"

"Fiona, is that really you?" Mr. Knox let out a big belly laugh. "Well, blow me down. You are a corker!"

"Listen, I need to talk to Mr. Montgomery. Is he here?"

Mr. Knox couldn't stop laughing.

Sigh. My patience was wearing thin. "Put a sock in it and tell me where I can find Mr. Montgomery."

"He isn't here," Mr. Knox gasped, still barely able to contain himself. He wiped his eyes with the backs of his hands.

I glared at him. "What does *Der Spitzel* mean in German?"

"Did someone call you a Spitzel?" He continued laughing.

"What does it mean?" I was tempted to slap some sense into him.

"Stool pigeon." He sucked in breath.

Stool pigeon! The dowager's last words were stool pigeon.

"As in spy." Amidst more guffaws, he took out a handkerchief.

I turned on my heels and marched down the hall.

Stool pigeon. The countess was identifying her murderer as a stool pigeon. A stool pigeon working for the Germans or the British? There was one person who might be able to help me find the answer. But first, I needed to talk with Captain Hall.

My heart sank as I approached the door to Captain Blinker Hall's office. I could see through the opaque window that the office was dark.

I had no choice but to try Captain Hall's flat at the other end of the building. Like others in the upper brass, he lived in a well-appointed flat on an upper floor of the far wing of Old Admiralty.

If the countess had been a German spy, either Blinker Hall would already know, or he would be the one to tell. And if anyone in the blasted War Office could prevent Ernest Elliott from hanging, it would be Blinker Hall.

I hurried down the long hallway, scanning the name plates as I went. Luckily, the flats were marked, or I would never have found Captain Hall's residence. Standing before the door, I had second thoughts. After all, he'd already told me to stay out of the criminal investigation. But the poisoned cordial directly involved Fredrick Fredricks. And then there was the address on the slip of paper Fredricks had given to Mrs. Roland, which I had committed to memory. I thought it best to leave the paper with Mrs. Roland in case her brother did return and the War Office wanted to follow him.

I took a deep breath and knocked on the door. It was a Sunday, but at least it wasn't the middle of the night.

Captain Hall opened the door. He was wearing his uniform. I wondered if he slept in it too. His eyelids fluttered as he stood with his hand on the door, as if he might shut it in my face.

"Sir, I have news." My heart was racing and my stomach was doing flips. *Hold yourself together, old girl!* "It's about Fredrick Fredricks, the South African big game hunter and American journalist."

"Is that you, Miss Figg, under that beard?" Captain Hall gestured for me to come in. "I knew I'd seen you before, but I couldn't place you." He smiled. "What have you learned?"

Once we were seated in his serviceable sitting room, I told him about the poisoned cordial.

He interrupted me. "You're not to interfere in domestic matters. Leave the murder case to Scotland Yard." He blinked even faster when perturbed. "The War Office can't get involved."

"But, sir..."

He scowled and shook his head.

"But, sir," I continued. "Fredrick Fredricks left an address with the shepherd's widow to give to her brother when he returns from the German prison."

Captain Hall quit blinking and stared at me. "What address?"

"In Paris. The Grand Hotel on the Champs Elysées."

"The French are our allies."

"The countess is a Saxe-Coburg—"

He interrupted me again. "So is our king."

"Yes, but could the countess have had German sympathies? I suspect she might have been smuggling in German spies."

"Go on." He sat on the edge of his chair.

"Well, let's say she was working for the Germans. And let's say she decided to stop...or worse, she became a double agent? Then they would want to get rid of her, right?"

"Interesting theory, Miss Figg."

I scratched at my beard, which was deuced uncomfortable. "What if the

Germans sent Fredrick Fredricks to silence the countess because she knew too much about their espionage operations in England? What if she was a double-agent? And he was sent by the Germans to take her out."

Captain Hall templed his index fingers under his chin. "They told me you were smart, Miss Figg."

Now I blinked.

"Given this was your first assignment, you were on a need-to-know basis." He relaxed his hands into his lap. "I'm afraid we couldn't tell you everything."

"Everything?"

"We've known for some time that the countess, recently become Mrs. Edith Wilkinson, was working with the Germans and bringing in their operatives. But we needed to learn more about her involvement and try to infiltrate her operation." He stood up and started pacing the small room. "A few months ago, our informant in the household reported that the countess had a change of heart. It seems one of her sons had found out and forced her to stop."

"You have an informant at Ravenswick Abbey?"

"Yes, Lady Mary Elliott."

"Lady Mary?" I gasped. "How can you allow her husband to hang for a crime he didn't commit?"

"There are larger issues at stake here. Issues of national security. I'm afraid I still can't tell you everything. You'll have to trust me."

That was exactly what I'd said to Lady Mary. Given Captain Hall had sent me on a dangerous assignment with blinders on, I wasn't sure I could trust him.

"Leave the Elliott case to me," he said finally. "I need you to quit playing Sherlock Holmes and find out Fredrick Fredricks's next move. Can you do that?"

"Yes, sir. I'll try."

He nodded, indicating our time was up.

I was halfway out the door when he called after me, "Miss Figg."

I turned back.

"Be careful."

Now he tells me!

Chapter Twenty-Two: The Diary

Monday morning, I distractedly prepared my toilette, dressed for the office, drank my tea, and ate my toast. Today was the moment of truth for Lord Elliott. Would I allow an innocent man to be sent to the gallows? To save him, would I have to come forward and reveal myself as Dr. Vogel and ruin my own investigation of the Great White Hunter, not to mention risk my job at the War Office. Captain Hall had forbidden me from interfering in the trial. He'd made it clear that the War Office could not get involved in domestic matters, and furthermore, my assignment was to gather intelligence on Fredrick Fredricks, not to "play Sherlock Holmes."

Clifford was the last best hope to save Lord Elliott. Had Clifford tricked Fredricks into finding the incriminating letter in the hatband?

Blast! I stopped in my tracks. I'd been a bloody fool. If Fredricks was the murderer, I'd sent Clifford on a dangerous mission, and worse than that, I'd revealed the whereabouts of a crucial piece of evidence to the traitor. In the process, I may have blown my cover. Good heavens...and put myself in the position to become Fredricks's next victim.

My imagination was running away with me. Why would Fredricks, a famous big game hunter turned reporter want to kill the countess? Why would a South African be working with the Germans? Why indeed! It occurred to me, I didn't know which side Fredricks fought on during the Boer war. I'd assumed he was fighting with the British... but what if he wasn't?

When I arrived at Room 40, the men were already gathered, heads bent over the table, presumably looking at another intercepted telegram. The excitement of the Zimmerman telegram had long worn off. The Americans had joined the Allies over a month ago, but so far that hadn't made much difference. They had yet to send a significant battalion or fleet to the Front. Mr. Grey told me the American army would grow now that they'd started conscription and made Puerto Ricans citizens so they could draft them too. Being sent off to war seemed a high price to pay for citizenship, but it's the price most men paid for citizenship these days.

"Miss Figg, come take a look at this telegram," Mr. Grey called from beyond the partition.

I filed the document I'd been holding in my hand and headed out to the planning table. Even though I was only an honorary member of the team, I was pleased when one of the men asked for my input.

"Oh, for the days of splendid isolation," Mr. Knox said, "when all we had to worry about was India and the other colonies. Then that bloody archduke had to go and get himself assassinated."

It was absurd that one man's death triggered the blasted war and hundreds of thousands more deaths.

"It wasn't as simple as that Serbian nationalist shooting the archduke, and you know it," Mr. Montgomery said. "Anyway, the question now isn't how we got into the war but how we'll get out."

"First the French armies mutiny and now the Russians. It's a bloody mess!" Mr. Knox ran his fingers through his fine hair.

"Has something happened in Russia?" I asked, staring down at the newspaper on the table. The headline read: "Lenin returns from exile." *So it wasn't a telegram.*

"We have credible information that now Lenin is back in Russia, his Bolsheviks plan a second revolution to take down the provisional government," Mr. Montgomery said. "If that happens, Russia will be out of the war and we will have lost an important ally."

"What do you think, Miss Figg?" Mr. Grey asked.

Never having understood the whole Russian situation, all I could think to say was, "Have you ever noticed the resemblance between King George and his cousin Tsar Nicholas? They look like twins!"

"What happened to Nicholas could happen to George," Mr. Knox said. "Now that would be a rum do."

"Do you really think what happened in Russia could happen here?" I asked.

"When people are starving, anything can happen," Mr. Grey replied.

"Golly, what a mess." I sounded like a bloody schoolgirl. I couldn't imagine England without its king.

"*Golly*, indeed." Mr. Knox mocked me.

For the rest of the morning, I absentmindedly shuffled papers around my desk until lunchtime. Sitting at the little table in the kitchenette, I took a bite out of my margarine sandwich, craving a slice of fresh tomato, or some bacon, or a nice soft cheese. *Blasted war!* Maybe Mr. Knox was right. Another year of war rations and we could see revolution in Britain too.

I wished Clifford would appear and whisk me off to the canteen or Old Shades. No doubt, he was attending the last day of the trial. I glanced at my watch. Three more hours until the afternoon papers came out. Then I'd find out whether Fredricks had found the letter and saved Lord Elliott...or done away with Captain Douglas. I was tempted to take off work and go to the trial myself. But, I didn't dare risk being recognized. After all, I'd been there as Dr. Vogel just last week, and I didn't have time to go home and change. Anyway, I didn't fancy putting on that horrible beard ever again.

I prayed for a miracle. I had no appetite for more death, whether at the gallows or on the Front...nor for another bite of greasy margarine. I rewrapped the rest of my sandwich, and was just getting up from the table when a familiar lanky form appeared in the doorway to the kitchenette.

"Ready for lunch?" he asked.

"Why, Clifford, you came!" So he was still alive!

He smiled. "Yes, and wait until you hear what happened." Clearly energized by the morning's events, he was nearly bursting to tell me. "I'll take you to lunch and tell you all about it. You won't believe how terribly clever I was."

"I can't wait to hear," I said. "Let me get my hat and brolly."

"Yes, it's raining buckets."

"The canteen, then?"

"The canteen. Come on, old girl." He led me by the elbow. "Have I got a story for you."

Over bean soup and treacle pudding, the captain recounted Friday night's events. I was dying to hear how he'd enticed Fredricks to return to Ravenswick Abbey and whether he'd discovered the damning letter and what it meant. I was also dying to tell him about the poisoned cordial, but I didn't dare. I was under strict instructions to maintain my cover for as long as possible and learn as much as I could about Fredricks, specifically his "next move."

"You should have seen Fredricks." Clifford grinned. "He dashed out of the Paddington house, called for a car, and took off. Later he sent a telegram instructing me to gather everyone at the house. He does love to play to an audience." He took a swig of beer, no doubt to wash down the horrid soup.

"Go on. Then what?" I was too eager to eat.

"Well, everyone came to the house, including Derek Wilkinson and Miss Bentham, who carried on as if she wouldn't stay in the same room with him. It was quite a performance, I must say. I was suspicious of her from the start, you see—"

Of course, they probably still thought their plan to poison the countess had worked. "What happened? Did Mr. Fredricks solve the crime?" I wished the blasted man would get to the point. This was no time for one of his long-winded stories...unless, of course, it was the story of Fredricks's real reason for coming to England.

"I was jolly clever and put the suggestion in Fredricks's head that someone had tampered with the dowager's hat—"

"You said that already."

"Oh, did I? Yes, well—"

"Everyone gathered at the house, and what happened next?"

"Everyone gathered in the sitting room and Fredricks made quite a show of dismissing the *"harengs rouges"* as he calls red herrings before getting into the meat of the case." Clifford gestured with his spoon as he spoke. "Fredricks loves to show off his talent with languages. You know he speaks five languages... or is it seven?"

I scowled at him.

"Oh sorry. Right." He laid his spoon on the table. "First there was Lady Mary and the candle grease—"

"Lady Mary's only crime is jealousy."

"Yes, how did you know?"

"Dr. Vogel's confession that he stole the letter on her behalf."

"Right. I'd forgotten about that."

"Why don't we skip the fish course and go straight to the meat, as you say." I waved my spoon at him.

Clifford's face fell. I knew how he loved to milk a story for all it was worth, but awaiting the outcome of a murder trial was testing my patience. "Did Fredricks find the letter or not? Was the trial dismissed? What happened to Lord Elliott?"

"Let me finish the story." He took another sip of beer.

"Quit nattering and get to it then!"

"Yes, well. Fredricks stood at the front of the room like a professor delivering a lecture and reconstructed the events leading to the dowager's murder. It was really quite impressive. I wish you could have been there. You would have—"

"Captain Douglas," I growled. At least I didn't have to watch the arrogant newspaperman acting like he'd solved the case all on his own. Although, listening to the captain waffle on without getting to the most interesting part of the story was almost as intolerable.

"Yes, right." He gave me a sheepish smile. "As I was saying, Fredricks made a great show of rehearsing the events leading to the murder. You should—"

I furrowed my brows and tightened my lips.

"Right, sorry."

Eventually, after some prodding and scolding, Clifford related Fredricks's reconstruction of the murder:

In the late afternoon, the countess had a row with Ernest over his indiscretion with Mrs. Roland. Incensed by her son's infidelity, she made a new will leaving everything to her new husband, Derek Wilkinson. Then, later, the countess destroyed the will she'd just made.

"Why would she destroy a will she'd just made, you ask?" Clifford seemed very pleased with himself.

"No, I didn't ask." Although I did wonder how the countess would have learned of her son's infidelity. I quite suspected it was a rumor started by her own husband Derek Wilkinson to turn her against her heir. I stirred my tepid bean soup. "Can't you skip to the end?"

"What fun would that be?" He smiled. "Anyway, you'll never guess how Fredricks solved the case. He was absolutely brilliant. I don't know how, but Fredricks knew about the paper. No one would think of that but Fredricks."

"You mean the letter?" I sat at attention.

"No, the writing paper."

"Oh." I closed my eyes and sighed.

"It was genius. Don't you want to hear about the paper?"

"All right, what paper?"

Clifford nattered on, describing Fredricks's "genius" without so much as a hint as to whether the big game hunter was really a spy, and without telling me how he persuaded Fredricks to go back to Ravenswick Abbey.

Instead, he told me Fredricks had speculated that the countess went to her husband's desk to get some writing paper to write the new will, having run out herself. When she found the desk locked, she opened it using her own key. It was then that she found the love letter, which the maid had seen her holding, and which her husband never intended for her to find.

"A love letter? Is this my letter or a second letter?" The multiplication of letters was getting confusing. The letter I'd seen was most certainly not a love letter. From a subsequent chat with Dilly Knox, who'd translated it for me, I'd learned it was far from a love letter. Rather, it was a warning, a warning of a threat to the dowager's life to be exact.

Geh Raus. Sie sind auf dich. Dien Leben ist in Gefar, which translated to *Get out. They're on to you. Your life is in danger.*

"So the countess knew about the liaison between her husband and Gwen?"

"So it seems. And this is where poor Lady Mary comes back into the picture." Clifford finished the rest of his beer. He'd retired his spoon and was now waving his serviette to punctuate the spicy bits of his story.

"You see," he continued, "Mary thought the letter was from Mrs. Roland, and she was determined to retrieve it from the dowager's handbag. She knew the countess would be sound asleep because the powder I found on the serving tray was actually—"

"Sleeping powder administered by Lady Mary herself. Yes, I know."

Clifford scowled. "How could you know that?"

I cleared my throat. *Yes, how could I know that? Dr. Vogel was the one who knew, not me.* "I seem to remember Dr. Vogel mentioning it...No matter. Continue with your fascinating story."

"I really can't believe Lady Mary would have behaved in such a deceitful manner," Clifford continued. "I rather resented Fredricks insulting her this way. I suppose she was driven to it by jealousy...otherwise, such a wonderful woman, you know—"

I gave him a stern look, and he stopped abruptly.

"Yes, well. Sorry."

"How did Fredricks figure out Lady Mary had drugged the tea with sleeping powders?" I gave up on the watery soup and looked to my pudding.

"That's a funny story, really..." He glanced into my eyes and his voice trailed off. "Right. I'll get to the point." Again, he restarted his story. "When Fredricks learned that blackguard Dr. Vogel had been at the house for tea the night of the murder, he put two and two together—"

"And got seven." *Of course!* Lady Mary said she'd hidden one of the teacups in the jade vase. Fredricks must have realized one of the cups was missing.

Clifford stared at me. "Are you clairvoyant?"

I laughed. "Just a good guess."

"Well, finding out one of the cups was missing led Fredricks to retest the milk, this time for narcotic instead of poison. I was right, too. I knew it was the warm milk all along. Sometimes Fredricks is deuced disagreeable. He purposefully led me astray with the milk. I really should have put a wager on it—"

"The poison wasn't in the milk, so you still would have lost that wager," I said with a sly smile. Anyway, why would an extra tea cup make him retest the milk? It didn't make sense. Then again, most of Fredrick Fredricks's conclusions about the case were wrong. Oh how I wished I could tell Clifford the truth and set the record straight.

"Right. Well, yes," he stuttered. "You'll never guess how the poison was administered!" Clifford looked pleased with himself.

"In her heart medicine?" I asked, knowing full well the poison was in the sloe-berry cordial, the little bottle having been delivered by the "brilliant" Fredrick Fredricks, himself.

"My word!" He looked stunned. "How did you know?"

"When I worked in the hospital dispensary, I learned a few things about poisons and medicine."

"I say, you are a cracking clever girl. I'd love to see you take on Fredricks." He chuckled. "He could use a good comeuppance."

"I see what kind of friend you are." I winked. *Yes, Mr. Fredrick Fredricks has met his match.* Whatever he was up to, the poseur wasn't going to get away with it.

"Fredricks said the milk was the key to the delay in the effects of the strychnine."

I was beginning to understand how Fredricks's lizard brain worked. "He thinks the narcotic in the warm milk delayed the strychnine reaction. That's why it didn't take effect right away." Of course, I knew otherwise. The fatal dose of strychnine had settled to the bottom of the medicine bottle, and it would have been another day before the countess took it. In the meantime, she couldn't resist Mrs. Roland's sloe-berry cordial, which did her in before any other murder attempt could be consummated. Too bad I couldn't tell Clifford any of this. He'd really be impressed with me then.

"Jolly good, Fiona!" Clifford threw up his hands. "Is there anything you don't know?"

"Too many things to list, I'm afraid."

"You're well ahead of me. Fredricks had to explain it to me three times before I understood."

"Yes, well, deductive reasoning may not be your strong suit."

His face fell and I reached over and patted his hand. "Rest assured, dear Clifford, you have many others."

Blushing, he smiled from ear to ear. "My word."

"I rather think your friend Fredricks tries to throw you off the scent with his *harengs rouges* and then chastises you when you believe him. He's a sly devil, your huntsman."

"He knew who had done it all along yet didn't confide in me. I was rather put out, I must say."

"I don't blame you. Now finish your story, if you please." Waiting for the captain to finish his story, I took a tentative bite of treacle pudding. The spongy cake with warm custard was one of my favorites. Surely even the canteen couldn't ruin treacle pudding. The gluey substance stuck to the roof of my mouth quickly proved otherwise.

"Oh, right. Of course." Clifford resumed, "Thanks to your intervention and my clever ruse, Fredricks found the letter Dr. Vogel had hidden in the hatband. You should have seen him! In front of everyone, he pulled the letter dramatically from his inside jacket pocket like he was some kind of magician. When he read the letter, Miss Bentham started shrieking and Derek Wilkinson tried to make a break for it." Clifford grinned. "It was all jolly exciting. The inspector from Scotland Yard was lying in wait, so the murderers didn't get far. Turns out those two were in cahoots all along, planning that Derek would marry the countess and then together they would poison her and elope with her fortune. Beastly business, I'm afraid."

"What?" I felt the pudding sink like a rock into the pit of my stomach. "He read the letter? What did it say?"

"I told you. It was a love letter from Gwen to Derek. And that's all it took for Fredricks to sus out the rest. That rotter Wilkinson murdered his wife."

"Fredricks accused Wilkinson?"

Clifford nodded. "Scotland Yard took him into custody."

"Clifford, what if I told you they didn't…" I sat on my hands to stop myself.

"Who didn't what?" he asked.

"Do you think attempted murder is just as criminal as actual murder?" I asked.

"Well, I suppose that depends."

"Depends on what?"

"The attempt."

"*Mens rea* or *actus reus*," I said under my breath.

"Men's what?" Clifford got a pained looked on his face, as if I'd mentioned *fluores menstruada* again.

"Guilty minds or guilty deeds."

"In the case of Derek Wilkinson and Miss Bentham, I'd say both!" He lifted his beer bottle in the air for emphasis.

Was it right to convict Derek and Gwen for committing murder even though they hadn't succeeded in carrying it out? If it hadn't been for the poisoned cordial, their plan may have succeeded and then they would be murderers. Still, unless I came forward with new evidence, they could hang for a crime they didn't commit.

"Fiona, are you listening?" Clifford's question brought me back into the moment.

"Oh yes. Right. The suspense is killing me!" I dropped my fork and threw my hands in the air. "How did you persuade your friend Fredricks to return to Ravenswick without betraying Lady Mary's secret? To my mind, that's the only mystery in this case."

"I was jolly good, wasn't I?"

"I don't know. What did you do? You still haven't told me!"

Clifford pulled a sheaf of paper from a satchel. "To find out, you'll have to read this." He shoved a leather-bound book across the table at me.

"What is it?"

"Seems I have a flair for writing." He was beaming. "*The Daily Times* is printing my account of the whole affair, in installments."

"When did you write this?" I lifted the book. It had some heft. I was impressed. "You couldn't have written this whole thing last night?"

"Good heavens, no. I've been at it since the beginning, you see. I guess you could say I kept a diary."

"Well, did Lord Elliott get off or not? Surely you're not going to keep me in the dark about that?"

"Yes. Yes, he did." Clifford smiled. "Thanks to you, old girl."

"A diary?" I took the leather book in both hands. "You didn't betray Dr.

Vogel…or Lady Mary?"

"Good Lord, no." He got that familiar hangdog look on his face. "Do you take me for an idiot?"

The jury's still out.

Chapter Twenty-Three: The End of the Beginning

After Clifford left the canteen and I finished the last bite of my treacle pudding—which wasn't half-bad once I got used to the texture—I snatched the diary off the table, and went back to Room 40. I stuffed the diary in my desk drawer and tried to forget about it. Yet, as I worked on perfecting my filing system, the brown book called to me. When I could resist no longer, I took a break for a cuppa and brought the diary with me to the kitchenette. I had butterflies in my stomach as I started reading. Perhaps I would finally get the dirt on Fredricks and some clue as to the real reason he was in England. If Clifford knew about the dowager's treason, or his dear Fredricks's secret note left with Mrs. Roland, he hadn't let on.

I read the first few lines. *What cheek!* Clifford Douglas said he was asked by the family to write an account of the case. *Horsefeathers!* I didn't believe it for a minute. I doubted any of them wanted their story in the newspaper, except, of course, for the pompous huntsman, who would probably lap up the publicity. For a spy, he adored being in the limelight.

I had to admit, Clifford was a good writer, but the diary was full of inaccuracies. I went back to my desk to fetch a red pen so I could make corrections.

Reading the diary, I learned more about Clifford Douglas than I did about the murder…or the Great White Hunter. First off, it was obvious from the way he described her "sleeping embers" and "fierce and feral soul bursting from a divine and elegant figure," that he fancied Lady Mary Elliott, a married woman. And the way he carried on about his *brilliant friend* Fredrick Fredricks, I wondered if he didn't fancy him too. When I read about his proposal to Lilian Mandrake, I burst out laughing.

Mr. Knox came to investigate. "What's so funny?" he asked.

"Nothing, really." I put my hand over my mouth. It was just too funny. I couldn't stop laughing.

"Let me in on the joke." He came closer so he could look over my shoulder. "I could use a good laugh."

I closed the diary. "Just a friend making a fool of himself."

"Aha! A love story. My favorite."

I bet it is your favorite, you cad. I'd heard the rumors about Mr. Knox's lovers, both women and men. Whereas Clifford Douglas's exploits were all in his mind, Dilly Knox was a man of action. I'd seen it in his eyes as both a woman and a man.

"Yes, well. This one's not for you." I took a sip of tea. "Anyway, it will be printed in the *Daily Times*. You can read it when it comes out." I made a sweeping gesture with my hand. "Now shoo."

After Mr. Knox finally left, I carried my tea and the diary back to my desk for more privacy.

I reread the part where Clifford proposed to Lilian. I couldn't help but giggle. He used the same lines on me. Clifford was nothing if not a romantic, saving damsels in distress. With this war on, if he went around proposing to every crying girl he encountered, he would spend a lot of time down on one knee.

The diary left me with the impression that I was right. Fredricks had dismissed whatever Clifford said and then led him astray with red herrings before circling back around to the place where they'd begun, thereby proving Clifford right in the end, but taking full credit, all while making the poor captain feel like a fool. With friends like that…

There was nothing in the diary to suggest Fredricks was a spy. Then again, there was nothing to prove he wasn't either. Given he was obviously smitten with the "famous hunter turned newsman," on that score, Captain Clifford Douglas was not a reliable source.

From the start, everyone in the household suspected Derek Wilkinson had poisoned his wife. Even his lover, Gwen Bentham, accused him as part of her act. And yet it took the great investigative journalist Fredrick Fredricks to *prove* it, which he did by producing the damning letter I'd disclosed to Clifford. Yet, the letter he produced was most certainly *not* the letter I found. Of that, I was certain.

Once the photograph was removed from the water bath in the darkroom of my mind, it was indelible. Now that I'd finally been able to conjure the purloined letter before my mind's eyes, I knew it was not a love letter but a warning from another German spy.

If Fredricks did find my letter in the hatband, he hadn't disclosed it to Clifford. Indeed, he conveniently substituted a love letter—real or forged. If the journalist found the German letter and didn't report it, then there is only one conclusion to reach. Fredrick Fredricks was the German spy.

I fingered the leather diary, wondering how much evidence I would need to gather—and how I would go about gathering it—to convince Captain Blinker Hall that the huntsman had killed Edith Wilkinson to stop her from turning over any secrets she'd learned from the Germans. I was sure my hunch was right and she had been aiding the Germans, had a change of heart, and became a double-agent. Captain Hall confirmed as much.

I flipped through the pages of Clifford's diary. I was dying to know how he persuaded Fredricks to go back to Ravenswick Abbey and look through the dowager's hats without spilling the beans about Lady Mary and me. I flipped through the diary looking for the telltale passage, which had to be somewhere near the end of the story.

Aha! I found it. Running my finger down the page, I read as fast as I could. The fastidious Fredricks was bemoaning not solving the case while polishing his knee-high combat boots, an activity he claimed relaxed him. Clifford remarked on the odd activities his friend found relaxing, such as polishing combat boots and brushing slouch hats or trading out grosgrain hatbands for leather ones.

A bit obvious, but hopefully effective. I read on:

"Why, I bet you hide your love letters in your hatbands."

"The volume of love letters I receive wouldn't even fit in this boot." Fredricks held up the knee-high combat boot he was polishing.

"But your ladies, where do they hide their love letters? Certainly not in combat boots."

Jolly clever, Clifford Douglas!

Fredricks laughed. "Right you are old man. Some of those ladies' elaborate hats could hide a dozen love letters." He stopped rubbing his boot and stared over at me, eyes wide.

"My God. That's it, *mon ami*." Fredricks dropped his boot and stood up.

"What is it, Fredricks?" I was feeling rather chuffed with myself. Miss Fiona Figg would be jolly pleased with me.

Yes, Captain Douglas, she is. I continued reading:

Perhaps she'll even let me kiss her.

My dear captain, I wouldn't bet on it.

"*Danke mein freund*, you've activated my lizard brain."

Fredricks and his blasted lizard brain. At least this time the supercilious newsman gave his friend the credit due him. *I salute you, Clifford Douglas very ingenious, indeed. You outfoxed the fox himself.*

I had a new admiration for the captain. He was clever, and more importantly in these troubled times, he was loyal. He didn't betray me or Lady Mary or even his nemesis, Dr. Vogel. I finally realized why he hated Dr. Vogel so much. He was jealous of Lady Mary's attachment to the doctor. I smiled and closed the diary. *Dear Clifford.*

"Miss Figg," Mr. Grey interrupted my musings. "A telegram for you." He handed me a slip of paper.

"What?" *Who would send me a telegram?* Suddenly, the room felt cold like someone had walked on my grave. I took the paper from his hand. "Thank you, Mr. Grey."

He nodded and left me to read in peace. In these times, telegrams were dreaded, for they usually contained bad news. I racked my brain to remember what relations I had at the Front.

The telegram was printed on thin paper and had been stamped several times by various officials. My hands trembled as I read it. I saw the name *Archie Somersby* and my pulse quickened. *Why would I be notified if Archie had died or been captured?* I exhaled audibly when I realized the telegram was *from* Archie not *about* Archie.

I scanned it and then read it out loud to make sure I'd understood. "Fredricks's parents and siblings died in the Boer wars. His fault. More soon. Love, Archie Somersby."

I reread the telegram several times before it sunk in. Fredricks was somehow responsible for the death of his entire family? Those two little boys and the baby girl in the photograph? And the dark beauty, was she his wife? What a tragedy. How did it happen? Killed in the war? By the Boers or the British? Or by Fredricks himself? My stomach turned imagining how the huntsman might have been guilty of killing his entire family.

A guilty conscience could explain quite a bit about Mr. Fredrick Fredricks—his fastidious obsession with order, his religious devotion, his secrecy, his soft spot for young maids, and perhaps even his becoming a spy. *Had Fredricks accidentally—or intentionally—killed his family? And why had he never mentioned his family to his good friend Clifford Douglas?* Then again, if the British had killed his family, that could most certainly turn Fredricks against us. *Yet, how was it his fault?*

It was all deuced mysterious, and I was determined to find out the truth about the secretive huntsman, who was much more than he appeared to be.

I reread the telegram again. This time, my eyes lingered on the signature, "Love, Archie Somersby." *Love.* My heart skipped a beat.

"I say," the familiar voice startled me out of my daydreams.

"Curses!" My hand flew to my chest. "You scared the life out of me." I slid the telegram into my desk drawer. "Don't sneak up on me like that."

"Right. Sorry, old girl." Clifford pointed to his diary. "What did you think of my writing?" He blushed.

"Lovely." Indeed, in addition to telling a good—if inaccurate—story, Clifford's account solidified Dr. Vogel's cover by making him a real person. "I hope you don't mind, I made a few corrections. For starters, Dr. Vogel was acquitted of espionage charges."

"Oh. Right. I'll change that before it goes to print."

"I was impressed by the way you tricked Fredricks into going back for the letter."

"That was jolly clever of me, wasn't it?" He grinned.

"It was brilliant!" *Too bad it wasn't the right letter.*

"I say." He blushed and stammered. "I-I say, would you come to supper with me tonight? I have a surprise for you."

Oh dear. I hope he's not going to propose again. I raised one eyebrow. "What sort of surprise?"

"Well it wouldn't be much of a surprise if I told you, now would it?"

"You've got me there." I laughed.

"May I?" He picked up the diary and put it into his satchel. "Shall I pick you up at half six?" he asked hopefully.

I nodded. *What could it hurt? It was only supper.* Anyway, perhaps I could pump him for information about Fredricks's family in South Africa.

On my way home from work, I stopped by Charing Cross hospital and made my way upstairs to the dispensary.

Daisy was perched on a stool at a high counter, filling an amber bottle with blue pills. She looked up and gave me a toothy grin. "Cor, you were right. The first cordial bottle was starkers. Not a trace of wax." She went to the medicine cabinet, removed one of the new cordial bottles, and brought it back to the counter. "See?"

I joined her at the counter and watched as she pulled the wax seal off and uncorked the bottle.

"Look." She ran her finger around the lip of the bottle. "When you pull off the wax, there are still visible traces." She took a sip.

"What are you doing? That might be poisonous!"

She laughed. "It's scrummers. Want some?"

Was she nuts? I shook my head. "You tested the other new bottle and it was clear of poison?"

"Don't be daft! You think I'd drink it otherwise?" She took another sip.

"If Fredricks added poisonous mushrooms to the cordial, could he have removed the wax so completely?"

"Piece of cake. Melt it off and then rub with mineral spirits." She held up the pinkish cork. "But the wax stained the cork. It absorbed traces of mineral spirits, too." She pushed it under my nose. "Smell."

A faint smell of turpentine hit my nostrils. I nodded.

She offered the tiny bottle to me again. "Last sip. Sure you don't want any?"

"No, thanks anyway." I held up my hand. "I'd better go. I'm going out tonight."

"With your handsome Captain Douglas?"

"How'd you know?"

"I'm a cunning woman, remember?" She winked. "Be good…and if you can't be good, be careful."

I arrived at my flat with only thirty minutes to change. I bathed and applied rose water to my wrists and neck. Wrapped in a towel, I went to my wardrobe. *I could do worse than Captain Clifford Douglas*, I thought as I flipped through my dresses. *Which one is appropriate for a June evening out with an officer?* I wanted something attractive but not alluring. I didn't want to give the good captain the wrong idea…at least not yet.

I paused at a blue-gray hobble skirt that put me in mind of the song "Alice Blue Gown," about the American Secretary of the Navy's daughter, Alice, who rode in cars with boys, smoked, and kept a pet snake. Secretary

Roosevelt reportedly said, "Either I can run the navy or tend to Alice, but I can't possibly do both." I chuckled. *Cheers, Alice Roosevelt!*

After long minutes of agonizing indecision, I chose a dark-plum two-piece with a lace bodice and straight, loose skirt that fell just above my ankles. I wore dark stockings and my favorite beaded slippers. Once I had my evening kit on, I went to my dressing table and applied my makeup—lipstick, rouge, and a touch of kohl.

Then came the wig. I tugged it into place and styled it the best I could. Captain Douglas had complimented me on my hair. God forbid he'd see the black spikes that made me look like a wild animal.

I'd done all I could for my appearance and still was more Poor Little Peppina than pretty. But it would have to do. I glanced at my watch. Captain Douglas, never punctual, should be arriving sometime within the next hour.

Sure enough, fifteen minutes late, there he was at my door, looking jolly handsome in his evening suit.

When the car pulled up in front of Kettner's, you could have knocked me down with a feather. I hadn't eaten at Kettner's since Andrew had proposed to me over champagne and oysters five years ago. It felt like a lifetime. I thought of poor Georgie growing up without his father. The war had taken so much from so many.

"You know," Clifford said as he helped me out of the car. "They say the owner was once chef to Napoleon III. And famous authors like Oscar Wilde and that bright young thing Agatha Christie have been spotted here."

"Is that why you chose it? Seeing as you're an aspiring author yourself?" I asked playfully.

"Well, no, actually..." he stammered. "You'll see."

"Right, the surprise." I wasn't one for surprises, but Clifford seemed so pleased. And he had kept my secret...and Dr. Vogel's too.

Inside, the restaurant was light and bright, with white plaster walls adorned with scalloped molding and generous mirrors framed with sculpted ribbons. The mosaic floor in the champagne bar was magnificent as light from the chandelier danced across it.

"This way, Captain Douglas," the maître d' said. "The rest of your party is already here."

The rest of the party! Clifford, the rotter, had tricked me. I turned to go but realized it was too late. Everyone was watching. I couldn't very well make a scene. I would have to bite the bullet and meet Fredricks and Lady Mary as Miss Figg. Yet, dressed in my finest, I felt as if Miss Figg was a disguise too.

Clifford escorted me to a circular table, around which sat the party from Ravenswick Abbey, minus the deceased mother and her accused murderers, of course.

"Everyone, I'd like you to meet a friend of mine." Clifford introduced me. "Miss Fiona Figg. She also works at the War Office."

The men stood up.

I nodded. "It's a pleasure to meet you all. I've heard so much about you from Captain Douglas."

Fredricks took my hand and kissed the air above it. *"Enchanté*, Madame Figg."

"Miss," I corrected him. The mistake gave me an uneasy feeling. He'd done it on purpose. "Mr. Fredricks—"

Still holding my hand, his eyes sparked as he gazed up at me and said, "You can call me Apollo."

"Miss Figg is an admirer," Clifford said. "She talks about you constantly. I thought it was high time you met."

Damn Clifford! Telling Fredricks I talked about him constantly. I had no choice but to play along.

"Yes. I've read your articles about female animals who dispose of their mates." I glanced over at Lady Mary. "Betrayal is not just a human weakness, it seems."

Lady Mary gave me a strange look, and a flash of recognition hit her pupils. *Blast it all!* She'd recognized me.

"I'm sure they deserved it," she said with a smug smile. "Philandering husbands—no matter what the species—deserve a dose of arsenic." She touched her husband's arm. "Don't you agree, dear?"

Ernest looked down at the serviette in his lap.

"Please sit down next to me, Miss Figg," Lady Mary said. "It seems we share a common interest in just deserts." She patted the seat next to her.

So, she hadn't recognized me, except perhaps as a sister who'd also been wronged by an unfaithful husband. I nodded and sat down.

"We're celebrating Ernest's release from that horrid business," Clifford said. "All thanks to—" He seemed to catch himself. "Ah, to my friend, Fredricks."

Fredricks smiled and nodded.

"Is it true, you're one of the greatest investigative reporters in the world, Mr. Fredricks?" I asked as I took the chair next to Lady Mary.

He tipped an imaginary hat. "And you are the charming Miss Figg who has filled the dreams of my friend Captain Douglas."

I blushed. "Captain Douglas is a man with many dreams, and I daresay his dreams can accommodate many...people."

Fredricks laughed.

After reading Clifford's dairy—to speak in his favorite language, that of clichés—I'd say he fell in love at the drop of a hat, either that or he was grasping at straws.

"And you, Mr. Fredricks, who fills your dreams?" I asked in a rather cheeky tone.

"Aside from charming young ladies like you," he said, bowing toward me and Lady Mary, "only wild animals and criminals."

"Perhaps you identify with them."

"Wild animals or criminals?" When he smiled the furry creature on his upper lip stood at attention.

"I'm sure Mr. Fredricks hasn't committed any crimes," Lady Mary said indignantly. "He saved my dear Ernest from the gallows. He's the dearest of men and we owe him the greatest debt."

Fredricks nodded and smiled. The arrogant chappy did love flattery.

"Yes, I heard you were brilliant, Mr. Fredricks. But to inhabit the criminal mind, mustn't you have something of the criminal in your heart?"

"Ah, well," he said, taking his seat. "Crime is my vocation, or perhaps I should say, the psychology of crime, which all comes down to animal instinct and the lizard brain."

"Your theory puts me in mind of Dr. Freud, who says we are shaped by our childhoods. Tell us about your childhood, Mr. Fredricks."

"Fredricks was never a child," Clifford joked. "He was born full grown."

"From Zeus's head?" I asked and then added under my breath, "the god of philandering husbands."

"Freud is a charlatan!" Fredricks pounded his hearty fist on the table so hard that it caused the wine in our glasses to tremble. "We cannot blame our own evil on our parents. Each man must take responsibility for himself. Criminals must be brought to justice."

Freud isn't the only charlatan. "Do you take responsibility for everything you've done in your life?" I asked.

"I do," he said with resolve.

"Then why not tell us about the innocence of your childhood?" I asked playfully.

"Do not confuse privacy with guilt, Miss Figg." When Fredricks stared across at me with those icy blue eyes, I wanted to slide under the table. *I'm being too pushy, I know, but I must press on.* This might be my last chance to interrogate the Great White Hunter.

"Stop being so serious, everybody," Lilian said, laughing. "We have an announcement to make." She tapped her fork against her water glass to get everyone's attention. "Tell them," she whispered to Ian Elliott, who was sitting to her right.

Ian's tanned countenance turned a lovely shade of mauve as he stood up. "Yes, we have an announcement."

"You're getting married," Fredricks said, pulling the rug out from under Ian's feet.

Did he have to spoil the surprise? What a pillock.

"No!" Clifford looked indignant. "There you're wrong, Fredricks."

Poor Clifford. Sometimes he was so clueless.

"You said he snubbed you," Clifford continued, really putting his foot in it.

"That's because I'm in love with him, you silly goose." Lilian beamed up at her fiancé.

"Oh, I say." Now Clifford was blushing.

"It's true. We're engaged to be married." With a confused look on his face,

Ian glanced around the table and then sat back down.

"Champagne!" Ernest said, looking around for the waiter. "Waiter, bring us some champagne."

He and Lady Mary were behaving like honeymooners, touching and giggling. Obviously, the trial had brought them closer than ever. I was glad to see Lady Mary so happy. Although I don't know if I could be so quick to forgive a philandering husband. Hopefully, at the very least, he did not have the French disease.

After champagne and oysters, followed by a delicious supper of roast and potatoes, we were a jovial party, enjoying conversation while we waited for pudding. This dinner must be costing the family a fortune. Although with his mother dead and Derek Wilkinson accused of murder, Lord Elliott was now a very wealthy man.

Once the next trial revealed Wilkinson did not commit the deadly deed, even if he had intended to do so, we would see where the fortunes fell.

"Mr. Fredricks, do you have any family nearby?" I asked innocently. "Will you go back to them after the war?"

Fredricks froze, a forkful of tart almost to his mouth. "I prefer to talk about the future rather than the past." The secretive huntsman took a bite, and then carefully wiped his mustache on a serviette.

I resolved not to let his rudeness stop me. "Where will you go next, Mr. Fredricks? Now you've recovered from your injuries and solved the murder?"

He sipped his coffee but didn't answer.

"We're off to Paris," Clifford said.

I stifled a cough. The address on the note Fredricks left at the farm was a hotel in Paris. "How exciting," I said, stabbing a forkful of Bakewell tart and struggling to maintain my composure. "Where in Paris?"

"*Hôtel Grand*," Fredricks said. "Do you know it, Miss Figg?"

"They have an absolutely smashing restaurant," Douglas said. "Although I suppose with this beastly war, everyone and their brother is on rations."

A spark ignited in my brain. The photograph I'd seen in the case under Fredricks's bed, it wasn't of his wife and sons. It was a picture of him and his brother with their mother. And the other picture must have been of his sister. *A devout mother, an entire family killed...* who was Fredrick Fredricks? I didn't know, but I was bloody well going to find out.

"Fredricks is introducing me to his great friend, the famous dancer, Margaretha Zelle." Clifford's voice was full of excitement. "You've probably heard her stage name—"

Fredricks cut him off. "I'm sure Miss Figg isn't interested in dancing girls." From across the table, the cunning journalist was regarding me with an appraising look. "You're very familiar, Miss Figg." His eagle eyes glimmered. "The shape of your nose—"

"I have one of those faces." I forced a smile. "Everyone thinks they nose me."

The party laughed, amused by my pun.

"Perhaps you too have a nose for crime." Fredricks tilted his head and put a substantial finger to his nose.

"I have a nose for truth." Without flinching, I returned his gaze. Then I spotted it. A tiny bead of spirit gum attached to the end of his mustache. Fredrick Fredricks was not who he seemed.

As we finished our pudding, I kept my eye on Fredricks. He was such a striking figure, and his mannerisms so exaggerated, he had to be acting a part.

Then again, perhaps I was mistaken, and it wasn't spirit gum on his mustache. Maybe it was just aspic or a bit of Bakewell tart.

Trying not to stare, I focused on the dodgy spot on his upper lip. I was sure it was spirit gum, and I should know.

Fredricks dabbed at his mustache with his serviette, gave a weak smile, and excused himself from the table.

Was the huntsman on to me? Or had he realized I was on to him?

Chapter Twenty-Four: The Bird Has Flown

Fredrick Fredricks never came back to the table. Clifford was beside himself, worrying his friend had been taken ill.

"Perhaps I should return to Paddington and check on Fredricks," Clifford said.

"I'm sure he's fine." Ernest Elliott waved for the waiter to pour more wine.

"I really think I should check on him." Clifford was fidgeting in his chair.

"Why don't we all go?" Lady Mary laid her hand atop her wine glass to stop her husband from pouring.

"We're celebrating!" Lilian held out her glass and Ernest obliged.

"Please don't inconvenience yourselves on my account." Clifford stood up. "But if you'll excuse me, I really think I must..." He glanced at me and then at Mary. "Perhaps you can see Miss Figg home?"

"Can't you join us?" Lady Mary turned to me. "We have an extra room ready if you'd like to stay the night."

"Oh no, I couldn't." The more time I spent with Lady Mary Elliott, the more chance of her recognizing me...although now that I knew she was an informant for the War Office, I was deuced curious to talk to her.

"At least join us for a nightcap," Clifford said with an inviting smile. "I'm sure Lady Mary wouldn't mind sending you back home in the car."

"Of course not." Mary took my hand. "You must join us. And Alfred can drive you home." She laid her serviette on the table. "Ernest, shall we?"

Begrudgingly, Lord Elliott got up from the table, settled the bill, and called for a hansom cab.

Curiosity about Fredricks won out over fear of Lady Mary, and I joined them in the cab.

When we reached Paddington house, we were informed by Annabelle, the parlor maid, that Mr. Fredricks had packed up and flown the coup.

"Good Lord!" Clifford paced back and forth in the foyer. "Why would he leave without telling me?"

"Maybe his newspaper called him away on another assignment?" I offered. Or maybe he knew I'd spotted the spirit gum on his upper lip and he'd fled. It dawned on me, he might even have recognized me and figured out he was being tailed. In that case, he probably knew I suspected he had poisoned the countess. Running away was further evidence of his guilt.

I joined Clifford in pacing the foyer.

"I think we could all use a nightcap." Lord Elliott beckoned us to follow him. "Jolly peculiar, just disappearing into the night. You'd think he was a fugitive."

"Indeed," I said, trailing the others into the drawing room.

In the middle of our speculations on what could have taken Fredricks off in such a rush, a telegram arrived with a message for Captain Douglas.

Annabelle delivered the slip of pink paper on a silver plate. "Sir, a telegram."

Clifford looked puzzled as he slid the paper off the plate. "I say!" He glanced up at me. "It's from Fredricks."

"What does he say?" I sat bolt upright.

The others went silent in anticipation.

"The cheek of the fellow." Clifford shook his head. "Listen to this." He held up the telegram and read, "Waiting at *Hôtel Grand*. Where are you? You should have been here yesterday."

If Fredrick Fredricks is already in Paris, who were we dining with tonight? And if we were dining with the huntsman, then who sent that telegram?

"What does he mean?" Lady Mary asked. "He couldn't be in Paris already."

"Does the blasted man expect me to arrive early to prepare for his grand arrival?" Clifford crumbled the telegram in his palm. "This time, he's gone too far."

"Has anyone checked his bedroom?" I asked.

"Follow me." Lady Mary led Clifford and me up the stairs. She opened the door and gestured inside. "Do you mind if I leave you to it? I have a beastly headache."

I patted her hand. "Take some headache powders and rest." I caught myself before I fell fully into the persona of Dr. Vogel.

"Thank you, Doctor," she said with a wink.

My cheeks burned. *Was she on to me or was that a joke?*

After Mary left us, I followed Clifford into the room. Now was not the time to worry about being alone with a man in a boudoir, even one who'd asked me to marry him.

Fredricks's room was neatly made up and completely empty, with absolutely no sign anyone had been living there for the last month. The bed was made military style, and every ornament or vase was standing neatly aligned and at attention.

I circled the room looking for clues. There wasn't a stray hair or crumb or speck of dust anywhere. The floor was spotless and the top of the dressing table was polished to a shine. Either Lord and Lady Elliott had excellent housekeepers, or Fredricks had left the place cleaner than when he found it. So clean, in fact, there was no trace of his existence. Fredrick Fredricks could just as well have been a phantom.

I heard a sigh of delight and glanced over at Captain Douglas, who was sipping dark liquid from a cordial glass.

"What are you drinking?" I asked, dashing over to join him at the small table in the sitting area.

"I say, it's delicious." Standing near the heavily curtained window, he held up a tiny bottle. "Fancy a taste?" He poured what was left into another cordial glass.

"Where did you get that?"

"It was sitting here." He pointed to the table. "Fredricks must have left it as a going-away gift."

"Stop!" I grabbed his hand.

"Apologies. How rude of me." He held out the glass he'd just poured. "I should have offered it to you first."

"It could be poisoned!" I took the glass by its stem and examined the viscous liquid. *Was this some kind of joke?* I sniffed the liquor—a sweet aroma with a hint of citrus hit my nostrils, but nothing untoward, at least nothing that my nose could detect. Mrs. Roland's sloe-berry cordial. The question was, with or without the addition of poisonous mushrooms?

"Fredricks may be deuced annoying sometimes, but why would he poison us?" Clifford chortled.

I had a hunch why Fredricks might want to poison me. "Trust me. Don't drink it."

The captain gave me a quizical look and then dabbed at his mouth with the serviette.

"Wait! Let me see that." I grabbed the serviette from his hands. I couldn't believe my eyes. In the corner of the serviette, stamped in thick black ink, was the figure of a cat.

"I say." Clifford examined the figure. "It's a black panther."

The insignia on Fredrick's pinky ring.

Clifford was using a long wooden toothpick to pick his teeth.

"Where did you get that?" I asked, pointing to the toothpick.

"What?"

"That thing in your mouth?"

"Oh, this?" He removed the toothpick and held it up. "It was in the wine glass."

"Are you daft? It's evidence."

"Evidence of what?" He gave me that hangdog look of his.

I shook my head. "Of the true identity of your friend Fredricks."

"True identity?" The captain wrinkled his brows. "He's a great hunter turned newsman."

I nodded. *A great fraud, more like.* I bit my lip. I was bursting to tell him, but I dared not explain my hypothesis for fear of betraying my top-secret assignment. My whole body tingled with excitement. I needed to report the black panther insignia to Captain Blinker Hall as soon as possible. I hoped to heavens the cordial Clifford just finished off didn't kill him.

I took a hanky from my handbag and gently removed the toothpick from Clifford's fingers. The thin wooden staff was about four inches long. It was dagger-sharp at one end and had a carved wooden pine cone on the other.

"Oh my giddy aunt!" *Was the arrogant huntsman so devious?*

"What is it?" Clifford asked.

"A calling card." I twirled the stick inside my handkerchief. I'd recognized the staff as a thyrsus, the symbol of the Greek god of wine and chaos, Dionysus.

"I say, what does it mean?" Clifford's eyes widened.

"Didn't Fredricks tell us his friends called him Apollo?"

"I never call him Apollo," he said indignantly. He fingered the edge of my handkerchief. "The panther and the staff. What do they mean?"

"Clifford dear, we've got the wrong Greek god."

The next morning, I got up early, hurried my toilette, and headed to the War Office. I was eager to tell Captain Hall what I'd found.

"A wooden staff and a black panther, you say?" Captain Hall's eyelashes were batting a mile a minute. "The panther is familiar, but the staff, that's new. Either that, or you're the first to notice it, Miss Figg."

I handed him the thyrsus and serviette stamped with the black panther, which I'd wrapped in a handkerchief.

He examined them. "So Frrr...the chap from Ravenswick Abbey is the elusive spy, Dionysus, after all."

"Just who is this Dionysus?"

"A notorious spy." He pulled a file folder from his desk drawer and handed me a sheet of paper encased in clear cellophane. "He always leaves the black panther insignia."

I studied the black panther stamp on the stationary. "Why didn't you tell me any of this before I took the assignment?"

"Classified information. Top secret." He slid the pencil behind one ear. "Anyway, we weren't sure this Frrr...chap was our man."

"So if the spy Dionysus poisoned the countess to stop her from becoming a double-agent and turning against the Germans..." I thought for a minute. "Is there really a Fredrick Fredricks—the South African hunter and American journalist?" I passed the stationary back to the captain. "And who sent the telegram from Paris?" I asked under my breath.

"Either Dionysus is a clever chameleon, or we're dealing with a ring of spies."

I hadn't thought of that, but it made perfect sense. I nodded.

"So was the fellow I met at Ravenswick the real Fredrick Fredricks or the infamous spy?" I narrowed my eyes in concentration. "Was Dionysus posing as Fredricks? Or is Fredricks our spy?"

"We're counting on you to find out, Miss Figg." He stood up, signaling our meeting was at an end.

I stood up too. "You can count on me, sir."

"Keep up the good work, Miss Figg." His lashes were fluttering as fast as my heart. "I want you to continue following this Frr, er, Dionysus character—or, characters. Find out how many of them there are and what they're up to."

"At least one of them is in Paris, sir." I straightened my skirt. "At the Grand Hotel."

"Well then let's quit chin-wagging." He waved toward the door. "Get over there right away."

"With pleasure, sir."

Two hours later—after one crucial stop—I was back at my flat, packing my suitcase for Paris. Obviously, I couldn't reprise my role as Dr. Vogel. I hung my two men's suits in the back of my wardrobe. And, the huntsman had seen me as Teresa the maid of the mountain. Or had that really been Fredricks? Perhaps the man in Paris was an accomplice. I packed the maid's outfit just in case.

Delighted, I carefully folded my new purchase from Angels Fancy Dress. I was jolly pleased with myself on this one. I'd found the perfect disguise for the Grand Hotel. No one would recognize me in this getup.

Standing in front of my wardrobe, staring at the boxes on the top shelf, I smiled to myself. I was faced with my usual dilemma, picking out the right hat. *Which hat is appropriate for top-secret espionage and outsmarting the great huntsman...not to mention his alter ego, the notorious spy?*

Aahhhh. What a relief. Selecting a suitable hat was once again the most difficult decision of my day.

A Note from the Author

If you enjoyed *Betrayal at Ravenswick*, please consider leaving a review on Amazon or Goodreads. Those reviews mean a lot to indie authors like me.

Acknowledgements

Thanks to my tireless editor and friend, Lisa Walsh, for correcting my typos and encouraging me from beginning to end. Thanks also to the brilliant Barb Goffman for giving me feedback on an earlier version. Thanks also to the folks at Level Best Books, who are a delight. Finally, thanks to my "partner in crime," Benigno Trigo for reading every word, and egging me on. Last but not least, thanks to my furry muses, Mischief, Mayhem, and Flan. It would be a lonely business without them clawing up my chair and jumping on my keyboard.

Cover: BNP Design Studio

Author Photo: Vanderbilt Photo Studio

About the Author

Kelly Oliver is the award-winning and Amazon Bestselling author of The Jessica James Mystery Series, including **Wolf**, **Coyote**, **Fox, Jackal**, and **Viper**. **Wolf** won the *Independent Publisher's Gold Medal* for best Thriller/Mystery, was a finalist for the Foreward Magazine award for best mystery, and was voted number one in Women's Mysteries on Goodreads. **Coyote** won a *Silver Falchion Award* for Best Mystery. **Fox** was a finalist for both the *Claymore* and the *Silver Falchion Awards*. **Jackal** was a finalist for the *Mystery and Mayhem Award* and for the Silver Falchion Award.

She is the author of the middle grade mystery series, The Pet Detective Mysteries. **Kassy O'Roarke, Cub Reporter**, the first in the series, won a Reader's Choice Award for Children's Mysteries.

Betrayal at Ravenswick, A Fiona Figg Mystery is the first in her historical cozy mystery series.

When she's not writing novels, Kelly is a Distinguished Professor of Philosophy at Vanderbilt University, and the author of fifteen nonfiction books, and over 100 articles, on issues such as the refugee crisis, campus rape, women and the media, animals and the environment. Her latest nonfiction book, **Hunting Girls: Sexual Violence from The Hunger Games to Campus Rape**, won a Choice Magazine Award for Outstanding title. She has published in *The New York Times* and *The Los Angeles Review of Books*, and has been featured on ABC news, CSPAN books, the Canadian Broadcasting Network, and various radio programs. To learn more about Kelly and her books, go to www.kellyoliverbooks.com.

CPSIA information can be obtained
at www.ICGtesting.com
Printed in the USA
LVHW031913110423
744071LV00001B/74